## PRA

## *Knights of the Round Table: Lancelot*

"Though Camelot is in the background, this tale is more a Dark Ages romance between individuals with a mutual past to overcome if both take the steps that love offers them . . . Lancelot is a fascinating character . . . Historical romance readers will enjoy this fine interpretation of the mists of Camelot."

—*The Best Reviews*

"The legends of Lancelot and his place in Camelot are well-known, but in *Knights of the Round Table: Lancelot*, Gwen Rowley puts a refreshingly unique spin on the myth . . . An intriguing twist on the famous legend, *Lancelot*, the first book in the Knights of the Round Table series, shows a totally different side of Camelot and should not be missed."

—*Romance Reviews Today*

"Fascinating . . . Rowley takes one of the focal stories of Western European literature and puts her own spin on it . . . [giving] us a surprisingly twenty-first-century Sir Lancelot."

—*The Green Man Review*

"Rowley passionately pens the romantic scenes between Lancelot and Elaine with simple grace and elegance . . . The whole book is written just superbly, and I loved every minute reading it."

—*Romance Reader at Heart*

"The enticement of Rowley's reimaginings of the Camelot legend is how cleverly she manipulates the myths surrounding Arthur, Guinevere, and Lancelot, adding touches of reality and twists of plot that leave us to wonder what might have been."

—*Romantic Times*

*Don't miss the previous novels in the Knights of the Round Table series . . .*

***Lancelot***

***Geraint***

# Knights of the Round Table

• • •

## GAWAIN

Gwen Rowley

JOVE BOOKS, NEW YORK

**THE BERKLEY PUBLISHING GROUP**
**Published by the Penguin Group**
**Penguin Group (USA) Inc.**
**375 Hudson Street, New York, New York 10014, USA**
Penguin Group (Canada), 90 Eglinton Avenue East, Suite 700, Toronto, Ontario M4P 2Y3, Canada
(a division of Pearson Penguin Canada Inc.)
Penguin Books Ltd., 80 Strand, London WC2R 0RL, England
Penguin Group Ireland, 25 St. Stephen's Green, Dublin 2, Ireland (a division of Penguin Books Ltd.)
Penguin Group (Australia), 250 Camberwell Road, Camberwell, Victoria 3124, Australia
(a division of Pearson Australia Group Pty. Ltd.)
Penguin Books India Pvt. Ltd., 11 Community Centre, Panchsheel Park, New Delhi—110 017, India
Penguin Group (NZ), 67 Apollo Drive, Rosedale, North Shore 0745, Auckland, New Zealand
(a division of Pearson New Zealand Ltd.)
Penguin Books (South Africa) (Pty.) Ltd., 24 Sturdee Avenue, Rosebank, Johannesburg 2196,
South Africa

Penguin Books Ltd., Registered Offices: 80 Strand, London WC2R 0RL, England



KNIGHTS OF THE ROUND TABLE: GAWAIN

A Jove Book / published by arrangement with the author

PRINTING HISTORY
Jove mass-market edition / September 2007


Cover illustration by Aleta Rafton.
Cover lettering by Ron Zinn.
Cover design by George Long.


For information, address: The Berkley Publishing Group,
a division of Penguin Group (USA) Inc.,
375 Hudson Street, New York, New York 10014.

ISBN: 978-0-515-14349-2

JOVE®
Jove Books are published by The Berkley Publishing Group,
a division of Penguin Group (USA) Inc.,
375 Hudson Street, New York, New York 10014.
JOVE is a registered trademark of Penguin Group (USA) Inc.
The "J" design is a trademark belonging to Penguin Group (USA) Inc.

PRINTED IN THE UNITED STATES OF AMERICA

10 9 8 7 6 5 4 3 2 1

*For Kat and Danny*

In destinies sad or merry,
True men can but try.

*Sir Gawain and the Green Knight*

# Chapter 1

• • •

SIR Gawain detested magic.

As Inglewood Forest loomed before him, it seemed the space between the trees was filled with shifting shadows and its very air was redolent of sorcery. But he steeled himself and galloped on, catching up to the king just outside the entrance.

"Did you really think you could sneak away?" he demanded, pulling up his charger beside his uncle's.

"A king does not *sneak*," King Arthur answered loftily. "I told you I meant to do this on my own."

"And I said I was coming with you." Gawain repressed a shudder as they passed into the cool dimness of the forest. "In fact, it would be best if you turned back and let me—"

"No," the king said sharply. "And if you ask again, I will send you back to Camelot."

"I am not asking," Gawain replied with straining patience. "I am telling you—"

"And *I* am telling *you*—I am *ordering* you to stay out of it. You cannot keep fighting my battles for me, Gawain, it just won't do. First it was the Green Knight, now it is this Somer Gromer Jour—"

"I am only doing what I have sworn to do—what every one of your knights has sworn—"

"Yes, but none of them stepped in and took the Green Knight's challenge, did they? I'm not saying I'm not grateful—you know I am—but it's enough. Somer Gromer Jour is my opponent, and I would thank you to let me deal with him on my own."

Gawain drew a long breath. "Arthur—"

"Ga*wain*," the king mocked him. "You should hear yourself—no, really! For a moment there, I could have sworn it was my old nurse talking. Next you will be after me to change my shoes and wear a flannel on my chest!"

Gawain's mouth twitched, but he repressed his amusement and fixed his uncle with a stern glare. Arthur merely grinned and spurred his horse ahead.

It was Arthur's way to face danger with a smile, and had they been riding into battle, Gawain's heart would have been equally as light. But this Somer Gromer Jour was clearly an unnatural creature, appearing out of nowhere as he had last year to challenge the king to private combat. And then, once Arthur was defeated, had the knight sought any sort of reasonable terms? No, he had posed the king a question so peculiar that no honest man would even think to ask it, and demanded that Arthur—on pain of death—present himself in one year's time with the answer.

*What do all women desire?*

How could any man possibly divine the answer to such a riddle? What would be the point?

The whole business reeked of sorcery.

"Arthur, this is serious," he said as he drew level with the king.

"And well I know it." Arthur cast a rueful look at his saddlebag, bulging with a thick tome bound in leather, the result of a solid year's worth of painstaking labor on both his part and Gawain's. "Who would have thought it would be so difficult to get a straight answer to a simple question?"

"Me. Women can no more say what they really want than a hen can fly to the moon! In fact, given the choice, I'd wager on the chicken."

Arthur's brows lifted. "Was that a joke? Oh, well done, Gawain, I was beginning to think that you'd forgotten how!"

"This is no laughing matter. Somer Gromer Jour has bested you once already—no doubt by use of sorcery—"

"No doubt," Arthur agreed wryly.

"And the task he set you is impossible, as well he knew."

Arthur acknowledged the truth of that with an exasperated sigh. He could hardly deny it after the past year, which they had spent—wasted, Gawain thought now—in canvassing the female population of Britain for the answer to Somer Gromer Jour's deceptively innocuous question.

"Impossible or not, I did accept," Arthur pointed out. "I have given my word, and I will keep it."

"*I* have given *my* word, too, and I refuse to stand by and let that man—that *sorcerer* who will not even give his proper name—take your life because you could not find the answer to his ridiculous riddle!"

"I don't think it will come to that," Arthur said. "We have a whole book here—"

"And for every answer in that book, we have its opposite, as well."

Arthur nodded glumly. "I thought we were onto something with the grand marriage. We had a lot of those."

"We did," Gawain agreed. "But it was not unanimous."

"Did you mark how many said they wanted to be widowed? A bit depressing, that. And then there were the nuns," he went on, aggrieved. "They put paid to wealth and beauty. As for wisdom—"

Gawain snorted. "I told you *that* one was a nonstarter."

"Damn it all, what do *you* think women want?"

"A man to tell them what to do," Gawain answered promptly.

"Yes, well, if you notice, we didn't get a single one of those."

"That's because women lack the wit to know *what* they want. Even if they did know, they wouldn't say. Women like their secrets, Arthur—they're cunning creatures."

"They can't be witless *and* cunning," Arthur protested. "You have to pick one."

"No, indeed, for they are both," Gawain assured him gravely. "Even the dullest will seek to deceive a man, and the more wit they have, the more dangerous they are."

Arthur sighed. "You are very hard upon the ladies."

"I speak as I find," Gawain answered with a shrug.

"This past year hasn't done you any good at all," Arthur said regretfully. "I was sure if you were to get out, meet some lasses who are, well, a bit different . . ."

"Did you think some simple goose girl would alter my opinion?" Gawain demanded, his lip curling in a contemptuous smile. "I knew quite enough about women before I started out, and greater knowledge has only confirmed my worst suspicions."

"Well, I still think it's a grand marriage they want," Arthur said a little grumpily. "It's what most of them said, isn't it?"

"Yes, but the question isn't what most women want—it is what all women desire. *All.* Which is precisely why it is impossible. Arthur, you *must* let me take this challenge for you."

"Must, eh? Who is king here, I'd like to know?"

"You are. And you will go on ruling so long as I draw breath."

Arthur laughed. "Oh, Gawain, I *am* fond of you! I honestly don't think it has occurred to you that *some* heirs would take a very different view of the matter. A *clever* nephew would be pushing me forward with one hand and arranging his coronation with the other."

"I will not rule—" Gawain began.

"You damn well will if I die without issue. That is what it means to be my heir. I chose you and I expect you to do your duty."

Gawain let out a long breath and said with straining patience, "That is what I am attempting to do, sire—"

"Oh, so now it's *sire*, is it?"

"—And what I *will* do. Arthur, I am taking this challenge."

"I forbid it," Arthur said. "And if you ask again—hello, what's this? Oh, damn it all, I think he's thrown a shoe."

• • •

AISLYN stood, resting a hand against the tree trunk, absently brushing a strand of red-gold hair from her eyes as she peered down at the forest path. Her heart stuttered when she glimpsed a flash of crimson between the leaves, still far off in the distance. King Arthur. It must be. And another rider, no doubt his squire. Though they were too far off to make out their words, she was almost sure she caught the sound of laughter. King Arthur must be either a brave man or an utter fool. Did he not realize he was riding to his death?

She settled down again, her back against the tree trunk, bare feet dangling above the road. Another few minutes and he would be upon her. What would she do then? Only a fool would throw away the security she had worked so hard to gain, and a fool Aislyn certainly was not. She'd been one once, but now she was . . .

The witch in the wood. That's what they called her. Someone to be approached only as a last resort. The peasants never spoke to her; they never even came as far as the door of the abandoned charcoal burner's hut she had taken as her own. If they had, she wouldn't answer. They left their offerings of food and cloth on the stump and when they returned, they found whatever potion it was they needed. It had been a good enough arrangement for the first few years, when she desired nothing but solitude, but now . . .

"Not much of a life, is it?" she asked a squirrel on the branch above her, but its only answer was a flip of the tail before it vanished up the trunk.

No, it wasn't much of a life, but at least she was alive. Which she would not be if Queen Morgause learned who had foiled her plot against King Arthur's life.

Of course Morgause was behind this. Aislyn knew her former mistress too well for doubt. The riddle was one Morgause had used of old, and the entire business had been carefully designed so no blood guilt would stain the queen's white hands. The challenge accepted freely by the king, the champion to do the deed itself—oh, it was clever, but Aislyn had never taken Morgause for a fool.

She was, after all, the reason Aislyn had spent five years hiding in this forest. Morgause still sought her former pupil—and the grimoire Aislyn had stolen from her, the queen's own book of spells—and would not give up the hunt until one of them was dead. So far Aislyn had managed to elude her, but what now? She, Aislyn, the witch of the wood, held a king's life in her hand. What was she to do with it?

To save him was to reveal herself, for even if Morgause did not guess from whom the answer came, she would bend all her considerable powers to the problem. Yet to simply sit and let the king ride past was tantamount to murder. Which would it be? His life or hers? Or was there a way both could be saved?

She had no proof, nothing but her own word against that of a queen who was, moreover, King Arthur's half sister. Would the king believe her? Even if he did, would he thank her for such information? Would he not want to hush up the entire matter . . . including the messenger?

She had asked herself these questions a thousand times over the past few days, and the answers still eluded her.

The sound of a horse's whinny shattered her reverie. They had stopped; the king was off his mount. The moment of decision was upon her. She alone could stop Morgause. She alone could save the king. And then where would she run?

"Oh, bugger it," she muttered, jumping down to land noiselessly upon the path. "I've nothing else to do."

The king hadn't seen her. She straightened, smiling as she opened her mouth to call out to him. She stood thus, her mouth agape, then turned and stepped behind a tree, peering cautiously around its trunk.

That was no squire with Arthur. It was *him*. The one person in the world Aislyn hated more than Queen Morgause: Morgause's eldest son, Gawain.

*He looks just the same* was her first thought; her second was that he had changed almost out of recognition. His hair was still as golden fair as ever, though he no longer wore it loose, but drawn back severely from his brow. Five years had stripped the last boyish roundness from his face; his cheekbones were more prominent, his jaw squared, and his mouth was set in a hard line, as though he had forgotten how to smile. She thought he might have gained an inch or two across the chest, though that could be a trick of her imagination, or the effect of the glittering mail he wore beneath a snow-white surcoat.

But he was still Gawain, still the fairest man she had ever seen, sitting proudly on his destrier—

*"Look, Aislyn!" he cried, his cheeks flushed as he leapt from the saddle to stand before her. "What do you think? Isn't he the most splendid horse you've ever seen? What shall I call him?"*

*"Oh! You want me—are you sure?" She was breathless, both from the honor and the way he smiled at her, his gray eyes shining. "Very well, then. He will be—"*

—Gringolet. Gringolet, nearly as famous as his master: Sir Gawain the Fair, they called him, Sir Gawain the Courteous—Sir Gawain, the Hawk of May, First Knight of Camelot, and heir to Britain's throne.

Sir Gawain, the faithless churl who had professed undying love for her—and then abandoned her to almost certain death.

Aislyn had scarcely noticed the other man, bent low over his horse's hoof, until King Arthur glanced up, saying, "It's all right. I think it's just a stone."

Aislyn had expected Arthur to be older, for she could scarce remember a time when he had not sat on the throne. Now she remembered that he had been little more than a boy himself when he was crowned; he still had some way to go before he would see thirty, and looked even younger than his years. He was not a handsome man—or perhaps it was unfair to judge him with Gawain so near—but he had a kind face.

If only it wasn't Gawain with him! She could not reveal herself to *him*, it would be madness, though almost worth the danger to see the expression on his face. Oh, how satisfying it would be to tell him precisely what she thought of him in words honed to perfection during five long and lonely years! The temptation was near unbearable, save for the fact that her satisfaction would be short-lived . . . as would she, most likely.

But now that she had seen the king, she would not let him pass without such help as she could give him.

Well, there was only one thing to do, though she sighed a little to remember the care she had taken with her appearance today. If she was going to meet the king—as she had been almost sure she was—she'd wanted to look her best. It had been a long time since any man had seen her as she really was, and she'd been looking forward to the king's reaction when she stepped out of the trees.

Leave it to Gawain to spoil all her fun.

Well, she amended, hurrying back to the oak where her satchel hung upon a branch, perhaps not *all*. Now that she came to think of it, this could be even more amusing than she'd hoped.

She mixed the potion with the ease of long practice and downed it in a gulp, grimacing at its bitterness. A small moan escaped her as it began to work, but she was accustomed to the pain of transformation now. A few moments later, she reached out a gnarled hand to fumble in her bag, and sighing, emptied the contents of a small vial over herself, her nose wrinkling in distaste as a sickening odor stung her nostrils. Taking up a stout stick, she turned back toward the path.

• • •

"I almost have it," Arthur was saying when Aislyn hobbled between the trees. The king's tawny head was bent as he probed the hoof with his dagger. "Son of a donkey! Stand still! I won't hurt you, if you would just—Gawain, hold his head for me, would you?"

Gawain dismounted and took hold of the bridle. The king's horse stilled instantly at his touch.

"It's deep . . . but if I can just . . . There!" Arthur set the hoof down and sheathed his dagger. "I don't think any harm's done, but—"

"Arthur, King of Britain!"

Arthur turned. Aislyn had to give him credit; he did not scream or even flinch . . . much. And he controlled his instinctive start almost instantly. He even managed a smile; a rather sickly smile, true, but she was impressed that he had made the effort. Most men, confronted with the crone that was Aislyn's particular creation, turned tail and fled.

"Grandmother," he said politely. "How may I serve you?"

"Oh, how courteous!" Her laugh was a truly hideous cackle, one in which she took great pride. "But it is I who desires to serve you."

"I thank you," Arthur said, and amazingly, he did look grateful. "But I have no need—"

"Do not be so quick to spurn my gift, Arthur, King of Britain, he who rides to his own death!"

No sooner had the last word left her lips when Gawain's sword was in his hands. He braced himself and cast a quick, assessing glance to either side of the path.

"Put up your weapon, Hawk of May! I bring not danger, but salvation to your king. Would you know the answer you have sought, King Arthur? I can give it to you!"

"You can? Well, I call that lucky—see, Gawain, I told you it would turn out well! How very kind of you, Grandmother." The king's smile was so unaffected and so charming that Aislyn felt the warmth of it even where she stood.

"Come here, Arthur King," she croaked, crooking one twisted finger. "What I have to say is for your ear alone."

"Don't do it." Gawain stepped before the king, drawn sword at the ready. "Sire, I mistrust this . . ."

"Lady?" Aislyn suggested.

"Witch," he finished flatly.

"Gawain, what are you thinking?" Arthur cried, pushing him aside. "Pay him no mind, good dame. He's a bit unreasonable about magic, but he means no harm."

"Does he not, my liege? I beg leave to differ. Men always seek to slay that which they fear."

Gawain lifted his perfectly sculpted chin. "I fear no woman."

Aislyn smiled. Arthur fell back a pace; Gawain paled, the sword trembling briefly in his grasp before he managed to control it. "Come here, my liege," Aislyn crooned, "come and I shall tell you the answer to your riddle."

"There *is* no answer." Gawain had recovered swiftly; he faced her, all belligerent male arrogance. "The question is impossible."

"I daresay it is—to such as you. But methinks your king has more wisdom."

Arthur took a few steps toward her, then halted, looking as though he might be sick. The stench, Aislyn had always thought, was a particularly good touch. She did not smile again—no need to terrify the poor man—but worked her jaw so the lower tusk slid against the upper with an unpleasant grinding crunch.

Arthur winced but held his ground. "Yes, Grandmother? What is it you want to tell me?"

So here it was. This had been amusing, but the moment she spoke, the fun would be over and the trouble would begin.

Once Morgause realized that the king had slipped through her grasp again, her anger would be terrible. Aislyn did not grudge the king his life—now that she had met him, she was glad to be of service—but she could not discount her danger.

*I might escape,* Aislyn thought. *I have before. But how much longer can I trust to luck?*

It was her problem, not the king's, one assumed of her free will, and there was no point in whinging about it now. What galled her was that Gawain should ride merrily back to Camelot, leaving her behind to face his mother's wrath.

Again.

*Aislyn clung to his stirrup, looking up at him through a haze of tears. "Don't leave me here—you can't!"*

*For a moment, it seemed Gawain hesitated, then he set his jaw and took up the reins. "Let go of me. Let go, damn you!"*

*He spurred his charger forward, and Aislyn reeled back, catching her hip upon the mounting block before falling to her knees. Too stunned to rise, she watched in disbelief as he galloped out of the moonlit courtyard with his cloak billowing behind him.*

No, not again. Not this time.

The plan dropped into her mind, perfect and complete. She would be as safe as she could be, and Gawain . . . The sound of her own laughter startled her, but the harsh cackle only made her laugh the more. Yes, she would do it. Let Gawain see how it felt to be betrayed by honor. Let him fully taste the misery of doing the right thing and losing everything that mattered most.

Let him spend a little time in hell and see how well *he* liked it.

"I have a favor to ask in return," she said to the king, who was eyeing her uneasily, no doubt as a result of her sudden outburst. "'Tis just a small thing, nothing of importance . . ."

"Name it and it is yours."

"I want . . . well, lately, sire, I've had the fancy to wed."

"To wed?" Arthur struggled manfully to control his mirth. "Why don't you come to court—as my guest, of course—my *honored* guest. Stay as long as you like—forever if that pleases you—and we shall look about for someone who might suit."

"I don't need to look about."

The merriment vanished from Arthur's face. "You don't?"

"No." She smiled again, and he reached out to support himself on a tree trunk. "Sir Gawain here is a bonny knight and he says he fears no woman. Well, says I, that's the man—the *only* man—for me."

"Grandmother," he replied carefully, "Sir Gawain is—well, he is a good deal younger—"

"Oh, I don't mind *that.*" She nudged Arthur in the ribs and winked. "I will soon teach him all he needs to know."

Arthur's pallor deepened. "I cannot permit this."

"What's it to do with you? He's a grown man, isn't he? Let's hear what he has to say."

"I'll give you anything else—gold, you would like that, wouldn't you? Or—or lands. A castle—"

"Him," Aislyn said firmly. "Or nothing."

"Then I fear it must be nothing."

She shrugged. "I still say you should ask him, but if you won't, you won't. Farewell, my king, and—well, I won't wish you long life or health, why waste my breath?" She patted his arm kindly. "Let's just leave it at a quick and painless death."

• • •

SOMETHING was wrong. Gawain could see it in Arthur's face as the king strode back to his horse. The hideous creature who had accosted them hobbled a few steps and stood by the side of the road, leaning on her stick.

"What did she say?" Gawain demanded.

"Nothing." Arthur swung himself onto his horse and urged it forward. "Hurry up, Gawain," he called over his shoulder, "we've wasted enough time."

Gawain leapt onto his charger and kicked it into a canter, his stomach churning as he swept by the stinking crone. "Hold up, Arthur! Tell me what she said!"

"Oh, some nonsense—it doesn't matter, you were right, she didn't know the answer after all."

Gawain glanced back uneasily. The hag still stood there, watching them, smiling—at least he thought it was a smile. With those . . . teeth . . . it was difficult to tell.

He shuddered and turned back to the king. "What nonsense?" he insisted. "What are you not telling me?"

"Leave it," Arthur ordered curtly.

"Did she curse you? Is that it? By God, if she did, I'll—"

"You'll do nothing. She's a bit mad, poor creature, but harmless. Let's forget her."

They rode on in silence for a time. Arthur gazed ahead, his expression abstracted, one hand tapping out a rhythm on his knee—always a sure sign that he was upset.

"Arthur, look at me. Something happened back there. Either you tell me what it is or I'll go ask the witch myself."

"You will not."

Gawain pulled his charger to a halt.

"Damn it, Gawain, I am the king! I *order* you to stay here."

"Then tell me the truth!"

"It was nothing—no, wait. She said that she would tell me if I—if I made her one of the queen's waiting women."

"And you *refused*? Are you mad?"

"Guinevere wouldn't like it," Arthur said. "Would you? Having to look at that face every day—dear God, those teeth! D'you think that was actual moss growing on them?" He shuddered. "And her stench! I don't know how I managed to keep my breakfast."

"I am sure the queen would put up with a bit of inconvenience to save your life!"

"Yes, well, perhaps—I mean, of course she would, but I won't ask it of her. And that's an end on it. Belike the old woman doesn't know the answer, anyway."

Gawain seized the king's bridle. "Arthur, you are the greatest king Britain has ever known, but you are a wretched liar. *What did the crone want?*"

"Oh, very *well*!" Arthur laughed. "It's so ridiculous, I didn't like to say—"

"Arthur."

"Shewantedyoutomarryher," Arthur said. "Now let's get moving."

"She wanted . . . to marry her? *Me?*"

"Come along, man, we can't sit here all the day."

Gawain did not move. "To *marry* her? To marry *her*?"

"Stop *saying* that. It makes me sick to even hear the words. Gawain, I would never ask you—"

Gawain jerked his horse's head around. "Do you think you have to? Of course I'll do it."

• • •

THE hag was still standing where they'd left her, leaning on her stick as though awaiting their return. *Witch*, Gawain thought again, and forced himself to look her in the eye.

She gazed up at him through tangled brows, her expression both amused and strangely knowing. What she knew, he could not imagine, and he found he did not want to try. Her face was a mottled red, wrinkled as a winter apple, and only two teeth—tusks, he thought with dull horror—remained to her, one pointing downward toward her protruding chin, the other nearly touching the wart upon the end of her nose. Filthy gray hair hung in a matted knot to her shoulders, which were bent and oddly twisted.

"I accept your terms," he said. "Give us the answer."

"Hold up a moment, laddie, I want to be sure we have things clear between us. I stay with you at Camelot. Don't think you can go packing me off to one of your manors in the back of beyond."

Gawain's jaw clenched. "Very well—that is, if your answer is correct."

"It is."

"Let's have it, then. Please," he added between clenched teeth.

"Not you," she croaked. " 'Tis for the king alone."

"Sire?" Gawain said, and Arthur, who had been staring at the crone, shook himself as though waking from a dark dream.

"Right." Arthur dismounted and approached her. Two steps away, he halted and looked back. "Gawain—"

"Go on, sire."

"That's right, Arthur King, you just bend your ear to me . . ."

She leaned close. A moment later, Arthur drew back and stared at her incredulously. "That's *it*?"

"Aye, that's it." She wheezed with laughter. "You didn't find it for yourself, though, did you?"

"No," Arthur said slowly. "No, I did not."

"Well, then, off you go. I'll be waiting here for your return."

"And you are certain I *will* return?"

"Oh, aye. That is, I'm certain you'll give that Somer Gromer Jour what he's after. Whether you return or not . . ."

"If your answer is the right one, we will be back," Gawain promised. "You have my word on it."

"And I'll hold you to it. Even if I have to walk all the way to Camelot to find you."

"That will not be necessary." Gawain could not bring himself to look at her again, but he bowed in her direction before turning Gringolet and starting down the path.

# Chapter 2

• • •

AISLYN eased sideways in the saddle, trying to find a comfortable position. The crone was well enough for an hour or two, but after a morning's ride, every joint throbbed like a separate toothache and her own stench was making her queasy. The thought of remaining in this form for even a few days was not a pleasant one.

Then she looked at Gawain and decided it was worth it.

He rode perfectly upright in his saddle, his face set in the expressionless mask he'd worn since he returned from the king's meeting with Somer Gromer Jour. He'd brought with him a pretty little mare for her, a gesture that she suspected sprung more from his unwillingness to have her share his mount than any generosity on his part. Still, it looked well, and he had been nothing but polite during the ride, once or twice going so far as to ask if she would like to rest.

It was a good performance. She wondered how long he could sustain it.

"We are nearly there," he said. "Camelot is just over the next rise."

*Aislyn knelt by her window, staring up at the moon, too happy to even think of sleeping. Camelot! She was going to Camelot! She hugged herself, wondering if it was possible to die of joy. She could imagine it so clearly, the two of them riding down the road, Gawain laughing as he took her hand—and there it would be, just as he had described it to her. The new rose garden—"It's only mud and twigs so far, but one day it will be beautiful"—the proud battlements and lofty towers, the bright—*

Pennants. There they were, splashes of color against gray stone, the standards of visiting nobility hung according to their rank with the crimson Pendragon banner over all, its golden serpent writhing as it snapped in the breeze.

It was all just as he had said, exactly as she had seen it in her dreams. And here she was riding over the crest of the hill with Gawain beside her, on the way to their wedding.

She gave an inelegant snort of laughter. If this didn't teach her to be careful what she wished for, she didn't know what would.

• • •

THEY did not go to the main entrance, but to a private courtyard apparently belonging to the king. It was a pretty little place, surrounded on two sides by low stone walls twined with trailing honeysuckle just coming into flower. It must smell lovely here, Aislyn thought with an inward sigh. Unfortunately, she could not smell anything but herself at the moment.

Just as they reached the entrance, Gawain halted. "Sire," he said. "A favor, if you would."

"Good God, do you think I would refuse you anything?" The king shot Aislyn a look of deepest disgust. "Name it and it is yours."

Aislyn's stiff fingers clenched on the reins. What was this? Had Gawain thought of a way out? Or did he only mean to be rewarded for his sacrifice?

Impossible to tell from his face. When had he become so adept at concealing his thoughts? "Then I would ask that you do not disclose to anyone what has befallen us today, save that you succeeded in your quest."

"Not *disclose*—? But—but how else to explain—" Arthur broke off abruptly. "Yes, all right. Whatever you like." And for the first time since they'd set out, he smiled.

Aislyn eyed Gawain suspiciously as they entered the courtyard. What was he up to? Was he going to attempt to buy her off? Have her banished? Wring her neck and stuff her down the well?

"Arthur!"

For the first time, Aislyn noticed a young woman sitting on a bench beside the castle wall. She leapt to her feet, the book she had been reading falling from her hands.

Raven hair waved softly about the pure oval of her face and her eyes were luminous between starry lashes as she ran to the king as though she meant to throw herself into his arms. Two paces from him, she halted, blushing—like a rose, Aislyn thought, a stab of bitter envy piercing her heart—and, taking her trailing skirts in her slender white hands, sank gracefully to the flagstones.

"My lord," she said formally. "I was—it is good to have you back."

The king, who had started toward her, halted, his arms falling stiffly to his sides. "Guin—my lady," Arthur corrected himself quickly. "How kind of you to wait for me."

"It was no trouble," Queen Guinevere replied.

What was the *matter* with these people? Aislyn wondered, staring from the king to the queen. Did they always act like two villagers in a bad pageant, or only when others were there to see?

Gawain swung himself from Gringolet.

"My queen," he said with frosty courtesy, going down upon one knee.

Guinevere wrested her gaze from the king to the golden-haired knight kneeling before her. "Sir Gawain," she said with all the enthusiasm of a woman presented with a posy of dead blossoms. "So you are back, as well."

Aislyn's gaze sharpened. *Either the two of you detest each other,* she thought, *or you're putting on a very good show. I wonder which it is?*

"Yes," Gawain said, rising and turning to help Aislyn from her horse. She groaned as her feet hit the ground and Gawain, surprising her, handed her the staff strapped to her saddle. "May I present . . . ?"

Only then did Aislyn realize that no one had bothered to ask her name. "Dame . . . Ragnelle," she croaked, using that of a demon in a pageant she'd once seen.

Guinevere backed up a step, raising one trailing sleeve to her nose, her lovely face twisted with disgust. "What do you mean by bringing this—this—"

"Guinevere," Arthur began, "let me explain. You see—" He broke off, obviously remembering his promise. "We can talk about this later," he finished lamely.

They were up to something. Gawain had a plan—of course he did, Aislyn should have known victory could never be so easy. He meant to—to imprison her. Of course! She should have thought of that before. Toss her into some dark dungeon, lock the door, and throw the key into the river—

"Dame Ragnelle and I are to be wed," Gawain said. "Today, if possible."

Guinevere's pink lips parted in astonishment. Arthur rounded on Gawain, anger and amazement warring on his face.

"These young men!" Aislyn cackled, hobbling forward to rest a claw on Gawain's arm. "Think a wedding feast can be conjured from the air! Me and you know better, don't we, Your Grace? But don't bother yourself, whatever you can manage will suit me well enough. Let's face it, dearie," she said, dropping Guinevere a wink, "at my age, I can't afford to stand on ceremony."

Guinevere's jaw dropped a little further. She turned to her husband, but Arthur only nodded, still looking at Gawain.

"If that is what Sir Gawain wants," he said, tight-lipped. "We shall, of course, oblige him. Won't we, my lady?"

"I—I—" Clearly at a loss, Guinevere stared from her husband to his nephew. "Are you quite certain, Sir Gawain?"

"Quite," he replied with such frigid dignity that Guinevere was silenced. "Would you be so kind as to see that Dame Ragnelle has all she requires?"

*"Me?"* The word came out as a squeak, and again, Guinevere looked to her husband. This time Arthur met her gaze straight on.

"I would consider it a personal favor, my lady." He drew Guinevere aside and added in a lower voice, "Don't say anything about the wedding yet."

"As you wish. Well, then, Dame . . . Ragnelle," Guinevere said with infinite distaste. "If you would step this way . . ."

"Ta, love." Aislyn waggled her twisted fingers at Gawain. "I'll see you in a bit."

She followed the queen inside and up a long corridor. "Not so fast," she grumbled, "I ain't as spry as I used to be." Guinevere slowed, allowing Aislyn to catch up to her.

The queen's face was a study of revulsion and curiosity. Eventually, as Aislyn had suspected it might, curiosity won.

"This is all so sudden," she said. She attempted a light laugh, though it came out somewhat strangled due to Aislyn's close proximity. "How long have you known Sir Gawain?"

"Known him? I can't say as I know him at all," Aislyn replied, which was true enough. Once she'd thought she did, but she'd soon learned the folly of that assumption. "What woman really knows her man before they're wed?"

Guinevere shot her a startled look. "True, but . . ." She hesitated, pearly teeth worrying her full lower lip. "How did you meet?"

" 'Twas a lucky chance." Aislyn cut off further questions by the simple expedient of smiling. Guinevere gasped, one hand flying to her slender throat. "I expect you're thinking I'm a bit old," she went on, "and I can't deny I had my doubts. But I said to myself—Ragnelle, I said, you don't get such an offer every day—or even every century. If it doesn't worry him, who are you to fuss?"

Guinevere gazed at her, her face working with some emotion Aislyn could not immediately name. The queen's lips trembled—was she about to weep? But no, a tiny giggle escaped her before she managed to compose herself. "Yes," she said. "I see. How very interesting."

Interesting indeed. So the act had been no act at all. No friend of Sir Gawain could possibly find this situation comical.

*That's something we have in common,* Aislyn thought, wondering why she could not bring herself to like the queen. But then, she doubted Guinevere had many women friends at all, not looking like she did. Aislyn remembered how that felt, and thought that under different circumstances, she and Guinevere might have gotten on well together. For she—like Guinevere, she suspected—had never known what it was to be jealous of another woman's beauty.

Until today.

Feeling oddly out of sorts, she stomped into a bare chamber with a large cask in the center.

Guinevere pulled a cord and a moment later, a serving girl arrived. "Fill the bath," the queen ordered. "Have you anything to wear, good dame?" she added to Aislyn.

"Happens I do. My bag's still on my horse."

"I will see that it is brought to you. If there is anything you need, just ask one of the serving maids."

*What I need is to change back before I really am as old*

*as I seem to be,* Aislyn thought moodily as the cask was filled. *What I need is to find some place Morgause won't look, and get there.* But she couldn't be safer than she was right here, and until she thought of something better, here she would remain.

The bath was filled and after much vehement whispering among the serving girls, one was pushed forward. She was a frightened little miss of perhaps fourteen, and gulping audibly, offered to help Aislyn bathe.

"Go along," she said roughly. "All of you. I reckon I can manage on my own."

Alone, she regarded the steaming bath, longing to immerse her aching joints in its warmth, but she had used the last of her foul asafetida potion earlier. On reflection, though, she thought the point had been made and sank into the water with a sigh, looking down at her slack breasts and wrinkled belly with a shiver of disgust.

*Queen Morgause of Orkney slipped her hand beneath Aislyn's chin and lifted her face. "You are very beautiful, my dear."*

*Aislyn swayed upon her feet, sick with disappointment. Had she failed, then? Did she have no gift for magic after all? Perhaps what she had done was not so unusual as she had thought; mayhap every maiden at this strange court could gaze into crystal water and see their queen and recite what she was doing, though that lady was in another chamber at the far end of the keep. Had she been inaccurate in her description? Or—sharp fear stabbed her belly—had she imagined the entire vision, her need to see overwhelming her good sense?*

*As the queen continued to regard her, she stood silent, willing herself not to weep. What was there to say? Yes, she was beautiful. To deny it would be futile; to express gratitude, a lie. But a fair face had availed her nothing when the battering ram sounded at the gates. It was power she had needed then; the power to rain destruction on the armored men streaming into the courtyard, but all she could do was flee the advancing enemy. What matter if she was the fairest maid in all of Britain? She was still a beggar at Queen Morgause's court.*

*"Do not scorn the power of beauty," Morgause reproved her. "Only a fool does not wield every weapon at her disposal." The queen released her and sat back. "You have a rare gift, Aislyn, as did your mother at your age. But as I told her then, there is no point in teaching you if you do not mean to carry on with it. Any of my knights would have you gladly, dowry or no."*

*"No!" Aislyn cried. "I do not wish to marry!"*

*Morgause's brows lifted. "Whyever not?"*

*"My father—when he died—you know what happened then! My mother could do nothing to prevent it. And I want no man to rule me," she added fiercely.*

*"What has that to do with marriage?" Morgause asked, amused. "I was married for many years, you know."*

*Aislyn made a helpless gesture. "But you are not like other women."*

*"No," Morgause agreed with a complacent smile, "I am not."*

*"I want to be like you," Aislyn said. "Teach me magic—take me into your service."*

*"Come, sit by me," the queen ordered, gesturing to the cushioned window seat beside her chair. "Some wine? And do try one of these oatcakes—"*

*Aislyn was caught between embarrassment and hunger as the queen served her. The weeks she had spent upon the road had left her so empty that she sometimes thought she would never eat her fill.*

*"Have another—here, take them all," Morgause said, handing her the dish. "There, now we are comfortable! I will teach you, and you will do me a small service in return."*

*"Anything!" Aislyn declared, speaking around a mouthful of oatcake.*

*"My eldest son, Gawain—you have heard of him, no doubt—was taken from me when he was but a boy. My half brother, Arthur, insisted that Gawain be fostered at his court, for he knew well it would break my heart to be parted from my child. Not content with that, Arthur has twisted Gawain's mind." The queen rose suddenly and paced her solar, her slender body taut and shaking with the force of her emotion. "He has turned my son against me," she said, the words catching in her throat, "against his clan. You will bring him back to us."*

*"Me?" Aislyn squeaked.*

*"Yes, you." Morgause stood before her. "So young and fair—and Gawain is his father's son. He will want you—I imagine most men do. You will say to him the words I give to you, you will teach him to remember his duty to his own. And in return . . ."*

*Morgause took Aislyn's hand between her own. "Oh, look here, child! I think—yes, I do believe I see a great future for you." Her fingertip traced Aislyn's palm. "What is this? A crown? Would you like that, child?"*

*"Yes," Aislyn breathed, almost dizzy with the thought. "Yes, madam, I would."*

*"You will find me very generous to those who serve me well," Morgause said. "As for those who do not . . ." She dropped Aislyn's hand, her eyes suddenly hard. "Let us hope you have no cause to find out."*

# Chapter 3

• • •

"I am not saying she should leave empty-handed," Arthur argued. "She can have a manor—*two* manors—a duchy—"

"She refused all those before," Gawain said patiently, "and I have given her my word."

Arthur flung himself into a seat. "I know, you are right, but have you considered that you are my heir? What if I die tomorrow? Do you seriously expect to put that—that—*thing* on the throne as queen of Britain?"

Gawain had considered this already, during the ride back to Camelot. It was the reason he had requested this audience with Arthur, fearing that the king had not thought of it himself. "It is a problem," he said.

"A *problem*? It's a bit more than that, Gawain."

"Then you will have to name another heir."

"Another—? Who, Agravaine? He'd have the clans at each others' throats in no time. Gareth? Gaheris? They're just boys!"

"No younger than I was when you—"

Arthur crashed his fist down on the table. "*You* are my heir and as your liege lord, I forbid this marriage."

"It is too late for that," Gawain said quietly. "We accepted her help—"

"You mean I did."

"I mean *we* did. No other choice was possible for us or for Britain. She named a price; I agreed to it. There is no honorable way to withdraw."

Arthur buried his face in his hands. "How could I have allowed this? How could I have let you—"

"I am not the first man to marry from expediency, or even the first to wed a woman older than myself. It is a common enough arrangement, Arthur."

"She's not old—she's ancient. She is . . . *loathly*. But I don't suppose she can live forever," Arthur said, the words coming muffled from behind his hands.

"I expect not."

"You could send her off to Orkney." Arthur raised his head, his expression brightening. "You'd never have to lay eyes on her again."

"That I cannot do," Gawain said. "I'm sorry—I thought you heard. It was a condition. She said that once we married, we could not live in separate households."

"And you *agreed*?"

"I did." Gawain looked down at his folded hands, his chest tightening at the thought of leaving Camelot. "If she is so repugnant to you," he said carefully, "I could go with her to Orkney—"

"No! It's bad enough I've spoiled your life, I won't have you exiled, too. I need you with me." Arthur sighed heavily. "I suppose we'll just have to put up with the loathly lady."

The pressure in Gawain's chest eased. "I am sorry, Arthur," he began.

"For what? Saving my life? Don't be a fool." The king stood and walked to the door. There he hesitated as if he meant to say more, but in the end he walked out without speaking.

Gawain stared at the closed door, then bent his golden head and rested his brow on his clenched fist.

# Chapter 4

• • •

AISLYN had just put the veil over her head when one of the queen's waiting women arrived to escort her to the hall. She didn't know the lady's name; the haughty bitch hadn't bothered to introduce herself, obviously not finding the crone worth the effort.

*So this is Camelot,* Aislyn thought, following the lady's slim, straight back and wealth of bobbing curls as quickly as she could manage on her aching feet. *I can't say I care for it so far.*

Her opinion was improved when she reached the hall. The company was very fine—as fine as ever she'd imagined. The ladies were all young and pretty—*though none are as beautiful as I,* a small voice whispered in her mind—clad in flowing gowns with ribbons and flowers twined into their hair. Their hands were soft, their faces bright with youth and innocence as they chattered together, their musical voices interspersed with many a burst of laughter as they glanced sideways at the knights.

The objects of their admiration lounged about with

studied unconcern, as dashing a collection of young bloods as Aislyn had ever seen. A few were dressed in tunics that rose daringly above the knee, a fashion she had not seen before but wholeheartedly approved, though most wore more conventional robes. Their deep voices provided a pleasant counterpoint to the light laughter of the ladies.

"You don't think it's the Saxons, do you?" Aislyn's escort cried, joining a small group of knights.

"What else?" one said, his face glowing with excitement.

Aislyn stood forgotten in the doorway, watching them go through the eternal ritual of courtship: a sigh here, a smile there; a scarf dropped as if by chance, its owner waiting anxiously until her chosen knight retrieved it or passed by, pretending not to see. She drank it all in greedily, the sounds and scents and brilliant colors, and longed with all her heart to be among them. Oh, to wear such gowns again! To braid her hair with silken ribbons and walk proudly into such a company—why, she could capture any of these knights with just a smile!

Every one of the five years that had been lost to her was like a coal burning in her heart. At twenty-one, she knew herself still beautiful, but she would be among the eldest of these maidens. The first blush of her youth was gone forever, stolen by a faithless knight, and nothing could ever bring it back.

A small ripple passed across the hall and silence fell.

"Good people." That was the king's voice, coming from the far end of the hall. Aislyn pushed through the crowd until she glimpsed him standing on the dais before his throne, looking as grave as though he was about to announce a death.

"I have called you hither," he said mournfully, "to witness the marriage of my nephew, Sir Gawain."

The ladies gasped. The men looked at each other with much shrugging and shaking of heads. "Where is Dame Ragnelle?" the king called out.

Heads turned; people stood on tiptoe, looking about. Aislyn drew a deep breath.

"Here I am, Your Grace!" she called. "Step aside, now, let me through."

The crowd fell back before her, leaving an aisle leading to the far end of the hall, where Gawain stood beneath the largest window Aislyn had ever seen, a shaft of sunlight burning in his hair. He looks like his own ghost, she thought, and for a moment her heart smote her. Then she remembered the night he rode away from Lothian—

*The cobblestones cut into her knees, but Aislyn scarcely noticed. She could not move. She could not think. She could only kneel where he had left her, each heartbeat like a hammer blow.* Gone. He is gone. What will you do now? *It seemed an iron band encircled her chest, pulling tighter, tighter . . . she struggled vainly to draw breath, but even when the last air had been driven from her lungs the relentless pounding still went on.* Fool. He has betrayed you. Where will you run now? *Grief gathered like a wave—and then it broke, crushing her beneath it as a wrenching sob tore through her and ripped her heart in two.*

—and smiled beneath her veil. On either side people were whispering behind their hands as she hobbled up the aisle. Let them wonder. Let them speculate. Whatever they were expecting, they couldn't possibly be prepared for what was hidden by this veil—the same veil she had once placed over her wealth of red-gold hair with trembling hands, imagining the moment when Gawain would lift it. How they would all stare, that foolish girl had thought, knowing she would strike them dumb.

Well, they'd be stricken dumb today.

At last, Aislyn reached Gawain. "Took me a bit, but I'm here now," she puffed.

"So am I." He looked down at her gravely, then turned to the priest. "Good Father," he said, "let us begin."

The words were said, the vows made. And then at last the moment came. With hands that shook only slightly, Gawain raised the veil.

Someone gasped. Another cried out in shock. Several ladies burst into tears. Gawain gazed down at her in silence, his expression showing nothing. This was it, the moment of her triumph. Oddly enough, it felt very like that moment in the courtyard, for her heart was thudding and she could not catch her breath. But this time she did not waste a moment weeping. Instead, she laughed, a harsh and ugly cackle that tore at her like rending sobs.

# Chapter 5

• • •

"STILL alive?" Queen Morgause spoke in her most dangerously soft voice. The two knights who had accompanied her champion exchanged nervous glances, and as one they stepped back from the entrance to her pavilion and melted into the shadow of the trees. "Did you tell me he is *still alive*?"

"Eh? What's that you say?"

Somer Gromer Jour—Lord of the Summer's Day, as she had named him in a flight of fancy—stood before the queen, resplendent in mail so finely linked that it rippled like water when he moved. His helm was of the bucket variety, silver-washed and gleaming, with only a narrow slit at eye level.

Morgause gripped the arms of her chair. "Did you say the king is not dead?" she asked, raising her voice.

The knight pulled off his helm to reveal a lad of some twenty summers, with curling auburn hair flattened to his skull. His face was pleasingly proportioned, his features regular, unremarkable save for his eyes, which were wide-spaced to an unusual degree. The effect was rather more attractive than otherwise, and at first glance he was quite a good-looking young man. Indeed, he was very nearly arrestingly handsome . . . though somehow he just missed that distinction. Feature by feature, it was difficult to say precisely why, only that there was something oddly lacking in the whole. Perhaps it was in his smile, eager and a trifle vapid, or his eyes, empty of any spark of intelligence and purpose. But Morgause had never been inclined to look deeply beneath the surface of any handsome face.

"What?" he said again. "Sorry, I can't hear anything in that helm."

"You feckless, witless fool!" she cried. "Do you dare tell me that you failed?"

"Well, he had the answer, didn't he?" Somer Gromer Jour—who usually went by the more prosaic name of Launfal—said defensively. "So I had to let him go, didn't I? I mean, that was the agreement, what?"

"The answer? *He had the answer?* But that is impossible!"

Launfal shrugged. "He did."

"Where," Morgause asked distinctly, "did he get it? Or did you not think to ask?"

"I asked," Launfal said hastily. "Of course I did. But he only said that was his affair and no part of our bargain."

"Oh, did he really?" Morgause sank back in her seat and drummed her fingers on the armrest of the chair. "Well," she said after a moment, "I think we both know there is only one place he could have found it."

Launfal's brow furrowed. "Is there? Where?"

Morgause sighed. For a moment she had forgotten to whom she spoke. "He had it from your sister, you brainless dolt!"

"Sister?" he repeated slowly. "What, you mean Aislyn? Why would it be her?"

"I *told* you—" Morgause broke off, realizing there was no point in reminding him of their earlier conversation. Launfal didn't understand half of what she said, and what he did understand, he soon forgot. Luckily for him, it was not for his mind that she kept him. "It doesn't matter now."

"I don't see how you work out it was her," Launfal said, his broad brow drawn into a puzzled frown. "He's been asking for a full year now, anyone could have—"

"He did not know it when he set out from Camelot, my informants were quite certain on that point. So somewhere on the way . . ." She rose swiftly to her feet. "*This* time I shall have her. Guards!" she cried. "Guards, to me! Saddle my horse, we ride at once! Not you," she snapped at Launfal, who had donned his helm again and taken a few steps toward the door.

"Eh? Did you say something?"

She seized the helm and pulled it from his head. "Not *you*!"

His full lips turned down sulkily. "I don't see why I shouldn't come. She's *my* sister, after all."

Morgause regarded him narrowly. "She is."

"Well, then, I think I should be allowed to go."

There were times Morgause wondered if Launfal could possibly be what he seemed. Once she'd even gone so far as to question his mother—her own servant—and Olwyn had said with undisguised contempt, "The boy is little better than an imbecile. He was a seven-month babe and never quite right in the head."

Morgause, braced for a lie, had detected none in Olwyn's voice or eyes. But still, there was something . . . wrong about Launfal today. She could not put it more clearly than that, but Morgause had not earned the title of Queen of Air and Darkness by ignoring her instincts.

"You could have been back here long ago, but you lingered, didn't you? *Didn't you?*" she demanded, her voice rising to a shriek. "You knew it was Aislyn! Admit it!"

He started back, a look of comical astonishment on his face. "Me? Of course not! The thought never crossed my mind!"

*Not many do.* Morgause's lips twitched, her suspicion dying as suddenly as it had flared. What had she been thinking? That he could possibly deceive her? That he would even imagine attempting such a thing? No, Launfal was as he was, no more and no less. And while he did not have much in the way of brains, that was part of his attraction. He was young and strong and beautiful . . . a man fashioned for a woman's pleasure.

"Then where have you been? The truth, now!"

He flung himself to the ground before her. "I was sick. You can ask the others if you don't believe me. They laughed," he added resentfully, "but they don't understand. I can't bear to displease you, and I was afraid that you'd be angry. But it wasn't my fault!"

Even as she cast an impatient glance over her shoulder, knowing she should already be on her way, Morgause could not resist the sight of him down upon his knees. "Say you aren't angry!" he begged. "You must!"

She looked into his eyes, so clear and empty, and saw herself reflected there: beautiful beyond the dreams of men, all-powerful and infinitely desirable. She drew the tip of one finger from his temple to his jaw, then dealt him a stinging blow across the cheek. "You presume too much."

He seized her hand and pressed it to his lips. "Forgive me, I did not mean—it is only that I cannot live without—"

"Yes, yes, I know. Very well, you are forgiven. But you are not coming with me. Wait here for my return."

"Yes, madam, as you wish. I won't stir a step."

Morgause reached the entrance to the pavilion and looked back with an exasperated sigh. "Oh, do get up, Launfal. You don't have to stay just there."

"Of course!" He scrambled to his feet. "Right. I'll just . . ."

He looked around blankly.

"Why don't you have a wash?" Morgause suggested. "Then eat something and go to bed."

"A wash. Food. *Bed.*" That was a word he never failed to understand. A pleasant warmth stirred in her belly as he shot her a heated look beneath half-lowered lids. "Don't be too long."

Morgause smiled indulgently. "No longer than I must."

• • •

LAUNFAL'S eyes were no longer empty as he watched Morgause walk away, but blazing in a face as bleakly beautiful as a winter's moor. Had Morgause bothered to look back, she would scarce have known him.

But Morgause did not look back. Launfal knew she wouldn't. Had she begun to guess how well he knew her she would have been astonished—and deeply affronted that she was not the mystery she thought herself. If she learned he had feigned illness to give Aislyn the chance to flee—had, in fact, delayed Morgause for another quarter of an hour with his nonsense—she would likely have him whipped. And she would watch every moment of it, drinking in his agony with the same expression she wore when he pleasured her in bed.

Oh, yes, he knew her. He knew her very well.

"God help you, Aislyn," he said aloud, then a hard smile touched his lips. God had abandoned their family long ago. They were in the hands of a demon now, one who walked the earth in a woman's form. "Run," he breathed. "Run fast and far."

Aislyn would. She had always been the clever one. And she would not look back, for she never had before. He doubted she even remembered she had a brother, let alone wasted a moment in wondering what had become of him.

And why should she? He was as much an imbecile as Morgause thought him. Who *but* an imbecile would have just thrown away his one chance to escape this life that was killing him by inches?

He'd planned it all so carefully, choosing the precise words with which to convince King Arthur that he had no intention of slaying him, had never harbored any such intent, and that he himself was a loyal subject in need of the king's aid. He'd have only a few moments in which to say those words, for Morgause's guards would be posted near at hand, but the king was said to be quick of understanding. He would surely realize it was the truth when Launfal did not attempt to exact the terrible penalty for the king's failure.

The one thing Launfal had not anticipated was that the king would not fail; that he would, in fact, have the very answer Morgause had sworn he could not know. Morgause had been certain that none but Aislyn could give it to him, and Launfal had been equally certain that his sister was long dead. Why he had been so sure he could not say, save for his belief that had she lived, she would have found a way to contact him, an assumption as ridiculous as it was pathetic.

All this had flashed through his mind in the moment the king stopped speaking. Launfal's careful plans were blasted into ruins, but even so, he might have managed to win the king's aid. The risk would have been nothing to him had it been merely his own life at stake, but now it was Aislyn's, as well, and he had not known where she was or whether to speak would bring her into danger.

And so his chance had slipped away, all for the sake of a sister who despised him. "Nit," she used to call him, and though now it seemed trivial, at the time the pain had been quite real. It wasn't so much the name, though it was hardly flattering, but that Aislyn knew how it hurt him to be mocked for his size. He'd made the mistake of showing it, and so the name had stuck, others taking it up until he nearly forgot he'd ever had another.

*Nit.* It no longer fit his stature, yet there was a certain truth to it, though *fool* would be closer to the mark. You would think that by now he would have learned that the first lesson of survival was to think only of himself. Everyone else knew it, after all, Aislyn first and foremost. It could only be some errant scrap of honor that had driven him to folly, the dying remnant of the knight he might have been.

Somer Gromer Jour—Lord of the Summer's Day. What a joke. He was lord of nothing but his own ruin.

But perhaps Aislyn would have better fortune.

# Chapter 6

• • •

THE stale heel of a loaf had been Aislyn's breakfast; her supper the night before, a handful of boiled oats and a few walnuts. She had long since forgotten what it was to eat for pleasure rather than to merely keep herself alive, and when the doors leading to the kitchens were thrown open, the scents were enough to make her dizzy. When the varlets began to stream into the hall with platters on their shoulders, her knees grew weak and her stomach rumbled noisily.

She and Gawain were seated at the high table—Gawain at the king's right hand and Aislyn beside him, with the young brown-haired knight who had stood up with Gawain to her right. She spared him only a quick glance before her attention was riveted by the dishes appearing before her—suckling pig, parsnips and onions swimming in oil, manchet bread and pots of butter, barley in a fragrant gravy studded with currants—

She gazed at it all, barely able to stop herself from seizing everything in sight. But why should she stop herself?

The crone wouldn't. Laughing inwardly, she grabbed a slice of pork and stuffed it in her mouth, moaning aloud as the various flavors of meat and pepper and garlic exploded in her mouth.

The tusks made chewing a disgusting business, but the horrified stares of her tablemates only added to her enjoyment, for she had quite destroyed their appetites. They merely picked at the delicacies, faces turned away. At the lower tables, conversation was muted, and several of the ladies sobbed openly.

Gawain ate nothing. That was no surprise. She didn't imagine he'd have much appetite just now. What did surprise her was that he didn't drown his troubles in drink. He lifted his goblet once, took a small sip, and put it down again, where it remained untouched for the remainder of the meal.

And it was very good wine, or so it seemed to Aislyn, who had not tasted any for five weary years. She finished one goblet quickly and a second more slowly, savoring each drop. When it was done, she reached for the flagon. Gawain's hand grasped it first and moved it beyond her reach.

"That is enough," he said.

"Eh? Who are you to—"

"Your husband." He set a pitcher of water beside her empty goblet. "Drink that if you thirst."

"Now, look here, lad, if you think you can tell me what to drink and when, you are mistaken."

"No, it is you who are mistaken," he said with icy courtesy, "if you think I will shirk my duty to protect you, even from your own folly."

"Protect—?"

"My lady will not demean herself or me by drinking to excess."

*His* lady, was she? Once those words would have been enough to make her weep with joy, but now she only fixed him a steely gaze. "I've been looking after myself for years, laddie. If you think I will obey—"

"As you have just promised to do so, I believe I am within my rights to expect it. Should you wish to discuss the matter further, we can do so privately, but I refuse to quarrel in public. No," he added, holding up a hand as she began to protest, "I have said all that I intend to say on the subject. If you cannot conduct yourself as befits your station, I shall have you escorted to your chamber."

Having delivered this pronouncement, he turned away, leaving Aislyn to stare at his profile in shock.

Was this really Gawain? When had he grown so prim and dreary? The first thing she had noticed about him long ago—well, the second really, the first being that he was over six feet tall with a face like a young angel and a smile like the rising sun—was his sense of fun.

When you were with Gawain, everything was an adventure, even if you were just walking through places you'd visited a hundred times before. Look, he said, and she looked to find herself in a world that was new and vibrantly alive. It was all so beautiful, the burn rushing over the stones in a streak of white, a curiously shaped boulder, the first blossoms on a cherry tree. He'd picked one and tucked it behind her ear, his fingertips brushing her cheek—

She had forgotten that day. She had made herself forget, because to remember hurt too much. That was the day they'd found the kittens, bobbing down the millstream in a sack. Gawain had spotted it, of course, for there was nothing that escaped his notice, and where anyone else would have passed by, he'd wondered what it was. Once he'd wondered, he had to know, and he'd fished it out and dried the kittens off—how he'd laughed when they climbed all over him, and she had laughed, too, sitting beneath the cherry tree . . .

That was the day he had kissed her.

*Don't look back,* she told herself. It was all long ago and best forgotten. Five years stood between her and the girl she had been then: five years to understand that she had lost all hope of security—let alone of happiness. Five years of flight, of exile in a dingy little hut, existing but only half alive.

Five years that Gawain had spent serving his king, surrounded by his friends, living the life he'd always wanted and winning fame and glory.

She turned to the knight on her other side, who had been listening to her exchange with Gawain with shameless interest. He was a year or two older than Gawain, she thought, with smooth, dark hair caught back carelessly at his neck. His face was lean, his eyes very bright in his pale face. Throughout the meal he had not spoken to anyone, but stared into space, his fingers tapping out a restless rhythm on the trestle. Now he did not shrink from her perusal, but regarded her with those unsettling eyes, nothing but curiosity in his expression. She had been introduced to him, but could not recall his name. Brandon, she thought, or Darmuid . . .

"Sir Dinadan," he supplied.

"Right." She was a bit annoyed that he'd followed her thoughts so easily, so she gave him her best smile. He leaned a little closer, gazing fascinated at her teeth. "A friend of Sir Gawain's, are you?"

His eyes flicked up to hers. "Yes," he said decidedly. "I have that honor. We met years ago, after the—" He lowered his voice. "—the rebellion."

"Which one?" Aislyn helped herself to his wine. He grinned, revealing unexpected dimples.

"The first one, just after King Arthur came to the throne."

Aislyn nodded. Some of Britain's most powerful barons had thought pulling a sword from a stone was insufficient proof of Arthur's lineage and had sought to relieve him of his crown. Gawain's father, King Lot, had been chief among them.

"Was your father one of the rebels?" she asked.

"Alas, he was." Dinadan took the wine from her. She opened her mouth to protest, but he merely sipped and handed it back, a show of good will that could not have come easily. She lifted it to him before she drank, acknowledging the gesture.

"Father always was a fool," he went on. "Afterward, many of the rebels' sons were sent to court to be trained as knights."

A nice way of putting it, Aislyn thought, when what they'd really been was hostages to their sires' continued loyalty.

"And you are still here," she said.

"Indeed. King Arthur is Britain's best hope against the Saxons," he said, and all the humor vanished from his expression. "That alone would keep me at his side. The Saxons are a curse," he added, raising his voice slightly. "I would see every one of them driven back into the sea."

"Not quite all, surely?" Aislyn glanced past him to the tall Saxon lord seated on his other side, who she vaguely recalled was one of the king's allies. The man stiffened, his eyes narrowing.

*"All."* Dinadan leaned back, an ironic smile curling his thin lips. "I mistrust these treaty troops," he said, not bothering to lower his voice. The Saxon glared at him, then turned pointedly away. "Gawain does not agree with me," Dinadan went on in a drawl, though his long fingers were busy tearing a hunk of bread to pieces. "All the king does is well done in his eyes. But years ago, when I was a child, I was taken prisoner in a Saxon raid upon my home." He dropped the bread and took the wine from her again. "Seven years of slavery are not easily forgotten."

"No, I expect they wouldn't be."

He smiled and waved a hand, banishing the subject. "Tell me about you and Gawain. How did you come to marry so suddenly?"

"True love strikes fast."

He laughed and heads turned in their direction. Aislyn fancied he rather enjoyed shocking them, and she warmed to him, feeling she had found a kindred spirit. "I must confess, lady, that I have no idea what to make of you."

"Good."

He offered her the wine again, but she refused. Though she'd never admit it, Gawain was right. She'd had enough. A bit more, in fact, and she might give into the temptation to share her jest with Sir Dinadan, who seemed to her a man who might enjoy it. Instead she turned from him back to Gawain.

Holy Mother, but he was a handsome wight. Different, though, from the lad she remembered. That Gawain had been a blooded warrior already, but merry-hearted, too, always ready with a jest. She had yet to see him smile today—small wonder, considering—but she fancied the change in him went deeper than this marriage.

They called Gawain the Courteous Knight, and she'd always wondered why, for though he'd been mannerly enough when she knew him, she would hardly have called that his defining feature. But no song had ever praised him for the qualities that had captured her five years ago: his impulsive generosity, his high spirits, the honesty that always took her unawares. Strange how honesty was always referred to as blunt. His had been sharp as a dagger, slicing through all her glittering ambitions to reveal them for the tawdry things they were.

Or no, she thought, resting her chin on her hand, it was the fierceness of his idealism that had won her. Many and many an argument they'd had over it, too; first because, mindful of her duty to Queen Morgause, she had attempted to draw Gawain away from King Arthur and back to the loyalty he owed his clan. Later she had argued for her own sake, for she could not believe in the new Britain Gawain described to her, a place where every subject, no matter what their station, was entitled to the king's protection. A land where a widow could not be driven from her home simply because she lacked the ability to defend herself against a greedy neighbor.

A land where justice was every subject's right, not a gift to be purchased at the cost of a girl's body . . . and her soul.

Aislyn had not dared to believe such things could really be. But argue as she would, no words of hers could quench the fire that consumed Gawain, and in the attempt she had only succeeded in catching his vision like a fever.

Sir Gawain the Courteous? That was far too tame a title for the young warrior she'd known. But it suited the man beside her now.

There was a look of chill austerity about him that matched the tales she'd heard of him of late. Sir Gawain the Chaste, she'd heard him named, and though at first she'd laughed, remembering certain passages between them, she had never heard another woman's name linked with his. His was too lofty a spirit to surrender itself to the dark urges to which all men were prey—or so the stories went—and no mere woman could ever win a heart so devoted to his God and king.

Not for lack of trying, Aislyn thought eyeing the weeping maidens throughout the hall. But Gawain did not seem to regard them in the least. Even when one forgot herself entirely and called out, "Mercy, sire! Whatever Sir Gawain has done, have pity on him!" he only glanced briefly in her direction, brows slightly lifted as she was helped, sobbing, from the hall. A ripple of uncomfortable laughter passed among the courtiers, but Gawain did not seem to hear it, save that his lips pressed a bit more firmly together.

A pity, Aislyn thought, regarding the grim set of his mouth. He'd had a most enchanting smile. He'd certainly enchanted her . . .

*And you're lucky you didn't die of it,* she reminded herself sternly.

She picked at the remains of her meal, but her hunger

had long been satisfied. She was just wondering how long they would have to sit here when the great doors opened and a warm, blossom-scented breeze rushed in. "Sir Lancelot du Lac," a page announced, and suddenly the hall sprang to life.

Guinevere sat up very straight, her face vivid with excitement. The king looked over toward the door, as well, his expression brightening. Aislyn craned her neck to see this newcomer, but he was surrounded by a group of knights, all talking at once as they gestured toward the high table.

*"What?"* The voice rang out across the hall. "You're joking!" And then she did see him; a slender, dark-haired youth in a fine crimson cloak. He saw her, as well. Astonishment and disbelief chased each other across his fine-boned features before he burst into a merry laugh.

Gawain went very still. Only a single muscle leapt in his clenched jaw as the youth approached the high table, moving with lithe grace across the floor.

"My lady," the young man said, sweeping Guinevere a bow. "What news is this I hear? Did I really miss a wedding?"

"Indeed," Guinevere replied. "Sir Gawain was wed this day." The two looked at each other, then away. Guinevere bit her lips and the young man gave a sudden burst of laughter which he tried vainly to pass off as a cough.

"Lancelot," King Arthur said, the single word a warning.

Every trace of merriment vanished from Lancelot's face. Gravely respectful, he made the king a bow. "Sire," he said. "I am glad to be back."

"And I am glad to see you," Arthur said, relenting enough to smile. "Later you must tell me all your adventures." He looked pointedly toward Gawain; Lancelot took the hint and turned.

"*Sir* Gawain," he said. "It seems congratulations are in order."

"Thank you. Lady Ragnelle, may I present Sir Lancelot du Lac?"

Lancelot bowed. "I'm so sorry to have missed the wedding. I'm sure you were a lovely bride."

Cheeky boy. "Either your sight is failing or you're making mock of an old woman," she retorted tartly. "Which is it?"

He blinked, disconcerted, but only for a moment. "Every lady is beautiful on her wedding day," he said with a charming smile.

"Well, you're a sweet lad, aren't you?" she said, amused. "Would you like to kiss the bride?"

Panic flickered across his handsome face. "I—I do not dare. Sir Gawain would not like it," he added, long, dark lashes veiling his eyes. "I would not want to offend."

Aislyn let out a snort of laughter and waved a hand. "Perhaps another time."

"What have you been up to, Lancelot?" Sir Dinadan asked. "Slain any dragons lately? Bested any giants? Rescued a few maidens in distress?"

Lancelot's smile altered; suddenly it was not so charming anymore. "I've been keeping myself busy. And you? Lost any tournaments lately? Or have you been too busy making nonsense rhymes?"

"As it happens, I do have a new song. I've been waiting for your return to sing it. I think you'll like it even better than the last."

Lancelot's dark eyes narrowed. "And *I* think you'd be wiser to keep it to yourself." He bowed curtly toward the queen and retired to a seat at a lower table, which quickly became the center of the hall. Knights and ladies crowded around him, talking in high, excited voices punctuated by bursts of laughter.

"Has he really done those things?" Aislyn asked. "Slain giants and whatnot?"

"He has indeed," Gawain assured her. "Sir Lancelot is a most accomplished warrior."

*He's no friend to you,* Aislyn thought, *and well you know it. Look at him there, laughing at your expense. Don't you care? Does* nothing *bother you?*

And then she thought of something that would.

"Well, that's all for me," she said, pushing aside her trencher. "Come, husband, let's to bed."

"If you like," Gawain said with maddening composure. "My lord," he added, turning to the king, "may we be excused? My lady is weary and wishes to retire."

Arthur choked on his wine. "I—I—oh, God, Gawain—"

"Please, Arthur," Gawain said quietly. "Don't. It's all right."

"Then yes," Arthur said miserably. "Go on."

"What?" Aislyn grumbled as Gawain took her arm and helped her toward the door, "Are there to be no songs? No jests and merrymaking as they tuck us up together?"

Gawain shot her a dark look. "I think not."

Oh, really? This was her wedding day; she could insist upon the proper form. She glanced over the hall, wondering which of the ladies was so far out of favor that the task of unclothing Sir Gawain's loathly lady would fall to them. As for the men . . . her gaze settled on Sir Lancelot. No one would have to order *him*; he'd be the first one on his feet.

She looked at Gawain again. His expression showed nothing, but that fair skin would always betray him. Two spots of brilliant red stained his cheekbones, as though he had been slapped into awareness of her rights. She could do it. She *should* do it. He deserved no less.

"I suppose I'm a bit past such frolics," she heard her own voice say. Cursing herself for her weakness, she smiled, adding, "I'd just as soon have you to myself."

And she had the satisfaction of seeing every drop of color drain from his face.

# Chapter 7

• • •

THIS cannot really be happening, Gawain thought as he walked down the passageway, slowing his steps to the halting gait of the—the—*creature* whose claw dug into his forearm. No, not a creature. It wasn't her fault she looked the way she did. She couldn't help the warts, nor the wrinkles or the hairs sprouting from her chin. Well, perhaps she could do something about *those*—and was there really any need for her teeth to be quite that sickening shade of green? But would it really make a difference if she plucked her jutting chin and polished her two remaining teeth to gleaming whiteness?

Sweat prickled at his neck and armpits. She is just a woman, he told himself firmly, old and bent with age. Her form is . . . roughly . . . human. And she had done King Arthur a great service today, one deserving of reward.

God help him. There must be some way out. He couldn't do this—no man could.

And yet he must.

Suddenly he remembered his first battle. The king's

army had marched far into the night before they found the Saxon raiders encamped by the smoking remnants of a village. Arthur's men had snatched a few hours of—not sleep, they were too strung up for that—time to rest the horses and see to their weapons.

The rain stopped just before dawn, though the sun struggled to break through the heavy clouds. Even when Gawain could make out his own comrades, the far end of the meadow was swathed in mist. He could hear the Saxons—the steady pounding of spear butts on the earth, the guttural war chants—and smell the grease they used to wind their fair hair into braids. The mist began to splinter, giving him quick glimpses of the enemy—but surely they were not so many as they seemed. That was an illusion. It must be. But then the sun burst forth and there they were, rank upon rank of enormous, bearded men. So many men. Three times—four—their own number.

That morning, standing across the field from the Saxons, the same thoughts had chased each other through Gawain's mind. *I cannot do this—yet I must.*

When the time came, he did.

He opened the door to his chamber and stood back to let it—her, *Ragnelle*, God help him, his *bride*—pass through.

Two paces in, she stopped dead.

"What—what are those?"

He followed her pointing claw—*finger*—toward the bed. "Cats."

Ambrose, the white tom, leapt lightly from the bed to wind about Gawain's ankles. Star and Motley soon followed, though Sooty only rose and stretched by way of greeting before turning herself in a circle and settling back down on his pillow.

"Don't you like them?" he asked, hoping rather wildly that she would ask for a separate chamber.

"I—I don't mind them," the crea—, no, *Ragnelle*, answered.

Gawain threw open the shutter. "Out," he said, and they went—all but Sooty, as always supremely disdainful of anything resembling an order.

"You, too," he said, scooping her into his arms. He ignored her resentful yowl and tipped her out into the night. What now? *You know what,* he told himself, *don't pretend you don't. This is your wedding night.*

*God help me. I'd rather face every one of those Saxons again. Single-handed. Weaponless. Blindfolded, with my hands bound behind my back.*

He cleared his throat. "Shall I send for a woman to attend you?"

"I've been getting in and out of my own clothes for years," Ragnelle said. "I think I can manage it tonight."

"Right."

He gazed out at the moon-washed courtyard, wondering how this had all happened. There must be something he could have done—or said—to make it turn out differently. But what? Where had he gone wrong? He couldn't have refused to save the king's life. He'd had to accept. Just as he'd had to accept the Green Knight's challenge years ago. He wished now that he'd let the fiend cut off his head. At least that would have been an honorable death.

"Well?" a voice said behind him. "Are you going to stand there all night?"

He turned. There she was, lying in his bed—*his* bed—her scanty white hair spread out against his pillow, her eyes bright beneath her tangled brows.

*God help me.* Drawing a deep breath, he crossed the chamber to the candle.

"Leave it." His bride cackled, watching him with avid eyes. "I want to see what it is I bargained for."

It was intolerable. Yet he had wed her. She was within her rights to ask that he show himself to her. That was the point, after all, of the public bedding he had denied her.

But he wished she'd let him blow the candle out. Warm light washed the bed, pitilessly revealing the gross, misshapen features of his wife.

• • •

CANDLELIGHT lent Gawain's hair a ruddy glow, that exquisitely fair hair that one popular ballad had compared to falling rain.

There were many ballads about Sir Gawain. Aislyn, disguised sometimes as a lad, sometimes as the crone, had often stopped outside the village alehouse, arrested by the sound of his name drifting from within, borne upon a cloud of music and stale ale. It was a weakness and she'd known it, but like the drunkard with his ale, she'd been helpless to resist.

She watched him strip off his tunic and hose. Of course she didn't have to look. She had seen him naked before and it wasn't a sight she was likely to forget, no matter how much she'd wanted to. He had already attained his height then—or most of it—but had still been a bit uncertain about managing his arms and legs. That slight awkwardness was gone; he was in command of his body, moving gracefully through a world that had been fashioned for smaller men.

His shoulders had definitely broadened, she thought; new golden hairs glittered on his chest. Her gaze drifted downward, past the taut plane of his belly. As though aware of her scrutiny, he turned his back, presenting her with an equally pleasing view.

There wasn't any harm in admiring his form. In *her* form, she couldn't do anything *but* admire him. Which was all to the good, because he was indeed the most admirable of men.

She'd thought the same five years ago, standing in the doorway of his chamber. She had gone to him that night at Morgause's bidding, to fulfill the very special task the

Queen of Air and Darkness had set her: to use first her body, then her magic to seduce Gawain and bind him to her will.

He had lain sprawled upon his bed that night, one arm crooked over his head, moonlight gilding his hair and his face innocent and peaceful. Now, as he turned to her, his expression was very different—hard, intent, completely focused on the task ahead.

He slid into bed beside her and settled back cautiously against the pillow. His breathing was unsteady, though he fought to control it as he stared fixedly at the canopy above. Gathering his courage. Steeling his resolve. Oh, she knew exactly what he felt. You thought you couldn't do a thing, but when you had no choice, you beat back the terror and revulsion and just did it. No one wielded the magic Aislyn commanded without mastering *that* lesson. But what would happen if she insisted he make love to her? Would he? *Could* he?

He turned to her, and suddenly she was aware of the warmth of his bare skin, inches from her own, and the scent that was uniquely his, one she had never quite managed to forget. She gazed into the crystal depths of his eyes, and a treacherous tide of warmth stole through her body as she remembered the last time they had been as close as this. What would it be like to feel his touch once more, his lips upon her . . .

*Tusks.*

She gave a snort of laughter. "Stop making calf 's eyes at me, I'm too weary to pleasure you tonight." As she turned her back on him, she heard him release a shuddering breath of relief. "Mayhap I'll be feeling spryer come morning," she added nastily and pulled the coverlet over her head.

# Chapter 8

• • •

GAWAIN wasn't there when she awoke. She hadn't expected him to be. But his cats were all curled up on the bed, watching her stretch and groan as she tried to work the kinks out of her stiffened joints.

Ambrose. Star. Motley. She had chosen their names that day so long ago. All except the last, the black cat curled up on the pillow beside her own.

*Gawain untied the knotted sack and the wool fell away to reveal four kittens lying motionless, sodden fur plastered to their fragile bones.*

*"Too late," Aislyn said.*

*"No, no, this one is breathing—" Gawain lifted the kitten. It looked very tiny in his palm as he stroked it with one fingertip.*

*"Why, so is this one," Aislyn said, picking up another. "And this . . ." She laughed as they began to crawl about on the rock. "Now what?"*

*Gawain smiled ruefully. "Aye, that is the question, isn't it? Could you . . . ?"*

*"I am your mother's guest," Aislyn reminded him. "I suppose I could take one, but I doubt she'd welcome all of these."*

*"She might, but she shan't have them." His brows drew together as he regarded the kittens. "I had a cat once, when I was a boy. I called her Sooty and she slept on my pillow. One day she disappeared. I learned that Mother had taken her—for what purpose she would not say. But I never saw poor Sooty again."*

*Aislyn stroked the tiny bundle of fur on her knee. She could easily imagine what had become of the creature, for cat bones—particularly those of an animal that merited the name of Sooty—were powerfully magical. Aislyn had used them herself, never thinking them more than an ingredient. Watching Gawain laugh as the kitten clawed its way up his sleeve, she wondered if she could ever summon that cold detachment again.*

"Hello, Sooty," she said now, and the cat yawned, revealing a pink throat and sharp white teeth, then put out a paw and tapped Aislyn on the chin.

Were these really the same cats they had found that day? Star had been named for the blaze on her chest, and Ambrose appeared to be pure white, save for that one black spot on his belly. They had to be the same. She had forgotten them, until she was well away from Lothian, and had often wondered what became of them. It had never occurred to her that with everything that happened that night, Gawain would have remembered them. He might have left her behind, but he'd thought to take the kittens.

Bastard.

She groaned as she sat up and swung her legs over the side of the bed. The crone was not made for riding; yesterday had taken its toll.

Her feet dangled far above the floor, large, flat feet with twisted toes and thick, ridged nails. Her own feet were rather nicer, she reflected. They didn't ache like this. *She* didn't ache like this.

*Stop complaining,* she ordered herself. *You're safe for now. Just finish what you came here for and you can be on your way.* Where, exactly, she would go was still a mystery, but she would think of something.

She always had before.

Grunting, she stood, one hand at the small of her back. A screen in one corner concealed a chamber pot; she used it and then dragged an overtunic from her bag. It was far too long for the crone, having been made to Aislyn's measure, but she pulled it on. There was no point in using the comb . . . though after a moment's reflection, she twisted a few strands of tangled hair into a lumpy braid.

*Gawain rose and picked up the sack of kittens, then held out a hand to help Aislyn to her feet as a gust of wind showered them with cherry blossoms. He brushed them from her hair, smiling down into her eyes. He was going to kiss her, she was certain of it. It was just as she and Morgause had planned.*

*But she had not counted on this strange confusion. He bent to her, and at the last moment, she realized she couldn't simply stand there like a block of wood, she had to tilt her head—and so she did, jerking stiffly to one side just as Gawain moved in the same direction. Their noses bumped—what was the matter with her?—and he drew back.*

*Anger and mortification swept through her. She had never been so clumsy in her life! But she was oddly breathless, almost dizzy—with annoyance, she told herself, though that did not explain the strange fluttering in her belly, as if a hundred butterflies were trapped inside, trying to escape. He smiled and bent to her again—and again she turned her face in the wrong direction at precisely the wrong moment.*

*He pulled back and regarded her quizzically. "I never realized this could be so complicated. Unless—would you rather I did not—"*

*"No! I mean, I wouldn't rather—that is, I would like . . . if you would . . ." What was she blethering about? Luckily, he seemed more amused than concerned by her raving. He bent slightly and set down the sack of kittens, then laid his hands gently on either side of her face.*

*"Let's begin again," he said, laughter in his voice.*

*And then he kissed her.*

*She had never known a kiss could be so sweet. Or that the mere touch of mouth to mouth could undo her so completely. She was falling, tumbling, a dizzying plunge that should have terrified her, but did not. For Gawain's arms were around her, as strong and solid as he was himself.*

*He kissed her cheeks, her eyes, and then her mouth again, and the hard, cold kernel of bitterness she had carried for so long in her heart dissolved like snowflakes in a flame.*

*It seemed that she had wandered through an endless nightmare, but now, at last she was awake. What cared she for dark magic and cold power? She had everything she'd ever wanted, right here beneath the cherry tree.*

*When at last they drew apart, they gazed deep into each other's eyes, and all their questions were asked and answered without a word. He pulled her hard against him then, his cheek resting on her hair, and her eyes filled as she buried her face against his shoulder. What had she just done? What was she to do now? Not the task Morgause had given her, of that much she was certain. But she didn't want to think about the future. She wanted nothing but to stay here forever, safe in the shelter of his arms.*

*His fingers trailed down the small braid at her temple, threaded through with green ribbon, and she lifted her head to look into his eyes.*

*She touched his cheek, his lips, and he smiled, kissing her fingertips and winding her braid through his fingers. He glanced down at it, began to speak, and checked himself.*

*"What?" she demanded. "What were you about to say?"*

*"I thought—a lock of your hair—knights carry them into battle, and I—but—"*

*"Take it," she said, laughing.*

*He drew his dagger. "Are you sure?"*

*"Here." She took the dagger from him and sliced through the braid. He accepted it and pulled it through his fingers, stroking the green ribbons that bound it before twisting it into a circle and tucking it into the purse at his belt.*

*"Aislyn, I—"*

*He hesitated and she held her breath, waiting for him to go on.*

*"I will carry it always," he said, and though it wasn't what she'd hoped to hear, when she looked into his glowing eyes, it was enough.*

A bitter smile curved Aislyn's lips as she finished braiding a lock of the crone's white hair and tied off the tangled love knot with a bit of string. She wished there was a looking glass, but of course Gawain couldn't be bothered with anything so frivolous. Still, she was sure she looked not only repulsive, but ridiculous.

Smiling, she entered the hall a few minutes later, where a single trestle table was erected at the lower end with bread and meat and cheese laid out upon it. Various members of the household helped themselves and carried their meals away with them, for only the lord and his family sat down to break their fast. The high table was empty save for Gawain, Sir Lancelot, and the king.

"Good day!" Aislyn said, plumping herself into the seat

beside Gawain. "I'm behind my time, it seems. But a new bride needs her rest, you know. Isn't that so, sire?"

The king stared at her, nonplussed. Sir Lancelot choked on his ale. Gawain shot her a dark look, but merely offered her a loaf of bread.

"The king was just telling me of his adventure yesterday," Sir Lancelot said, breaking a rather awkward silence. "Go on, sire, what did Somer Gromer Jour say when you gave him the answer?"

Gawain stiffened beside her; he and the king exchanged a quick glance, then Arthur said carelessly, "Oh, nothing really. What was there to say?"

"The whole thing seems rather silly," Lancelot remarked. "What was the point of it?"

"I don't know," Arthur said. He gazed at Aislyn, frowning, then shrugged. "Perhaps one day we will learn more of this fellow, whoever he might be, and his purpose."

Gawain was looking at Aislyn, as well, with an expression she could not fathom. "So what shall we do today?" she asked brightly.

"The queen is planning an entertainment in the garden," Sir Lancelot said, his sober expression belied by the merriment in his dark eyes.

"What, with dancing and all?" Aislyn said, thinking that a few more aches would be well worth the opportunity to dance upon the green. The same thought seemed to be in Gawain's mind. He pushed his half-eaten porridge away, looking queasy.

"Sir Gawain and I are going hunting," the king said firmly.

"Today?" Ragnelle rested her hand on Gawain's arm. "Oh, sire, you wouldn't be so cruel. It'd be a rare shame to part us so soon after the wedding. Don't you agree, Sir Lancelot?"

Sir Lancelot, thus appealed to, went very red and was

seized by a sudden fit of coughing. Arthur scowled at the young knight, and Sir Lancelot choked out a hasty excuse before he fled.

"Must've been something he ate," Aislyn remarked. "Are you finished?" she added to Gawain. "Then why don't you show me about?"

"But—" the king began.

"We'll see you in the gardens later, sire," Aislyn said, fluttering her fingers. "Mayhap we can have a dance."

Gawain said nothing, but she thought she heard his teeth grind as she led him from the hall.

"So what *did* he say?" she asked when they were alone in one of the galleries. "Somer Gromer Jour?"

Gawain paused, leaning one broad shoulder against the stone wall as he regarded her through hooded eyes. "He seemed completely stunned for a moment, then he said, 'My sister told you that.' Tell me, have you a brother?"

*Launfal.* In league with Morgause? No, it couldn't be; not Launfal! He'd always been such an innocent. But innocence did not last long at Morgause's court.

"Happens I do," Aislyn said, "though it's been some time since I've seen him. He would be about my age, for there was not even a year between us. D'ye think he might have been Somer Gromer Jour?"

Gawain shook his head. "No, he was a young man. Judging by his voice and bearing, I would guess him no more than one-and-twenty."

Which would be Launfal's age, or near enough. Stupid little nit, how *could* he have gone over to the enemy? It was difficult to believe that her frail, unworldly little brother had succumbed to Morgause's blandishments. Aislyn might have done so herself, but she'd always believed Launfal too good to be taken in by evil. Of course, it had been five years since she had seen him and people changed. If he was Morgause's creature now, he had changed more than most, and at the thought an odd little pain lanced through her, somewhere in the region of her heart.

• • •

ONCE they reached the gardens, Aislyn cast off her melancholy and flung herself into the queen's revels with abandon. She refused Gawain's offer to serve her, but snatched an iced cake from a platter. "A new bride needs her nourishment," she said thickly, stuffing another morsel into her mouth. Those near enough to hear turned to stare at Gawain in horror, and he went brick red, his eyes narrowing into ice-gray slits. Aislyn met his gaze defiantly as she accepted a goblet of wine from a page. She lifted it in his direction before she downed it in a single draught.

"My lady," he began, tight-lipped as she tossed the empty goblet to the startled page and helped herself to another from a passing squire's tray.

"Ooh, music," she cried, "come, Sir Gawain, let us dance!"

"No," he said curtly. "Why do we not sit—"

She lifted her skirts to reveal her spindly shanks and cut a little caper. "Sit? Today? No, no, I'm feeling far too merry!"

Before he could reply, she spun away into the center of the green, knocking into a knight, who stumbled forward, catching his balance on the nearest lady, who drew back with an indignant squeak.

"Pardon!" Aislyn called cheerily, elbowing her way into the center of the green. Her dance, she thought, was a masterpiece of buffoonery. As she whirled and capered, the other dancers drew back to watch. Most of the knights attempted to contain their merriment, but in the end, they couldn't help but laugh. The weepers—those half a dozen maidens who had wailed throughout the feast the night before and were now huddled red-eyed and dejected in a bunch—were reduced to fresh tears, though this time of merriment.

Gawain simply watched, his face like stone. When Aislyn at last succumbed to exhaustion, he stepped forward, gave her his arm, and led her to a secluded turf bench set beneath an arching trellis overhung with vines. She leaned on him and sank onto the seat with relief. Holy Mother, but her back was aching! And her legs, and especially her feet. Even her toenails hurt.

"Can I get you—" Gawain began.

"No."

She belched behind her hand, cursing the crone's weak stomach. All the wine and rich food weren't sitting very well. And that frolicking about hadn't helped matters, either.

Gawain must be praying she would keel over . . . which seemed terrifyingly likely at the moment, for her heart was pounding like a kettle drum. But he gave no sign of the rage he surely must be feeling and merely looked at her with something that in any other man she would have taken for concern. It was a show, of course, a trick. But who did he think he was fooling?

Not the king, who was looking almost as ill as Aislyn felt herself. Surely not the queen, sitting a bit apart from the others with Sir Lancelot, the two of them whispering behind their hands. Not Sir Dinadan, either, who fixed Aislyn with his bright eyes, his expression so reproachful that she could not hold his gaze. It could only be himself Gawain deceived. No one else believed his ridiculous pretense of sympathy.

Aislyn least of all.

"Well, that was jolly," she said. "It's been some time since I had such fun!"

Sir Lancelot led the queen to the center of the green.

Others followed, arranging themselves in two lines. As the music began, Lancelot called, "We've room for one more pair, Sir Gawain! Do you and your lady join us!"

Something flickered in Gawain's eyes, and for a moment Aislyn thought that this was it, he was finally going to lose his temper, but then he mastered himself and said, "I think not."

Aislyn was tempted to press the point, but she could not bring herself to do it. All she wanted now was to find some cool, shady chamber where she could soak her feet.

"Would you like to retire for a time?" Gawain asked.

"What, and miss the fun? Or do you just want me out of the way so you can dance with one of them?" she said, jerking her chin toward the weepers.

"I do not dance," he said indifferently.

*Liar.* She'd seen him outdance every man at the court of Lothian; whirling around the targe, leaping to land neatly with one foot on either side of the spiked shield. She'd danced with him herself, their bodies moving in unison to the pipes and drums until dawn dimmed the torchlight. They had gone laughing to the stables then, and raced their horses over the hills, the rising sun on their faces and the wind in their hair . . .

Even the memory exhausted her. It seemed like something that had happened to someone else in a far-off age; a girl she could remember, but one that seemed to have no part of her.

Gawain belonged to that time. *Her* Gawain, the dazzling young knight who had galloped into Lothian five years ago and laid waste to the glittering edifice of her ambition. The man beside her now was a stranger. She did not love him—she didn't even like him. A great weariness overwhelmed her until she felt as ancient as the crone's form she wore. What point was there in punishing either of them for things that had happened in another life to two entirely different people?

"I think I will have a lie-down," she said. "Nay, you

needn't come with me." Without looking at him again, she hobbled from the garden.

• • •

BY the time she reached Gawain's chamber, Aislyn could scarce drag herself inside. *What am I to do now?* she thought, dropping down upon the bed. Her jest had fallen flat; she had no desire to linger here at Camelot . . . and yet, there was nowhere else she would be safe. *If I were to change back and confess all to the king* . . . Yesterday, that might have served, but today it was too late. She and Gawain were wed . . . or no, he was wed to Dame Ragnelle . . . it was all muddled in her mind, and she was no longer quite certain who she was . . . Sighing, she closed her eyes and succumbed to sleep.

It seemed but a moment later that she bolted upright to find the chamber filled with shadows.

"Who's there?" she cried.

Gawain started back, stumbling over one of the cats. It yowled and vanished through the window in a streak of black and white. "Ragnelle! I didn't see you."

She slid from the bed, groaning as her feet hit the floor. "Why were you cursing?"

"I barked my shin. Go back to sleep."

She squinted against the sudden light of a candle, taking in his disheveled hair and flushed cheeks. He sank onto the trunk and rubbed his shin.

"Out making merry, were you?" she asked, eyeing him with interest.

"Not particularly, no."

"You look sodden," she said. "And here I thought you never drank to excess. Beneath your dignity, isn't it?"

He rested his elbows on his knees. "I am not sodden. But after today, I haven't much dignity left to lose."

So he *had* minded. Well, that was something, anyway. It was a comfort to know that her suffering had not been entirely in vain. "Ah, well," she said, sitting down upon the chair, " 'twas all in fun."

"Fun? Oh, right. Particularly the part about a bride needing nourishment," he said, raking his hair back from his face.

She chuckled. "Aye, that was amusing."

"Was it?" he said coldly.

"Oh, go on," she said, exasperated. "Why don't you say what you are really thinking?"

"You have no idea what I am thinking."

"I'll wager that I do. I made you angry today, didn't I? Go on, admit it. And then there's that Sir Lancelot," she went on, without giving him a chance to answer. "Why don't you give him a good hard smack? You know you want to, and I daresay it would do him good. But no, you just let him go on, making jokes at your expense! You'd best take care or people will start wondering—" she broke off, realizing that she'd said more than she intended.

"Wondering *what*?"

"Well, wondering if you're as brave as all the tales make out."

He gave her a level look. "No one has ever had cause to complain of my behavior on the battlefield."

"What's all life but a battlefield? Yet you let that boy mock you, and you just sit there and do nothing! Don't you care what people say?"

"Not particularly, no."

"Even if they're saying you're afraid of him?"

"Anyone who could believe *that* knows nothing of me," he answered with a flash of pride. "But look you," he said, leaning forward, his expression intent. "The knights of Camelot are not mere fighting men, we are brothers. And Camelot itself is not just another castle, it is a—a beacon. You've heard of the king's justice, have you not? That isn't just a phrase, it is a living force that touches every one of his subjects. When we, the king's companions, go out into the world, we carry his vision with us—his law, his justice, his mercy—into every corner of Britain. We cannot allow petty quarrels to divide us. We must be *one*."

For a moment, Aislyn could see it once again, Gawain's shining kingdom built on justice and mercy . . . and then common sense returned. Once that Camelot had been her dream, as well, but when she had reached out to grasp it, she had learned how fragile dreams could be.

"Pretty words," she scoffed.

"The vows we have taken—to the king and to each other—are real. They're not just pretty words, they *matter*."

"Not to Sir Lancelot," she pointed out.

"If one of my brothers in arms treats me with discourtesy, the shame is his, not mine. But each man must look to his own honor. What *I* have sworn, I do."

Aislyn gave it up with an inward shrug. Talking to this new Gawain was like talking to a man encased in mail—no words of hers could make an impression. "So did you at least have a dance after I left?"

He shook his head. "I told you, I don't dance."

"Why, are you left-footed? Or did you never learn? Or is it just beneath you?"

He scowled. "I do not care to dance. Is that a crime?"

"Not a crime, but—"

"I do not play hoodman's blind or forfeits, either. Or sing pretty ballads."

Aislyn's mouth twitched. That, at least, was true, though he'd sung her one or two soldier's songs that had made her laugh, even as she blushed . . .

*Stop,* she told herself. *This isn't the same Gawain, remember? And you don't like this one.*

But still, she was a little curious. "What's the matter with you, anyway? Here you are, a bonny young knight of three-and-twenty, and a prince into the bargain! You have everything a man could want, and yet you mope and droop about, as merry as a rain cloud at a picnic."

"I enjoy myself," he said defensively.

"When?" she demanded. "How?"

"Well, when . . ." He frowned. "In battle."

"Killing people is fun?"

"No, I didn't mean that. It's just that I feel . . . useful then. It is," he said carefully, "something I do well."

"Aye, I've heard that. But we're talking about *merriment*." She rapped his knee with her knuckles to emphasize the point. "Having a laugh with your mates, flirting with the lasses . . ."

"You want me to flirt?" He smiled without humor as he turned back the coverlet. "That's odd advice for a wife to give her husband."

"I'm an odd wife," she said. "So where have you been all this time since I left you, then? The truth."

"I fell asleep in the chapel."

She rolled her eyes. "Have you ever thought of taking holy orders?"

He smiled briefly, surprising her. "One must have faith for that, and I . . ."

"You are not a good Christian knight?" Aislyn demanded mockingly.

"I serve my king; my soul is my concern. If indeed I have one," he added in a lower voice.

Aislyn barely stopped herself from reaching out to him. This was a change she had not expected; some of their most passionate arguments had been the result of Gawain's refusal to agree that belief in some invisible deity was the refuge of the weak and childish. Despite the combined prayers of her family and household, the God Aislyn had been brought up to believe was omnipotent had been either unwilling—or worse, powerless to help them. That their house priest had attributed this to some fault on their part only added insult to the injury.

*"Ach, I don't mind the priests much, either." Gawain said, gazing into the rushing water of the burn. "They are always shut away in stuffy chapels, prating of the evil in the world. But it seems wondrous fair to me," he said, looking about the forest clearing in which they sat, his eyes at last resting upon her. "And I think that Morgana—that is my aunt, the duchess of Cornwall—has the right of it. She says we are all in the hands of the Great Mother, and she told me that one day, I would see Her for myself. I didn't credit it then, but now—" Color flooded his face and he bent to pick up a stone, which he flung into the pool below. "Well, I think I know now what she meant."*

Strange that it should hurt her to realize his simple faith was lost to him. She had never been able to share it, but it had given him such joy that she could not but regret its loss for his sake.

"Then why go to the chapel?" she asked.

He looked achingly young for a moment, a bewildered sorrow in his eyes, but then he shrugged, his expression hardening. " 'Tis quiet there; a good place to think."

"And to sleep," she observed and he smiled wryly.

"That, too."

"Can I ask you something?" she said, surprising herself, and he shrugged again, stifling a yawn. "You are the king's heir. Should you not have taken a bride years ago?"

"If I had, we would not be here now." He lifted his gaze to her, his expression bleak. "I never meant to wed."

"Never?"

"Once, I'd thought to, but . . . no." He fell back upon the feather mattress.

Aislyn pulled herself to her feet and looked down at him, her heartbeat quickening. Was it possible he regretted what he had done five years ago? That he still had some feeling for her after all? *Leave it,* she told herself, *let it go, it doesn't matter now . . .*

"Why didn't you?" She held her breath, waiting for his answer.

Gawain laid his forearm over his eyes. "She died."

She must have made some sound, for he said roughly, "No more. For pity's sake, Ragnelle, just let me sleep."

# Chapter 9

• • •

AISLYN sat, clutching the arms of the chair, each breath an effort. What difference does it make? she asked herself. He isn't the same. It doesn't matter if he's mourning some dead lass.

"Once I meant to marry . . ."

*Once.*

It all rushed back so clearly, the nights she'd spent kneeling by the window, imagining Gawain declaring himself to her. She'd gone over it a hundred times, the words he would use, what she would say, how happy they would be. For five years, she had been certain he was on the brink of asking her before that terrible night.

But he had never meant to marry her at all.

She didn't know how to feel or what to think. The great love of her life had been a mere infatuation on his part. It was some other woman who had changed him from the merry lad she knew to this grim stranger.

Yet had he not always been a stranger?

She had risked Morgause's wrath for a man she had not

known. For his sake, she had very nearly lost her life. Everything she had done and been and felt since that night had been based upon a lie.

He had never loved her.

Her breath rasped in her throat as she stared at him, marking the long, straight limbs, the broad chest and flat belly, the angles of his face, and the moon-bright hair that spilled across the pillow. Yes, he was beautiful, but his beauty was no more than a shell. She had never known the man beneath, and if she had once loved him desperately, her love was nothing to the hatred that consumed her now.

She stood, hobbled over to the chest, and took up her bag. It didn't take long to mix the potion, and when it was done she gulped it down in a single draught.

She had forgotten how much it hurt. She fell to her knees, biting her lips against the pain as bones lengthened, straightened, as skin stretched and joints popped.

At last it ended. She stood, throwing off tunic and undergown, then raised her arms over her head and felt each muscle stretch. Oh, it was good to be herself again! She ran her hands across her face, fingertips tracing her own nose and lips and eyes, reveling in the smooth suppleness of her skin. She smoothed the shimmering waves of hair falling over breasts and hips to curl about her knees.

Padding barefoot to the bed, she looked down at Gawain. Dark golden lashes lay motionless against his cheeks. Save for the slow rise and fall of his chest, he could have been the effigy of a knight carved of alabaster and touched with gilt.

Just so had he looked that night in Lothian when she had gone to his chamber, sent there by the queen.

*Aislyn had never seen Morgause in such a temper. The queen's face was livid and her eyes glittered with the wild light of madness.*

*"Did your supper with Sir Gawain not—not go well?" Aislyn faltered.*

*Morgause's laughter was like a shriek. "Well? No, it did not go well. My son is a traitor."*

*Something about the way she said the word chilled Aislyn's heart. "Oh, madam, no!" she cried. "He is confused—"*

*"Do you dare defend him?" Morgause seized an alabaster pot from her dressing table and flung it. Aislyn ducked; the pot shattered against the wall behind her head. "Or do you only seek to excuse your own failure?"*

*"I need more time," Aislyn said desperately. "I am certain I can convince him—" Her words ended in a cry when Morgause slapped her hard across the face.*

*"Be still." Morgause sat down at her dressing table and dropped her face into her hands. "Gawain is Arthur's man; he told me so himself. He dared to look me in the eye and say he will serve that misbegotten bastard unto death."*

*"I am sorry, madam," Aislyn said carefully. "I did my best."*

*"Your best," Morgause spat, "was not good enough." She raised her head and gazed into the mirror, her eyes holding Aislyn's. "But you shall have another chance."*

*"Yes, madam, thank you, madam." Aislyn gabbled, backing toward the door. "I am certain that given a few more days—"*

*Not that she needed a few days or even one. All she asked was a quarter of an hour in which to beg Gawain to take her from this place.*

*"Tonight," the queen said, "you will go to his bed and you will bind him. Then we shall see what his pathetic notions of honor and loyalty are worth."*

*"B-bind him?"*

*"The spell. You know the one I mean, do not pretend you don't." The queen whirled and caught Aislyn by the arm, sharp nails digging into the soft skin of her wrist. "Once*

*Gawain is mine to command, Arthur will not hold his throne for long. You wanted a crown, Aislyn, did you not? Well, here is your chance to prove yourself fit to wear it."*

*The crown of Orkney, Aislyn thought numbly, that was what I hoped for, not that of Britain. How could she have been so blind to Morgause's true intent?*

*The queen's eyes narrowed. "Do not fail me," she hissed. "Or I promise that what life remains to you will seem far too long."*

*Aislyn nodded. "You can rely upon me, madam."*

*"Then go. Do what you must." Morgause's smile did not reach her eyes. "You can leave the rest to me."*

• • •

AISLYN *trembled as she stood in the doorway of Gawain's chamber, wondering if Morgause's magic was powerful enough to give warning of her impending treachery. But she drew in a long breath and gathered her courage in both hands, determined to confess everything to Gawain.*

He has to know, *she thought. He would understand that she had never meant to deceive him, that she had only said what she had been told to say—and not said those things she had been ordered to conceal. Once she explained how it had been for her, how helpless she had felt when she arrived at Lothian with nothing but her own wits standing between her and a life of servitude, he would realize that she'd really had no choice.*

*He would surely believe that she had not known Morgause was planning to overthrow King Arthur—although she should have realized it long since, and had she not been blinded by the dazzling prospect of a crown, she would have.* And what would you have done? *a small voice demanded mockingly.* Until you met Gawain, would you have cared?

*She liked to think she would, for Arthur was reputed to be both wise and just, virtues that Morgause clearly lacked.*

*But she could not be certain. Nor did it matter now; whatever she might once have thought or felt, she knew that she would never in this life allow Gawain to be used to such an end—or to any end at all. Better to slay him outright than consign him to such a fate. Should he be bound by magic, the man she loved would cease to exist, and in his place would be a shell with no will but hers—or to be exact, Morgause's.*

*And to think Morgause claimed to love her son.*

But I love him! *she told herself, stepping into the chamber and moving swiftly toward the bed.* And he loves me. He will take me from this dark place, sweep me off to shining Camelot, and protect me from his mother's vengeance.

*Never had a fool been so deceived.*

Now she knelt beside him on the bed and leaned over him, her hair falling about his face as she brushed his lips with hers. He stirred and sighed, and she kissed him again. This time he responded, still half-sleeping. She teased his lips apart and his eyelids fluttered, then snapped open.

"Aislyn?"

"Shh." She put a finger to his lips.

"But—"

"You are dreaming," she said, touching the space between his brows.

"Aye." He sighed, relaxing back upon the pillow, gazing up at her with a smile. Well, at least he welcomed her into his dreams. For tonight, he would not think of that other one at all. When he woke, he would be bound to her, body and soul—and she would be gone. Then he would finally understand what she had endured for five long years.

He touched her lips, her cheeks. Then his hands wound in her hair to pull her down to him.

He had always been so gentle with her, so sweetly hesitant, as though she was made of some exquisitely delicate substance he feared to shatter. But there was nothing gentle about the way he kissed her now. He did not ask, he demanded, and her whole heart leapt in answer. His hands were warm as they slid up her sides to trail over her breasts, teasing and caressing until she moaned aloud.

He turned, carrying her with him, not breaking the kiss. She wound her legs around his back, thrusting her hips upward to meet him as he filled her in one powerful surge. She cried out; her nails raked his back and he thrust again, more deeply, and again.

*This* was what she'd dreamt of through those aching, endless nights, *this* was what she'd longed for all unknowing. Two were one, perfect and complete, a feeling so intense that she cried out again, a wordless cry of wonder that he echoed as he arched against her.

It seemed she floated back to earth, back into awareness of herself and him, held fast in each other's arms, their legs entwined. His lips moved over hers in a lingering exploration that was echoed by the movement of light fingertips tracing the contours of leg and hip and breast. She made a low sound in her throat and he laughed, then pulled her to him, burying his face against her neck, holding her so tightly that she could feel the beating of his heart as if it were her own. But he had said himself that his heart had never been hers. It belonged to another, one whose death he still mourned.

*Finish it,* she thought, *complete the binding. Take from him his will, destroy his precious honor. Make him yours forevermore.* The spell was as clear in her mind as it had been five years ago, for Morgause had forced her to repeat it until each word was indelibly branded in her memory. Aislyn had not used it then, but she would now. She *would.*

She lifted herself on one elbow and looked down at him. "These eyes see naught but you, this tongue speak of naught but you," she whispered, touching his eyelids, then his lips. "This heart yearns only for . . ." He sighed, turning toward her in his sleep, fingers twining in a lock of her hair as his lips moved to form her name.

*Do it,* she ordered herself, then leave him to pine and sigh, every moment an agony of longing for what he can never know again.

"Man to maiden," she went on, her voice shaking, "heart to heart and . . . and . . ."

*He never loved you,* she thought as hot tears slid down her cheeks. *He only took you because he believed it was a dream.*

*Finish it.*

But when she looked into his face, she knew that she could not.

*I must go,* she thought. *I cannot stay here.* She rose and poured water from the pitcher, then cleaned herself and him, touching his brow and murmuring a soft command when his eyelids fluttered. He would never know. He would remembered this night only as a dream . . . if he remembered it at all. She sat down beside him and stroked the hair back from his face, then bent to kiss his lips once more. His arms slid round her and drew her down. She laid her head on his breast with a little sigh, her tears falling on his skin as she listened to the slow beat of his heart.

*Soon,* she thought, *soon I will go. Soon, but . . . not . . . quite . . . yet.*

# Chapter 10

• • •

AISLYN dreamed that she was home again, standing in the hall with her mother and her brother, both of them looking to her as the battering ram pounded against the gates. "We must flee," she said, and raising her voice, she turned to the people gathered in the hall. "Flee!" she cried. "The gates are breached!" Taking her brother's hand, she ran through the hall and into the passageway leading to the kitchens . . .

Something touched her face and the dream began to fade. Yawning, she stretched and found herself staring into the green eyes of a cat. Sooty, she thought, reaching out to stroke the gleaming fur—and froze, staring at her hand, her own white hand, as a fist hammered at the door.

Gawain lay beside her, eyes closed and hair tangled over his brow. He stirred, muttered something—

And Aislyn was rolling out of bed, seizing her bag as she dove behind the screen. Her hands were shaking as she pulled pouches and bottles from the bag, dropping them in her haste.

"Who is it?" She started at the sound of Gawain's voice, still thick with sleep.

"'Tis I, Gawain—Morgana. Don't tell me you are still abed?"

Morgana. *Morgana? Holy Mother, help me,* Aislyn thought, measuring powder into a cup with shaking hands. Morgana, duchess of Cornwall, Gawain's aunt . . . and the most powerful sorceress in Britain.

"A moment," Gawain called, and Aislyn heard the bed creak as he stood. "Ragnelle?"

"Here," she croaked, stirring frantically before she downed the potion.

"Are you all right?"

"Aye, 'tis just—" She bit her lip against a groan. "Something I ate."

"Morgana," he called, "a moment, if you would. My lady is . . . indisposed."

"Very well."

Aislyn looked down at her hands. It was done, she was once again the crone. Wiping the sweat from her upper lip, she peered around the corner of the screen to see Gawain pulling a robe over his head. Oh, why had she not gone away last night? She never wanted to see him again, and particularly not like this, with his hair tousled and his eyes heavy-lidded, whistling as he bent to find his boots.

"Toss me my shift, will you?" she said, speaking past the tightness in her throat.

"Are you well?" he asked, obliging her.

"Oh, aye." Perhaps he didn't remember. She knew it would be best that way, and yet how could she bear it if he did not? She hesitated, then asked, "How did you sleep?"

"Very well." His smile faded as he looked toward the bed, and when he blushed, she could not tell if she wanted more to laugh or weep. Before she could decide the door opened.

"Are you decent yet?" a light voice demanded.

"Aye. I'm sorry to keep you waiting," Gawain said, rising as a dark-haired lady came forward to embrace him.

"That's all right," she said, stepping back and peering anxiously into his face. "Are you well, Gawain?"

"Oh, aye. And you?"

"Quite. Is this your lady?"

The duchess of Cornwall looked nothing like her sister, Morgause. Morgana was not much taller than the crone; her features were even but unremarkable . . . save for her eyes, which were dark and very fine.

"It is," Gawain said. "Morgana, may I present my wife. Ragnelle, this is my aunt Morgana, the duchess of Cornwall."

"Your Grace." Aislyn bowed her head briefly.

"Dame Ragnelle." Morgana's eyes widened. For a moment she looked on the verge of either tears or laughter; her lips trembled before she compressed them firmly. "I am sorry to have missed your wedding."

"It was very sudden," Aislyn said, forcing herself to hold Morgana's gaze.

"So I heard." Without turning her head, Morgana said, "Gawain, I will stay and help your lady dress. Do you go break your fast and we will find you in the hall."

"Morgana," he began, "I—"

"Don't worry, I won't bite her." Morgana laughed lightly. "I merely want to get acquainted."

Gawain looked at Aislyn, his brows raised in silent question. "Go along," she said, nodding toward the door. "We shan't be long."

When he was gone, Morgana sat down on the bed. "My sister, the queen of Orkney, is fortunate in her sons. I am fond of all my nephews . . . but Gawain most of all."

Aislyn hobbled over to the trunk and opened the lid. "I expect you're thinking it's an odd match—"

"Why would I think that?"

Aislyn pulled out her overtunic of green wool. "You're

jesting with me," she said with an uneasy chuckle, "but it's nothing I'm not used to."

Ambrose leapt up on the bed and Morgana stroked him between the ears. "I'm not jesting," she said mildly, gazing down at the cat. "Why should I think the match is such an odd one?"

Aislyn stared at her, nonplussed. "Well, I am a bit older."

"You are not." Morgana raised her head. "Oh, come now, did you think *I* would be taken in by your disguise?"

"Disguise?" Ragnelle attempted a laugh. "Who would disguise themselves as *this*?"

"That is the question, isn't it? Why don't you give me the answer, Dame Ragnelle—or whatever your true name is."

Aislyn dropped the overtunic.

"Sit down," Morgana ordered, "and tell me why you have deceived the king and court, and most particularly my nephew."

Her voice was still pleasant, but now there was an edge to it. Aislyn sat down beside her on the bed.

*Careful, now,* she told herself. From all Morgause had said of her sister Morgana, the two had not been close for years. But nobles were strange; no matter what their private quarrels, they stuck together, particularly against those who might bring scandal on the family name. Best to leave Morgause out of this entirely.

"Do you know," she began cautiously, "of the king's meeting with Somer Gromer Jour?"

"I do."

"As it happens, I knew the answer the king wanted, so I set off to meet him on his way. When I saw Sir Gawain was with him . . ."

This was the tricky part, for she dared speak nothing but the truth to as powerful an enchantress as the duchess.

"Sir Gawain is the noblest of all King Arthur's knights," she said, choosing each word with care. "But 'tis common knowledge that he has no good opinion of women. It seems there's hardly a tale told of him where he doesn't find some chance to point out how treacherous we are. Of course, he's not the first man to say *that*, but his words carry more weight than most."

She halted a moment, waiting to see if she had chosen carefully enough. The duchess nodded and said, "Go on."

"I grew weary of hearing Sir Gawain's words in the mouth of every man who wants to keep his wife or daughter in what he's pleased to call her place," Aislyn continued. "So I thought—'twas but a jest, Your Grace, a—a lesson to him, if you would, to teach him to be more careful in the future."

Had she done it? Nothing she had said was a lie . . . she had merely left out certain words in the hope Morgana would supply them for herself.

"I see." The duchess looked down and smiled at Ambrose, who was curled up, purring, in her lap.

Aislyn had just dared to draw a full breath when Morgana went on. "That was a very interesting story, though more, I fear, for what you omitted than what you actually said. Are you sure you have nothing to add?"

Aislyn widened her eyes. "Such as what, Your Grace?"

"Such as where you learned to wield such enchantments, for a start. This spell is not one picked up from any village wise woman."

"My mother had some learning," Aislyn began. "Before her marriage, she studied—"

"Who taught you this spell?" Morgana interrupted.

Aislyn's shoulders slumped. "The queen of Orkney."

"Ah, so you know my sister! I should have guessed. Did she send you here?"

"No! Indeed, Your Grace, she did not! Some years ago, she took me on as—well, as her apprentice—"

"Morgause with an apprentice? Holy Mother, have mercy."

"—And when I left her, I . . . well, I brought a book of hers along."

"Where is it?"

Aislyn retrieved the grimoire from her bag and handed it to Morgana. The duchess leafed through it, her brows rising almost to her hairline. "It is Morgause's hand, and she would never willingly have let this from her sight. How long have you had it?"

"Five years," Aislyn admitted.

"And she has not found you in that time? You must be quite talented."

"Thank you, Your Grace. I never meant to steal it," she hurried on, "I thought it was my own and did not realize my mistake until it was too late. You won't—will you tell her where I am?"

"No," Morgana said. "I will not."

"Thank you—" Aislyn began again.

Morgana snapped the book shut and handed it to Aislyn, who dropped it back into her bag with a long sigh of relief. "That is," Morgana continued, "if I am satisfied with the rest of your answers. Now, tell me the real reason you wanted to punish my nephew."

"I met him in Lothian," Aislyn answered, "and he scorned my love." Before Morgana could press her for details, she hurried on, "I am sorry for what I did to him, Your Grace. I know now that it was wrong. I had already made up my mind to leave."

Morgana stroked the cat, her expression pensive. "Then why are you still here?"

"Well . . ." Aislyn swallowed hard. "I meant to go this morning."

"Did you indeed?" Morgana glanced at the twisted bedclothes, then turned her dark eyes on Aislyn. "What spell," she said, "did you use upon Gawain last night?"

Aislyn felt her face grow hot. "I—I only made him think that he was dreaming." Seeing the horrified disgust in

Morgana's eyes, she added quickly, "I wasn't like this! I changed back to my own form. No harm was done."

"No harm?" Morgause regarded her thoughtfully. "So you think I should let Dame Ragnelle walk away?"

"I won't come back, I promise."

"And then what will happen to Gawain?"

Aislyn shook her head, uncomprehending. "He will be free."

"He is wed to you. Without proof of his wife's death, he will be bound to her forever."

Aislyn had not considered this before. "Then I will renounce my claim on him and bid him have the marriage annulled."

"On what grounds?"

"Non-consummation." Aislyn bit her lip in mortification as Morgana glanced significantly toward the bed. "But—but he does not know," she stammered. "He thinks it was a dream—"

"What you have made him believe does not alter the truth." Morgana put her hand on Aislyn's, looking hard into her eyes. "There is more to magic than mastering spells, and I fear your knowledge has far outrun your wisdom. Given who your teacher was, that is hardly a surprise, but the responsibility for your words and deeds is yours alone."

"I will make it right," Aislyn swore.

"How can you? It is beyond your power to undo what has been done or unsay the lies that you have spoken."

"But I'll end the marriage—he will be free!"

"Lies come easily to you, don't they?" Morgana went on as though she had not spoken. "You have not yet learned what a burden they can be." She smiled suddenly and patted Aislyn's hand. "I am going to give you a great gift."

"You—you are? Thank—"

"I am going to make your lie the truth."

"What? What lie?"

"That's the trouble with lies," Morgana said, shaking

her head sadly. "One leads to the next, and soon it is impossible to keep them all in order. But we shall simplify matters. You wanted to be Dame Ragnelle—very well, then, Dame Ragnelle you are and shall remain." Aislyn gasped, sudden pain bending her double, though it was gone before she could cry out. "There," Morgana said. "Now there is no lie to trouble you."

"You cannot mean—you wouldn't—"

"I do and I have. Did you really think you would escape unscathed after such an affront to Gawain's honor?"

"But—but how can it help him if I am left like this? He is miserable—"

" 'Tis a bit late for *that* to trouble you." Morgana's lips curved in a smile. "Dame Ragnelle is very old. I daresay he will outlive her and wed again."

Aislyn clutched the bedpost. "You cannot leave me like this!"

Morgana's brows lifted. "Can I not?"

"Please," Aislyn whispered. "I was wrong, I know that now. I will tell him everything—"

"Too late," Morgana said, rising to her feet and brushing the cat hair from her skirt. "That is the way of life, I fear. You know a thing should be done, yet you put it off, and then the chance is gone. You will not tell him anything of this. Oh, you can try, but you will find it impossible to speak the words. You are Dame Ragnelle and always have been."

"Your Grace," Aislyn said, "have mercy—"

"As you did when you forced my nephew to marry a hideous crone? No, *don't* weep. It does not become one of your years."

Outrage snapped Aislyn's neck straight. "I am not weeping."

"Better." Morgana nodded her approval. "Perhaps there is something to you after all. Oh, very well, I will give you a chance to undo what I have done . . . in part. Should

Gawain kiss you—a true kiss, offered with love and accepted in kind—then shall you revert to your true form for half of each day."

"But that is impossible!" Aislyn cried. "He will never kiss me—not the sort of kiss you mean, not as I am now!"

"It doesn't seem likely, does it? But love has a way of overcoming obstacles."

"Love?" Aislyn laughed wildly. "He detests me!"

"I daresay. What do you feel for him?"

Aislyn opened her mouth to say she disliked him, but then she remembered the wild magic that had flared between them last night. "I don't know."

"Then you had better find out, hadn't you?"

# Chapter 11

• • •

"DO you have need of me today, madam?" Launfal asked.

"Why?" Morgause, seated at her writing table in her chamber at Lothian Castle, did not look up from the parchment she was reading.

"I had a mind to go down to the practice yard."

"I don't think that would be a good idea," Morgause said absently, waving one hand in dismissal. For a moment the temptation to seize her wrist and snap it was so strong it frightened him. These impulses had been coming more frequently of late, a black tide that washed away all rational thought. He lived in fear that one day the tide would simply take him—and if it ever did, he would not stop until he'd killed her. He would be a dead man anyway, why should he go to hell alone?

But he had not yet abandoned all hope and sanity, so he deliberately relaxed his fists before he spoke again.

"The exercise would do me good. And if you have nothing else for me to do—"

"I didn't say *that.*" She glanced up at him with an arch smile that chilled his blood. "I know I have been neglecting you of late," she went on, "but I may have time for you when I am finished here."

Her definition of neglect was not one he shared: a mere two days had passed since he had last been called upon to pleasure her. Other men might scorn him, believing he led an easy life, but none of them had experienced Morgause in bed.

"That would be wonderful!" he said warmly. "And if you do, you can send for me—"

She looked up at him directly then. "*Send* for you? Why should I? What *is* this about?"

"I need to get out," he said, deciding that a touch of honesty would not come amiss. "To breathe the fresh air."

"Do you?" She gazed at him thoughtfully, brushing the feather of her quill across her lips. "Well, Launfal, if my service is so wearisome, you could always return to the fields. There is plenty of fresh air there. *And* exercise."

*Yes,* he thought, *send me back. Anything but this!* But once again, he bit back the words. If he went back among the varlets now, it would be over. He would never leave this place. Never become a knight. Even the faint hope of achieving that dream would be at an end, and without his dreams . . .

He could not bear to go back to the life he had known after Aislyn had vanished and he and his mother had fallen so abruptly from the queen's favor. Between one day and the next, Launfal had found his status changed from that of guest to the meanest servant. His mother, the one time she had dared to speak to him, said only that they must both adjust to changed conditions. But she, at least, still dwelt among the queen's women, while Launfal, with no place in the strict hierarchy of the castle servants, was the lowest of the low.

He was given the most difficult and noisome tasks, and

his ignorance of how to perform them earned him frequent beatings. The friends he had made among the squires no longer knew him, and he could not even speak to his new peers, for their language was so unfamiliar that he might as well have landed in a foreign country. They understood him well enough—had, in some cases, served him in the past—but now took a vicious pleasure in pretending they did not.

Twice he had run off and twice been taken before the steward and whipped. "Try it again, lad," the steward had growled the second time, "and you'll be branded."

That put an end to his attempts to escape. No man so marked could ever hope to become a knight.

Launfal learned to fight then—not the noble feats of arms he had dreamed of, but silent, deadly struggles over half an onion or a bit of cheese. Even when he won, it was never enough to fill his belly, and he lived for the moment he could crawl beneath a mound of straw and lose himself in dreams of the day this would all be over and he would be back where he belonged. If that hope was lost to him, he might as well be dead.

Now he forced himself to laugh as though Morgause had made a joke, though he knew her to be serious. "Wearisome? Oh, madam, you shouldn't say such things! 'Tis only that you've been so occupied of late . . ."

"And do you think to find companionship in the practice yard?" she asked, still regarding him with that unsettling intensity. "I seem to recall that the knights have been unkind to you in the past."

They despised him to a man, called him the queen's whore and worse—not troubling to lower their voices, either, for they had learned he would not fight back, though they did not know what held his hand.

Morgause had forbidden him to fight. She did not want his face marred, nor for him to be incapacitated when she had need of him. "I ask very little of you," she had said the one time he disobeyed her, "but if it is too much, you need only say so."

That had been a mere two years ago, though it seemed an age. He had still retained some innocence then, enough to believe her capable of human emotion. "Oh, no, madam, I am pleased to serve you," he had said earnestly, "it is only that I would like to serve you as a knight."

Morgause had laughed. "A knight? You? Oh, no, Launfal, you are quite unsuited to *that* role! If your service to me irks you, then you shall return to your place among the varlets."

He still remembered the shock of that, as though she had struck him across the face. "But—but you said that was a mistake!" he had stammered in bewilderment. "You said you never meant for me, a knight's son, to—"

"I?" She raised her brows, looking at him as though he had gone mad.

Had he known her better, he would have stopped right there. But he had not yet realized that to Morgause, truth was not an absolute, but a weapon she wielded according to her whim.

"It was the night you first brought me to your chamber, do you not remember?" that innocent, ignorant boy had protested, as though she could be moved by reason. "You must! You sat just there—surely you recall—and said you were sorry, that you hadn't known I was sent to live among the servants, that—"

"Lower your voice," she said coldly.

"But you must listen—"

"*Must*? How dare you speak to me like that? Your disobedience—your gross ingratitude and impertinence—have wounded me deeply. *I* am queen of this demesne, and *I* shall set the terms of your service. If I say you are a varlet, then so you are. Do you understand me?"

And then, at last, Launfal did understand. Her soft words and apologies that first night had all been lies. Now that those lies no longer suited her, she had changed them for a different set. There was but one grain of truth in what she'd told him: she was indeed the queen, and her word was quite literally the law.

Two years had passed since that realization and Launfal was still alive, a victory won at the cost of a thousand betrayals of himself. Did one more really matter?

*Yes,* he thought, looking at her sitting at her writing table. *Yes, it does matter.*

Morgause smiled indulgently, and throwing down her quill, she stood. "Oh, very well," she said. "I can see I *have* neglected you, but I shall make amends."

The black tide swept over him again, and again he beat it back as she approached him slowly, no longer the queen but a woman bent upon seduction. How could she not know how she revolted him? In the days since their return from Inglewood Forest, it had become almost impossible to hide.

His anger died, leaving the familiar bewilderment in its place. He had always tried to be a good son, a good brother—even a good servant when such had been his lot. Yet despite all his efforts, God had been blind to his plight and deaf to his prayers.

There is no God, he thought. Heaven holds only stars and empty air. There is nothing but ourselves.

Morgause was close enough that he could smell the scent she favored, one that had once delighted him and now made his stomach twist. *I cannot do this,* he thought, *or no, I could. I have before.*

*I* will *not.*

He straightened, and for a moment she hesitated, a flicker of uneasiness passing across her face.

"Madam," he began, and was interrupted by a knock upon the door.

"A messenger from Camelot," the serving girl said, and Morgause forgot him instantly as she swept from the room.

Launfal waited only long enough for her footsteps to vanish down the passageway before he slipped after her and out a side door, not bothering to take even his cloak.

• • •

HE made it only as far as the orchard before he was halted by a squire from the queen. He thought briefly of making a run for it, but now that he had determined to leave at any cost, his mind was working with cool precision.

*Wait,* it said. *Your chance will come.*

"The queen is in a rare mood," the squire said as they walked back to the castle. "It seems Sir Gawain has wed without her leave—they're saying there's something odd about his marriage."

Morgause was pacing her chamber, two knights standing by the window and eyeing her warily. Her face was mottled with hectic color, her eyes narrowed into slits. Launfal had once told her she was beautiful in a temper, but like most of what he said to her, it was a lie.

"I leave for court tomorrow," she declared.

*And I?* Launfal wondered, his heartbeat quickening. If once he reached Camelot, he would be free. King Arthur was said to be both just and merciful; hearing Launfal's tale, surely the king would take pity on him. And if he was left behind, he would be free, as well. Who would bother with the queen's whore when the queen was gone away?

Perhaps there was someone up in heaven after all.

"Be sure to have them pack the amber gown," he said casually, sprawling in a chair and plucking a handful of cherries from a dish. "It is wasted here."

"The amber—?" She whirled to face him, and the fine hairs on his arms lifted when she burst out laughing. "Oh, you are good."

"Am I?" He tried to smile, but his face was oddly stiff. She sat down on the arm of his chair and drew a finger down his cheek.

"You'll never guess what the messenger told me," she said teasingly.

"That Sir Gawain is wed?"

"Mmm, yes, but there was more." Her hand slipped beneath his chin and she lifted his face to her. "It was about Somer Gromer Jour—do you remember him? Apparently when the king gave him the answer, he said something very curious. Can you tell me what it was?"

Launfal's heart began to thunder in his chest, but he forced himself to hold her eye. "No, madam. I cannot recall having said anything—well, perhaps I cursed a bit, but—"

"He said"—Morgause leaned close—"now, what were the words? Oh, yes, I remember. He said, 'my *sister* told you that.' "

Launfal swallowed audibly. He *had* said those words—blurted them out in shock—though he hadn't known he had been overheard. His mind raced, trying to find some explanation that would not sound too ridiculous, but he could only shake his head, attempting to look puzzled. "No," he said, "I don't recall—"

He saw the blow coming and turned his head to the right, so Morgause's palm merely brushed his cheek. "You lied to me that day. How many other times have you lied?"

"Never! Oh, very well, I did think it might be Aislyn, and I didn't tell you because it would only have upset you."

"And yet you knew full well I was looking for her."

"I did, but—I mean to say, she *is* my sister, and—"

This time he failed to anticipate the slap. It snapped his head back with such force that his skull hit the wall behind him with an audible crack. One of the knights—whose presence now seemed ominous—laughed.

"After all that I have done for you, *this* is how you repay me! I took you from the stables and gave you all any man could desire." She stood abruptly. "But it is finished. I have been growing weary of you for some time now, and this is the final straw. I am through with you."

Launfal stood, as well. His cheek throbbed and his skull was tender, but if that was the worst of it, he'd gotten off lightly. "I—I am sorry that I no longer please you," he said, nearly gagging on the words. "But I hope—that is, if I ever—" Gritting his teeth, he went to his knees. "For the sake of what we once had, I pray you give me leave to go to—"

"Go? You are not going anywhere! Oh, Launfal, and here I thought you were only *pretending* to be witless! You do not honestly think I will allow you to leave here?"

Hot blood rushed to his face and pounded in his temples. "Why should I not?" he said, rising. "God knows I have earned *some* reward from you."

She made to strike him and he grasped her wrist, pulling her hard against him. Desire flared in her eyes, and later he thought that one kiss might have melted her—at least long enough for him to consider his options. But his blood was up and he could only think how ridiculous she looked gazing up at him like a moonstruck calf—and in the next moment it was too late, for he had made his fatal mistake.

He laughed.

Morgause wrenched away from him. "Sir Ewan, Sir Col," she said coldly, "seize this man. He has laid hands upon the queen."

"Is that a crime?" Launfal said, still laughing. "Then I should have plenty of company in the dungeons!"

His arms were taken and pinned behind him, but he ducked away as Morgause aimed a blow at his face. "You find this amusing?" she hissed.

"No," he said, his chest still heaving with something that had gone beyond laughter. "I find it pathetic—almost as pathetic as I find you."

"Hark the churl who dreamed of knighthood! But you

are mine, Launfal, my property to do with as I will. Lest you forget it again, I will put my mark on you. Hold him down," she ordered curtly, and turned to thrust a poker—or no, dear God, it was a branding iron—into the heart of the fire.

Launfal fought, but the two knights were both large and strong. When they had forced him to his knees, Morgause wound her fingers through his hair and jerked his head up. "Such a pretty lad," she mocked, "such a pity." She fumbled one-handed for the iron and Launfal let himself sag in the grip of his captors. They shifted, fumbling for a better grip, relaxing their hold on his hands as they hauled him upright.

"Please," he whispered, "madam, don't—not that—"

"What, you do not want to bear my mark? Now I call that ungrateful."

As she passed the glowing brand before his face, Launfal found he did not have to feign the tears rising to his eyes. He shrank back against the two knights, knocking them off balance. "Don't mark me," he whispered. "Anything but that."

Morgause drew the iron back. "Anything? Well, I suppose we could geld you instead."

The terror was like ice. "No!" he cried, "mark me—please, madam, I—I would b-be honored to wear your brand, I will serve you m-most loyally, I swear it." He straightened, shifting his weight forward as he lifted his head and shook the hair back from his face.

"I say he should be gelded," one of the knights said.

"Wouldn't be much of a loss, though, would it?" the other answered, and they both laughed.

Their hands relaxed fractionally—not enough, but it was the best chance Launfal would have. He forced himself to remain perfectly still as the brand approached his face, but just as its tip seared his flesh, he lunged awkwardly forward and seized the burning end one-handed, twisting it from Morgause's grasp. Still on his knees, he flipped it and swung blindly behind him. The knight on his left fell back with a shout.

Launfal wrenched himself to his feet, bringing the iron around with all his strength. It struck the second knight full in the face and he went down like a stone. The first knight staggered to his feet and drew his sword. Before it had cleared the scabbard, Launfal felled him with a single blow. Morgause picked up her skirts and ran for the door, but he was there before her, the smoking iron at her throat.

He gestured toward the chair. "Sit."

His cheek hurt, but it was his hand that was the trouble, for it was seared to the bone. The pain and the stench of charred flesh made him want to vomit.

"Give me your scarf," he ordered harshly, and awkwardly, juggling the iron and setting his teeth against the pain of his seared palm, he bound her wrists to the arms of the chair. She attempted to rise once and he stepped back, the iron raised.

It would be so much simpler to kill her. More practical, as well. No matter how well he bound her, she would soon be free to raise the alarm. But the truth was that he *wanted* to kill her. He had wanted to for a very long time and he would never have another chance.

She looked into his eyes and sagged back in a faint that he doubted was genuine. Even if it was, what difference did it make? He could kill her just as easily unconscious.

The iron trembled in his grasp as he lifted it, then with a curse he let it fall and bent to jerk the knots tight about her wrists.

He bound both knights and relieved them of their weapons. The daggers he tucked into his belt; one sword he flung from the window, and the other he kept in his hand as he made for the door. It had been a long time since he'd held a sword. He had forgotten how good it felt. How right.

*Enjoy it while you can,* he thought, *for you won't have it long.* But at least he would go down fighting, not whipped and starved like an animal. He eased out the door, checking the passageway in both directions before heading for the back stairway.

He clattered down the twisting stairs at a dead run, halting with a gasp when he rounded a corner and found himself face-to-face with a young man who gave a startled cry, the book he had been holding falling from his hand.

"Launfal!" Prince Gaheris said, half laughing. "You gave me a start! Where are you—"

He fell silent, his eyes widening as they moved from the sword in Launfal's hand to his face.

Of the three princes still in Lothian, Launfal had always liked Gaheris best; in part because he was Morgause's least favorite of her brood, but also for himself. In another life, he'd sometimes thought, they might have been friends.

"What have you done?" Gaheris whispered. "Did you—is she—"

"Alive. Unharmed," Launfal said harshly.

He froze, looking toward the upper corridor, where the sounds of raised voices and running feet could be heard. He would *not* be taken here, trapped like a beast in its lair. His one remaining goal was to make it to the courtyard, where he would sell his life as dearly as he could.

"Move," he ordered Gaheris, raising the sword's point to his chest. "*Now.*"

Gaheris's gaze snapped back to him. "Come with me," he ordered and plunged through a curtained doorway leading to a storeroom. "Hurry," he hissed over his shoulder.

Launfal hesitated for the space of a heartbeat before he followed.

# Chapter 12

• • •

MORGANA found Gawain in the hall, sitting with a knight who rose as she approached, bowed to her, and hurried off.

"What ails your friend?" she asked, sitting down beside Gawain.

"He thinks you'll turn him into a tree if he offends you."

Morgana gazed after the retreating knight with interest. "Is he so offensive?"

Gawain shrugged. "Dinadan has never learned to guard his tongue. When he sees a jest, he cannot help but share it."

"How unfortunate for him. But tell him he needn't run next time. I have never yet turned any man into a tree—or anything else, for that matter."

After today, she could not say the same of women, but she felt no need to share that information with Gawain.

What Morgana had told Aislyn was true: she was extremely fond of her eldest nephew. What she had not said was that Gawain often annoyed her greatly, or that they had quarreled the last time they met. But now, looking at him, she felt only pride in how well he was bearing up under his disastrous marriage and could not recall why they had argued.

"Welladay," she said, gently chiding. "I turn my back, and now look at the trouble you've gotten yourself into!"

He smiled, albeit a trifle wryly, more in acknowledgment of her tone than of her words. Morgana was not so much older than he was himself, but had always taken her status as aunt very seriously.

"I wed. It happens. And it might as well be Dame Ragnelle as anyone."

"Does your mother know of this?"

He shrugged. "I suppose she'll hear sooner or later."

"And then she'll come to meet your bride for herself."

Of course by then, this whole charade would be finished. Despite what she'd said to Aislyn, Morgana had no intention of leaving her as a crone forevermore. She had meant to give the girl a fortnight or so in which to attempt the impossible, just time enough for Aislyn to repent the folly of her actions. Now she wondered if it was fair to make Gawain suffer even for that long.

"Mother won't come. I don't want her here and she knows it."

"And you think *that* is enough to keep her away?" Morgana laughed.

"It has served so far. Now tell me what has kept *you* away for so long. Where have you been?"

"Here and there," she said.

He frowned. "It isn't right for you to be traveling about the countryside on your own. It isn't safe."

"I can look after myself. And I have work to do."

"Work!" he said, dismissing all her years of study and labor with a wave of his hand. "You should marry."

*Now* she remembered why they had quarreled.

Angry as she was, she felt the old puzzled sorrow rise in

her when she gazed upon her nephew. Much of Morgana's childhood had been lost amid the turbulent romance between her mother and Uther Pendragon, but once Gawain was born, she had reclaimed at least a part of it. As a child, he had been her shadow, and they had spent many a day wandering the wood or lying in the meadow practicing birdcalls and watching clouds drift by.

Then Morgana had entered fully into her own studies, but she had followed his adventures with no small measure of pride. The Great Mother of them all was watching over him, she knew; testing him, training him, presenting him with the very lessons he had chosen to learn during this life. Whatever might befall Gawain, his spirit never shrank from it, but rose to meet each new challenge. Even when he had gone to meet the Green Knight and it seemed certain he would not return, he had laughed at those who would have sent him off with tears.

But some years ago, Gawain had undergone a strange and puzzling change, and her attempts to win his confidence were fruitless. He no longer looked to her for wisdom or valued her advice, nor was it only she he turned from. Ragnelle spoke truly on that score; Gawain was notorious for his contempt for all things feminine. And despite all Morgana's prayers on his behalf, the Goddess seemed to have turned her face from him, as well.

"Do I hear aright?" she said, half laughing. "Are you giving *me* advice on marriage?"

"Why not?"

"Tell me, Gawain, have you lain with that . . . woman you have wed?"

"What goes on between us is no business of yours or anyone's. It is an honorable union."

"It is a denial of life," she said flatly.

He snorted. "And here I thought your Goddess is in all women!"

Morgana stared at him. "What did you say?"

He did not deign to repeat himself, but it did not matter. She had heard him well enough. And he had spoken a simple truth that took her breath away.

The Goddess *was* all women—maiden, mother, crone. Gawain could not see Her face in his mother, and that was no surprise, given what Morgause was. His obstinate refusal to take a maiden to wife was proof enough that he was blind and deaf to Her in that form, as well.

And that left only the crone.

A slow chill wound down Morgana's spine. She had thought she did her own will when she enspelled Ragnelle, but now she realized she had been prompted by the Goddess. She knew not what would come of her actions, but that was not in her hands. She had done what she was meant to do.

"Come, Gawain, let me kiss you before I go."

"Go? But you've just arrived!"

"I needed to speak with the king, and now I must away. But I will see you again at Midsummer," she said, rising to her feet and setting her lips to his brow. "You know I wish you nothing but good fortune."

He smiled, then, with something of his old affection. "And I you. Take care, Morgana."

"I always do." She looked at him a moment, then said, "Your lady—no, don't frown, I will say no more against your marriage, for it is done. But Dame Ragnelle fancies herself something of a witch, I fear. Do you take her bag from her and lock it in your trunk. It is dangerous for her to be meddling with magic."

Gawain nodded. "I shall."

She turned to go, then halted and looked back, feeling there was something yet undone. Her lips and fingertips tingled, and she spoke before she had any idea what she meant to say. "If you would know happiness, you have only to give your lady that which all women desire."

He looked up from his porridge, brows raised. "Not that

silly riddle again! Go on, then, tell me what it is all women desire."

"I cannot tell you. You must discover it yourself."

He waved a hand. "I've already wasted a full year searching for that answer, and in the end, Dame Ragnelle did not deem me worthy to hear it. So I am afraid I cannot oblige her even if I would."

"Mark me well, Gawain," Morgana said, and heard the echo of another voice that spoke through her. "This is more important than you can imagine."

"If it's so damn important, she should have asked me plainly. I have no time for games and no patience for them, either."

"This is no game, but a task given to you to accomplish."

Something in her tone must have reached him, for he sighed. "Very well, Morgana. If I ever do stumble across the answer—which seems unlikely—I will consider the matter then."

# Chapter 13

• • •

BY the time Aislyn reached the hall, it was deserted. She hobbled stiffly through the courtyard to the gardens, where the queen and her ladies sat sewing.

"Ah, Dame Ragnelle," Guinevere said. "What can I do for you this morning?"

"I was looking for the duchess of Cornwall."

"She has already left us," Guinevere said.

"Where did she go?"

"I cannot say." Guinevere looked past Aislyn, her face brightening. "Perhaps my lord can tell you."

Aislyn turned to see Arthur walk into the garden with half a dozen of his knights. Gawain was among them. Aislyn's breath caught when she saw him; warmth suffused her face as she remembered him last night, shaking with passion in her arms.

His gaze passed over her, pausing only briefly to acknowledge her existence before moving on. She felt oddly bereft, but he could hardly be expected to connect her bent and withered form with the woman who had curled against him, her head pillowed on his shoulder as he whispered love words into her hair, and—

*Stop. It wasn't real, he didn't know . . . oh, holy Mother, what have I done? What am I to do now?*

"My lady," the king said, bowing to Guinevere. "I must away to Kent."

"Oh, but the tournament—!" Guinevere began.

"I know, and I am sorry, but there is no help for it. I must take counsel of King Aesc at once. Sir Gawain alone will accompany me, and we shall try to return before the end."

"Is the duchess of Cornwall gone?" Aislyn said to Gawain as he approached.

"Yes, she could not stay. What did she say to you before?"

"Not much," Aislyn lied. "Do you know where she was bound?"

"Morgana goes where she will. But she will be back for the feast at Midsummer."

Midsummer? Oh, no, that was far too long to remain as she was!

"Gawain," she said. "About the duchess of Cornwall. She—she—" Aislyn's throat closed like a snare, trapping the words she meant to speak.

"Yes?" Gawain said, glancing over toward the king.

"I am—I was—" Damn Morgana! Whatever she had done, it was working all too well.

Gawain drew on his gloves. "My aunt advised me to take your bag from you," he said, "and I have done so."

"My bag? But I need that!"

"For what?"

"I—I—my old bones ache sometimes," she said, "and all my remedies are in there."

"You can get anything you need from Lady Enid," Gawain said.

Not devil's trumpet, Aislyn thought, sown at the dark of the moon and harvested on Midsummer's Eve. Nor her pierced wolf's tooth or the water she had gathered on the first day of May at the very moment the sun fell upon the black lake, bearing it back home beneath the golden bridge without speaking a word to anyone.

But she could hardly tell Gawain that.

"I want my own remedies!" was the best she could manage.

"I am sorry, but my decision is final."

She glared at him, then remembering Morgana's words, assumed a meek expression. "Whatever pleases you, husband."

He sketched her a small bow. "God keep you," he said, and turned to go.

"Wait!" she cried, hurrying after him.

"Yes?"

"I—I—can I have a kiss?" Aislyn blurted out.

Several people standing nearby laughed, and Aislyn's face grew hot with mortification. Of course he would not kiss her. It was a wonder he could even bear to look upon her. Most men would not have endured the crone for even this long; why Gawain had was a mystery, and to ask for more was a risk she dared not take.

Yesterday she had wanted nothing more but to see him lose control of his temper, but now, as he turned back, the grim set to his mouth filled her with fear. What if he sent her away to Orkney—or worse, to Lothian, where his mother dwelt? He could. It was well within his power, and no one would blame him in the slightest. The only thing preventing him was a promise.

Men broke promises. They did it every day. Gawain had what he'd wanted from her: the king was safe. He'd have to be mad to keep her by him when he could be rid of her with just a word.

He gazed down at her, then shook his head and sighed a little before bending to brush his lips across her brow.

Aislyn looked down at the crone's horny toes protruding from holes she'd cut in her slippers. She wiped her eyes across her sleeve as she retreated to the secluded turf bench where she had sat with Gawain. It was still in shadow at this hour and she sank down upon it, watching as the king and Gawain departed.

It hadn't worked. But then, it wasn't exactly a *loving* kiss she'd had from Gawain. That he'd done it at all was a surprise—and a good sign, she told herself. She doubted he could have managed it the first day he'd met the crone.

*Me,* she thought. *I* am *the crone now.*

*Don't weep. It does not become one of your years.*

She had to act. And she would. She slumped against the back of the bench. As soon as she figured out what to do, she'd do it, but just now, she didn't have even the beginning of a plan.

The other knights lingered to talk to Guinevere's ladies. The queen dismissed the two girls beside her as Lancelot approached. He nodded to them as they went, then cast himself on the grass at the queen's feet.

The light voices and laughter of the knights and ladies floated through the sun-splashed garden, mingling with the fountain's song and the birdsong up among the branches of the trees. One merry group had gathered beneath the shade of a willow close beside the gate. Sir Dinadan was in the center, and between bursts of laughter, Aislyn caught the sound of his voice raised in song.

*—the clever wight,*
*To guess the name of this noble knight,*
*Who can talk the day into the night,*
*Speaking only of himself, alas!*
*He loves no one but himself.*

The queen bent over her tapestry frame and Lancelot closed his eyes, arms crossed beneath his head. Aislyn thought they looked like an illumination in a book: the lady and her knight.

"What's ado with King Aesc?" the queen asked. "I thought that was all settled long ago."

"It was, but now that Aesc has made peace with his kinsmen of Wessex, they are after him to repudiate his treaty with Arthur and join with them against the king."

"What, to turn traitor to my lord?" Guinevere said indignantly. "After all he has done for King Aesc!"

"So far Aesc is standing firm," Lancelot said, "and he is doing what he can to bring about an agreement between his kinsmen and the king. Still, Aesc is but one man, and you know how proud those Saxons are. There are many among his own people who are not entirely happy to be under Arthur's rule."

"I'm sure my lord will sort it out," Guinevere said vaguely.

"I offered to go with him, but he *would* take Sir Gawain."

"Of course he took Sir Gawain. To get him away from . . . her."

"Have you found out why he married her?" Lancelot asked, lowering his voice.

"Not a thing. And you?"

"No one knows anything," he said, and laughed. "Save that he must have done something awful to merit *that*. I wonder what it was . . ."

"We are bound to find out," Guinevere assured him. "Such a dark deed cannot be forever hidden."

"I suppose the king knows," Lancelot mused. "And has forgiven him—of course."

"Of course. He would forgive Sir Gawain anything."

Lancelot turned over on his side and propped his head in his hand. "So that's another tournament our first knight will miss."

Guinevere smiled down at him. "Poor Lance! Well, you'll beat everyone else."

"I've already beaten everyone else." He plucked at the grass. "And Sir Gawain refuses to fight me."

"It isn't only you," Guinevere said fairly. "He never accepts private challenges."

So he still held to that belief. Aislyn remembered him saying long ago that he thought them foolish. "A melee is one thing," he had said then, "because that's a chance to learn your strengths and weaknesses—and those of your companions. But these private jousts are all for show, and good men are sometimes injured—and that's a wicked waste if they are called to battle."

She had thought it sensible then, though only now did she understand how unpopular an opinion that was to hold at court.

Lancelot rolled over on his back. "Ah, well. He can't avoid me forever."

"No, he can't."

Aislyn sighed and began to lift herself from the bench, but she dreaded walking through the knights and ladies beneath the willow. Dinadan was still on his feet, and to judge by the laughter, his song was going over well.

*A shield that gives you strength tenfold,*
*Presented by a maid in gold,*
*Who did his beauty once behold*
*And promptly fell down dead and cold.*
*For he would not return her love, oh, fie!*
*He loves no one but himself.*

Guinevere looked over at them, frowning, and Lancelot lifted himself on his elbows. "Why, that damned impudent—" he began.

"Sir Gudrun is here," Guinevere interrupted him.

Lancelot waved a hand, beckoning to the tall, light-haired Saxon who had sat beside Sir Dinadan at Aislyn's wedding feast.

"Oh, Lance, must you?" Guinevere said. "He is so tiresome."

"Weren't you listening to anything I said before?" Lancelot said as he scrambled to his feet. "He is King Aesc's brother; now be—good day, Sir Gudrun!"

Guinevere looked up at the Saxon, smiling. "We were just discussing the tournament. Will you compete?"

"Oh, yes, lady," Gudrun said. "I am to ride on Sir Lancelot's side. Is that not so?" He nudged Lancelot in the ribs and they turned to look across the garden.

*He's off to battle like a shot,*
*With a sword, a shield, a lance, a—what?*
*Oh, come good people, you must wot*
*His noble name by now; that knight*
*Who loves no one but himself—not he!*
*He loves no one but himself.*

One look at Lancelot's face was enough to prove that he, at least, wotted well the subject of Dinadan's song. He and Gudrun exchanged a glance, then burst out laughing.

"What?" Guinevere said, gazing perplexed from one to the other. "Do you find Sir Dinadan amusing?"

"Oh, very," Lancelot said. "Good day, lady, we've much to do before the tournament."

"Yes, indeed, we do," Gudrun agreed, and the two of them went off together, smiling.

•

# Chapter 14

• • •

IT was a small company that set out for Kent to meet with King Aesc, chief among Arthur's Saxon allies. A mere dozen men-at-arms followed the king and Gawain through the gate and down into the village. People lined the road as they went by, cheering and calling out greetings, which Arthur returned with somewhat less cheer than was his wont. As they passed into the wood, the king gestured for Gawain to ride ahead with him.

"Is aught amiss?" Gawain asked when they were out of earshot of the others.

"You tell me," Arthur answered, looking at him closely.

"Then no, there is naught amiss at all," Gawain answered with a smile.

"How you bore Dame Ragnelle yesterday was more than I could fathom," Arthur said. "I think you must have the patience of a saint!"

"She is a trial," Gawain admitted, "but I think she has lived a hard life. It's rather sad, really, that she finally has the things she's longed for and is too old to enjoy them properly. I daresay I'd be ill-humored myself if I were her."

"That's taking a very charitable view of the situation."

Gawain shrugged. "What else is there to do?"

They rode in silence for a time, while Gawain tried to find some way to cheer the king. But there seemed no more to be said upon the subject of Dame Ragnelle, and though he attempted to turn the talk to King Aesc and the growing problem of his Wessex kin, Arthur was oddly subdued. At last the king made an excuse to ride back to the men-at-arms.

Gawain was sorry to see him go, but at the same time, he was relieved. This was exactly why he had asked Arthur not to reveal the reason he had married Dame Ragnelle. The last thing he wanted was anyone else looking at him with that furtive pity and concern.

Ah, well, he comforted himself, Arthur is a sensible fellow; sooner or later, he will accept what cannot be changed. Now that Gawain knew that Dame Ragnelle wasn't about to press her marriage rights, he did not much mind her. Oh, she was still as ugly as the day was long, but even now he didn't view her with the same revulsion as he had on their first meeting. And if she embarrassed him from time to time . . . well, at least she wouldn't put horns on his head, as so many young brides had done to their besotted knights. If a bit of awkwardness was the worst she had to offer, he could live with it without too much distress.

The forest gave way to neatly tilled fields, and the scents of leaf and mold to that of fresh-turned earth. A light rain began to fall, though the sun still shone to the east. For a moment a dazzling rainbow arced over the fields before the clouds parted and the sun once more beat down upon Gawain's head. In the next field over, fat raindrops splashed upon brown soil, and the rainbow shone palely to the west before vanishing once again, only to blaze forth in the eastern sky.

It was on just such a changeable spring day that Gawain

had first ridden to Camelot, his heart filled with all manner of terrible forebodings.

He had been weaned upon the tale of Uther Pendragon, who had murdered Gawain's grandfather, the duke of Cornwall and Uther's loyal subject. On that same night, Uther ravished the duke's wife, Igraine, after having himself magicked into the duke's likeness so Igraine believed it was her own husband she lay with. Nine months later, Arthur had been born.

That Uther had truly loved Igraine, had married her, and made her queen of Britain might have absolved him of some measure of his treachery in the eyes of the world—but not in the eyes of Igraine's eldest daughter, Morgause.

Morgause claimed to have loved her father, the murdered duke. Whether she had or not, Gawain never knew, for he had known little of loving-kindness at his mother's hands. It was hatred that defined Morgause, hatred first of Uther and later of the son he had gotten on Igraine. That hatred shaped the fate of Morgause's husband, whom she urged to rebel against the newly crowned King Arthur. It had shaped Gawain's, as well, when at fourteen he was wrested from his home and sent as hostage to Arthur's court when the rebellion failed.

Gawain had expected his wicked uncle to be malformed, no doubt as a result of hearing him constantly referred to as "that misbegotten brat." But even if Arthur appeared to be a genial young man, he was still the son of the Pendragon, that personification of all evil. And Gawain was the grandson of the duke of Cornwall and Igraine.

There was that between him and Arthur that could never be forgotten: the blood of a loyal man, the rape of a good woman, a stain of dishonor that could only be washed away by death. So let Arthur call him "nephew" and treat him with all outward courtesy, as though he were a guest rather than a hostage. Gawain was far too canny to be so easily deceived. They had been born to be enemies.

Only . . . Arthur did not seem to understand that.

*It is a trick,* Gawain had thought that lonely first year, as he held himself proudly aloof from Arthur's overtures of friendship. *He acts out of political necessity,* he told himself the second year, when Arthur named him as heir and took him on progress. *He is a fool,* Gawain decided soon after his sixteenth birthday, when Arthur began to lesson him in battle tactics, though once he grasped the essence of Arthur's strategies, he could not call him fool for long. And when he understood that, to Arthur, military victory was not an end, but only the beginning of his vision for Britain, he no longer knew *what* to think.

That was the worst year of all.

Gawain knew what he *should* think. Given their shared history, the odds were good that one day he would become Arthur's rival for the throne. As he, Gawain, was neither halt nor witless, but a warrior of undeniable promise, Arthur had but two choices: have him killed or make of him an ally.

Gawain supposed he should be grateful Arthur had not chosen the first path, though there were times during that terrible year when he almost wished Arthur had. Better to die than to betray his kin and clan.

That Arthur was a kind and admirable man would have been bad enough—but not an insurmountable obstacle. There was no shame in respecting an enemy or even liking him. But Arthur was more than a man—he was a king like those of the old tales, as wise as he was strong.

"We must put aside the old ways," Arthur said to him one night, when they sat alone in his chamber over a game of chess, "the old blood feuds and hatreds handed down from one generation to the next. You have Sir Whatsis who argues with his neighbor over a disputed boundary—oftimes a matter of a few acres!—and so they come to blows, and before you know it, Whatsis's son is at daggers drawn with his neighbor's son, and so on and on. Of course, the argument is not always trivial . . ."

Their eyes met over the board. Met and held for a long, long moment.

"But the point remains the same. Why should we—why should any man," Arthur went on deliberately, "waste his life in avenging wrongs that happened long before he was born? What purpose does it serve to compound an error into infinity? And who really suffers for it? The poor lads who go off to die over some stale quarrel they do not even understand—and the farmers whose lands are trampled, so come winter all go hungry. And when Sir Whatsis is needed to fight the Saxons, he doesn't give his mind or heart to the real threat. No, he whinges on about how his neighbor got the better encampment—or that *his* men cannot possibly be stationed beside *those* men. Oh, it might sound like a mere annoyance, but when you have a dozen Sir Whatsises—a hundred—it can grind an army to a halt. And what, I ask you, is the point?"

Before Gawain could answer that the point was honor, Arthur hurried on. "And then you have that Bruce Sans Pitié who feels free to help himself to any maiden who catches his eye—and no one dares to say him nay because he is a noble! Where is the justice in that?"

Gawain opened his mouth to protest that every lord must hold sway over his own demesne, but Arthur gave him no chance to reply.

"Don't you see, we have it in us to create something entirely new—a Britain united under a single set of laws. And those laws won't be based on some old man's bile, but on justice—and not only for the knights and lords. Indeed," he added with a wry smile, "I often think that if it comes about at all, it will be despite them. These old men with their old grudges—they cannot see beyond the ends of their own noses or grasp that anything is more important than their petty quarrels. But the future doesn't belong to those old men, Gawain, it belongs to us, and together we can make of it anything we will."

Gawain tried to reconcile the two loyalties warring for supremacy over his heart, but they were so opposed that any treaty seemed impossible. Matters came to a head over his knighting, an occasion Arthur wanted to mark with elaborate celebrations. In the space of six months, Gawain gained three inches and lost half a stone, and finally sent a message to his parents begging them to negotiate for his release. The reply, written in his father's hand but no doubt dictated by his mother, was short and sharp. He was grown to a man's estate, it said, and they expected him to act accordingly. "Do what you must," it finished.

Ten days later, Gawain knelt before the king and rendered Arthur his oath of fealty. Once the deed was done, he did not look back. An oath taken was taken. A promise made must be fulfilled.

So it was with Dame Ragnelle. He wished Arthur understood that there was nothing to be gained by complaining of what could not be changed. But Arthur was a romantic, something Gawain had not been for years.

His thoughts drifted back to a dream he'd had last night—a strange dream, very vivid. He was tempted to relive every moment of it, but he wrested his mind firmly to the present.

No matter how enticing a dream of love might be, in the end it was no more than an illusion, and no one knew the danger of illusion—and of love—better than Gawain. But they are one, he reflected, for love is always an illusion, a trap to lead good men to ruin and disgrace. Give him reality any day, even if reality was a muddy road beneath a darkening sky, with a difficult negotiation to look forward to and Dame Ragnelle to welcome him home when it was done. For right here, right now he was awake, aware, utterly himself and completely in control of his own thoughts and actions.

It might not seem much to other men, but to Gawain it was enough.

# Chapter 15

• • •

AISLYN was in a foul temper by the time she stumped up the stairway toward the royal pavilion. She had spent the past two days searching for her bag, and once she realized it must be in the trunk, in trying first to pick the lock, then using every spell she knew to open it. All she had to show for her trouble was a broken bodkin and a headache.

She would far rather have been resting—hiding—in her chamber, but as the queen herself had sent a page to bring her to the tournament, she thought it prudent to attend. Guinevere sat beside Arthur's empty throne, and on her left hand was Sir Lancelot, brave in a scarlet cloak and cap with a long white feather that curled over one shoulder.

"Are you not competing, Sir Lancelot?" Aislyn asked, surprised to find him there.

When Lancelot turned to her, the wind caught his plume. Guinevere batted it away from her face.

"Since the king is gone away, our gracious lady asked me to judge the outcome," Lancelot replied politely.

"Lance," the queen complained, "can you not remove that dratted cap? The feather keeps getting in my eyes."

"Remove it? Madam, I would have you know this cost me a small fortune. I will turn my head away."

He was in high good spirits, as was Guinevere. The two of them were whispering like children, then breaking into gales of laughter. Aislyn's spirits lifted a trifle, for it had been years since she had seen a tournament, and never one half so fine as this. The knights were gathering below, Sir Kay's on one end of the field, Sir Pellinore's on the other. She leaned forward in her seat when the marshal dropped his scarf and the two sides charged.

Gawain had been right. It was like a battle. They came together with a fearsome clash, and it was impossible not to be caught up in the excitement. "Oh, well done, Sagramore!" Guinevere cried. "Sir Kay is down—he will have hard words for his groom tonight, I trow!" Aislyn turned this way and that, trying to follow Guinevere's pointing finger, but it was such a press of heaving steeds and shouting men that she wondered how Sir Lancelot could possibly decide the winner. She turned to ask him—only to find another man sitting in his place, wearing the scarlet cloak and cap.

A great burst of laughter erupted from the audience and she saw a knight ride into the melee, wearing— She blinked and rubbed her eyes, but she had seen aright. The knight was wearing a yellow gown over his armor, the skirts ruched up over his legs and fluttering behind him as he galloped into the fray.

It had to be Sir Lancelot. The tales of his prowess had not been exaggerated, Aislyn thought. He rode like a fury, knocking knights aside as though they were straw men, only to pull up his charger before two knights who were engaged. One fell; the other—Sir Dinadan, she realized from his shield, turned to find Lancelot ready to engage him.

Aislyn was on her feet now, hands twisting as she waited for the charge. Lancelot put heels to his horse, but at the last moment he turned aside, making a show of smoothing down his skirt as Dinadan's steed swept by him. Having arranged the billowing fabric to his satisfaction, Lancelot lifted his spear as though ready to engage his opponent, giving an exaggerated start when he realized Dinadan was no longer facing him. He raised himself in his stirrups and turned his head this way and that, one gauntleted hand shading his visor as he sought his vanished opponent.

The other knights had drawn back to watch, and the stands rang with cheers and laughter as Lancelot finally spotted Dinadan and with a flourishing bow, invited him to joust.

It was over in a moment. Dinadan went down amid a burst of laughter from the crowd. Guinevere sat forward in her seat, a hand pressed across her mouth and tears of merriment streaming down her cheeks.

Ah, well, Aislyn thought, Dinadan *had* asked for it. She was relieved, though, when he stood and waved to the crowd, then with a bow as exaggerated as Lancelot's had been, saluted the victor before mounting his horse and turning for the sidelines. He was halfway there when Lancelot and another knight—Aislyn could not see who it was—came up on either side of him and escorted him off the field and into the forest.

"Where did they go?" she asked Guinevere.

"Off to drink, no doubt, and make up their quarrel."

Aislyn wondered why they couldn't wait for the feast to drink together; it seemed odd that Lancelot had abandoned the field when he surely would have carried off the prize, which turned out to be a two-handed cup filled with silver coin, presented by the queen to a rather stunned-looking Sir Sagramore.

Maybe Lancelot was so wealthy he did not care, though he must be very wealthy indeed to turn down such a prize as that! She'd have to ask Dinadan about it at the feast.

But Dinadan was not in his usual seat in the hall. Nor was Sir Lancelot. The first course was finished, and the second, before Dinadan arrived, though Aislyn did not recognize him at first. He was escorted on either side by Sir Lancelot and another man—the Saxon, Gudrun—who held him firmly by the arms.

And he was wearing the yellow gown.

His armor was beneath; it gleamed through the many rents in the saffron fabric, which was stained now with earth and what looked like blood. She could not read his expression, for his head was bent, his tangled hair obscuring his face.

"My queen!" Lancelot cried. "I have brought a new damsel for your service!"

"G-good my lady," Guinevere choked, "you are welcome here. Come, sit by me."

Dinadan wrenched free of his captors. He turned, gathering the tattered hem, but on his first step he stumbled, half falling in a dreadful parody of a curtsy.

Knights beat upon the tables with their fists, convulsed with mirth, and the ladies shrieked with laughter. Guinevere bent double, one arm clasped across her middle, half sliding from her seat. Aislyn was reminded of a bear-baiting she had seen as a girl. Everyone had laughed at that, as well—but she had run off to be sick behind a bush.

She felt the same nausea now, the same pity and rage. But this time, she could do something about it.

She stumped into the center of the hall and stood before Lancelot, hands fisted on her hips.

"What's this you're playing at?" she demanded. "For shame, Sir Lancelot, to treat a brother knight so!"

Lancelot looked momentarily taken aback, but he soon recovered. "Why, Dinadan, it seems you have made a conquest! Does Sir Gawain know of this?"

"Watch yourself, lad," Aislyn said quietly. "Your tongue is outrunning your manners—and your sense."

"What is this?" the Saxon asked, raising his hand. "Begone, before I fetch you a clout to remind you of your place."

Aislyn eyed him up and down. "Am I meant to be frightened? Of *you*?"

Lancelot caught the Saxon's wrist. "Gudrun, don't," he said in a low voice. "The king wouldn't like it." He glanced about the hall, then smiled. "Lady Ragnelle, if you want this . . . damsel for your own service, you only need appeal to our gracious queen."

The queen exchanged a glance with Lancelot and smiled. "Lady Ragnelle," she said, "I will grant thy boon."

Aislyn rolled her eyes and reached for Dinadan's arm.

"In return for a favor from you," the queen said.

"What's that?" Aislyn asked suspiciously.

"We all *so* enjoyed your dance the other day," Guinevere said. "Do you perform it again for us, I beg you."

Dinadan raised his head. One eye was swollen nearly shut and blood oozed from a gash on his cheekbone. "Don't," he said to Aislyn. "I can take care of myself."

"Quiet, you," Gudrun growled, jerking him away. "Let the old woman dance for us. Go on," he cried, raising his voice, "Dance!"

Aislyn didn't know why she should mind. She'd been more than willing to make a fool of herself in the garden. But somehow that was very different than someone else forcing her to do it.

"Either you dance," Gudrun added, pulling Dinadan forward so abruptly that he stumbled, "or *he* does."

Aislyn cast a look about the hall, certain that someone would protest. But all she saw were the avid faces of people half starved for amusement, people who had lived so long in luxury that they had forgotten what it was to be poor and powerless—if they had ever known.

But Camelot wasn't supposed to like this! It was meant to be different. Better. A beacon, Gawain had called it, and only now did she realize how very much she had wanted to believe him.

But he'd been wrong. This place was rotten to the core. When she could simply walk away, it had been easy to laugh at their pretension, but now it wasn't funny anymore. Tears rose to her eyes, tears of helpless fury and shame and of sorrow for Gawain's dream of Camelot.

"Well?" Gudrun demanded. "Why are you still standing there?"

Aislyn nodded. No point in slobbering, she told herself. Get on with it.

She put her hands on her hips and tipped her head back to look up at the queen. "Where's the music? You can't expect me to dance without music!"

Gudrun clapped his hands. "Dance!" he cried. "Dance!"

Others took up the cry, crashing fists or tankards on the trestles to the rhythm Gudrun set. "Dance!"

When Aislyn set her jaw and hopped from one foot to the other, they howled like beasts. She had just taken her second step when a voice sliced through the tumult like a blade.

"What in God's name is going on here?"

Aislyn stumbled on the next step as she whirled, her heart lifting when she saw Gawain's golden head above the flushed and sweating crowd. His face was set, only the flashing of his eyes betrayed his emotion as he strode between the trestles to stop before the dais. "Madam," he said, bowing to the queen, "the king sends you greeting and bids me say he will be with you on the morrow."

He turned, his gaze passing over the group in the center of the floor. "Sir Lancelot," he said. "Pray explain the meaning of this."

Lancelot's cheeks were poppy red, but he managed an insolent smile. "It is a merely a jest," he said. "A joke between friends."

"A *joke*?" Gawain repeated incredulously, his gaze moving from Dinadan to Aislyn. "A *jest*?"

"We were having a bit of fun," Lancelot went on. "A thing *you* wouldn't understand."

A few people laughed, but the laughter was uncomfortable. They knew they had done wrong. Yet they were angry, too, like children caught out in some mischief. They would not thank Gawain for this, she thought, nor forget how he had shamed them tonight.

"You are right, I don't understand," Gawain answered. "Perhaps Sir Dinadan would explain."

"Ask your lady," Dinadan said tightly. He tore the remnants of the gown from his shoulders, stepped out of the puddled fabric and walked from the hall. The people, silent now, parted to let him pass.

Gawain turned to Aislyn, his brows raised in question.

"They were making mock of Sir Dinadan," she began steadily enough, "and I—but then . . ." She blinked hard, and when her vision cleared, she saw Gawain raise his hand and slowly, with great deliberation, strip off a glove.

For a moment, Aislyn thought—hoped—that he would strike Lancelot across the face with it, but he merely let it fall onto the yellow gown.

"Sir Lancelot," he said with icy courtesy, "will you meet me in the lists tomorrow?"

Lancelot bent to pick up the glove, looking as though he'd been handed the keys to paradise. "Sir Gawain," he answered with a sweeping bow, "it will be my pleasure."

A cheer greeted Lancelot's words, and Aislyn shook her head. Fools. Fools and children, that's all they were. And now they had found a new champion, one who would not challenge them to be better than they were, but pander to the worst in them.

If Gawain was aware of the cheering, he gave no sign of it. "My lady," he said, offering his arm.

Was he *mad*? He could have made a magnificent exit, head high and dignity intact. That was impossible with her hobbling along beside him. But he did not hurry her. The moment they were through the door, the laughter burst out, Lancelot's rising above the rest.

Gawain was silent as they walked through the corridors to his chamber. "Please excuse me," he said when they reached the door.

"Where are you going?"

"To the chapel."

"Aye. But don't you be staying up too late, now."

"I won't."

She watched him go down the hallway. "Sir Gawain," she called after him, and he turned, the torchlight falling on his face. "Mind you beat that rascal tomorrow."

"I will do my best, but . . ." He smiled and his shoulders moved in the slightest of shrugs. "In destinies sad or merry, true men can but try."

Of course he will win, she told herself as she stepped into the chamber. He is the best, isn't he? If there is any justice in this sorry world, Sir Lancelot doesn't stand a chance.

She stripped to her shift and hoisted herself onto the bed with a groan. She was weary half to death, her joints afire. If only she had her bag, she could have brewed something to ease the pain. But Gawain had taken it from her. Anger flared anew, then died when she remembered him striding into the hall, and in her mind, bugles and banners heralded his entrance.

What a tangle it all is, she thought drowsily, wrong and right so twisted together that it is impossible to pick out the knot. That Lancelot is dangerous . . . Gawain himself is dangerous . . . yet she could not deny that she'd been proud of him tonight.

He would not lose tomorrow. He *could* not.

'Tis but a joust, she told herself, drifting on the edge of sleep. Two men riding at each other with sticks. It doesn't matter who knocks the other down. There was no reason to feel that the fate of Camelot was hanging in the balance . . .

And yet she did.

# Chapter 16

• • •

THOUGH it was the last match of the day, no one had slipped away early to the castle. Princes and duchesses, lords and ladies, knights and squires and pages and damsels—everyone, down to the meanest varlet or kitchen slut who could bribe or sneak their way into the stands were on their feet and shouting as Lancelot and Gawain rode to the royal pavilion to make their bows to king and queen before the joust.

They reached the royal pavilion at precisely the same moment. As neatly as though they had rehearsed it, they bowed their uncovered heads, gold and sable moving in perfect unison.

King Arthur stood. He had returned this morning, and Aislyn had not seen him until he joined her and Guinevere in the royal pavilion. He was very grand in his crimson robe with the jeweled crown upon his brow.

"Kindly bear in mind," Arthur said, his keen glance evenly divided between the two knights, "that this is a courtesy match. We shall be most displeased if any injury results on either side."

He was already displeased. That had been clear from the moment he arrived. He had hardly spoken two words to his queen, though Aislyn suspected he'd had plenty to say to her in private. She certainly looked like she'd been scolded soundly.

Lancelot nodded, acknowledging the king's words. Aislyn wondered if it was fear or excitement that blanched the color from his face. Only Gawain looked himself, impossibly handsome and cool as a mountain tarn.

Arthur sat down. Having been dismissed, the two knights cantered back to their respective ends of the tourney field and accepted their lances from their squires. Lancelot was upright, leaning slightly forward, his lance held straight before him, while his mount—a breathtaking white stallion—pranced restively beneath him. Gawain sat easily in the saddle, as close to slouching as his armor would permit. His steed, Gringolet, stood flat-footed, looking as bored as his master.

Aislyn watched the marshal's hand rising, rising—the stands were so silent now that she could hear the rapid thudding of her heart. And then the hand fell.

Gringolet took off like a shot from a crossbow. Lancelot's mount was a bit slower off the mark, but soon found its pace. The two met at a flat gallop, and a cry went up as their lances crashed and splintered. Gawain reeled but kept his balance. Aislyn was on her feet, cheering as Lancelot's shield spun through the air and he was knocked backward, feet flying from his stirrups, arms pinwheeling in a futile attempt to gain his balance. He was falling, falling . . . Aislyn fell abruptly silent, her mouth still open as Lancelot hung suspended, the force of his fall arrested as though an invisible hand had seized him by the collar. And then somehow he was upright again, clutching his horse's mane as the animal slowed and stopped at the end of the lists.

The crowd went wild, stamping and screaming as Lancelot's squire hurried forward to retrieve his shield and present it to him, along with a fresh lance.

That *couldn't* have just happened . . . but it had. "Impossible!" the people cried. "A miraculous recovery!"

It *had* been impossible, that much was true, but Aislyn had seen the impossible before. She had *done* the impossible by transforming herself into a twisted hag and wedding the fairest knight in Camelot. She knew exactly how she had done it, too, as surely as she knew what had happened here today.

There was power in a name. And the name for what she had just witnessed was not *miracle*, but *magic*.

The marshal signaled the beginning of the second joust. This time Lancelot did not hesitate. He and Gawain met at a full gallop; again, their lances splintered and both knights reeled, though both kept their stirrups and their balance.

The crowd was turning. Aislyn could feel it. They sensed something was amiss, even if they could not say what it was. Now as many cried Gawain's name aloud as Lancelot's as the two knights accepted fresh lances from their squires.

A hush fell as the marshal cried the third and final ride. Aislyn was still on her feet, drawn taut as a bowstring. This time, she thought, *this* time Gawain must prevail. His cause was just, his skill so great that he had withstood a magical assault not once, but twice. He couldn't lose now. He *couldn't*.

The marshal's hand fell. Gringolet surged forward—and stumbled over a piece of splintered wood. It was a small stumble, and the stallion recovered almost instantly, but Gawain's balance had been thrown. Aislyn saw him recover his grip on his lance and straighten in time to meet Lancelot squarely. Against any other knight—any *earthly* knight—he would surely have prevailed . . .

But not against Sir Lancelot.

He turned Gawain's lance point easily with his shield, while his own hit straight and true, knocking Gawain backward with such force that he flew from the saddle to land in a cloud of dust upon the field.

"The victory to Sir Lancelot du Lac!" the marshal declared.

"No!"

Aislyn did not realize she had cried the word aloud until King Arthur looked over at her, a frown creasing his brow. "That was wrong," Aislyn said to him. "You know it, don't you?"

"It was unlucky that they missed that piece of wood," Arthur agreed. "But the match was fair."

*"Fair?"* Aislyn cursed her hag's voice; now, when she most needed to speak firmly, it rose into a shriek. "It was nothing of the sort! It was sorcery!"

Arthur leaned toward her. "How *dare* you?" he demanded in a low, fierce voice. "Sir Gawain has enough to bear; do you seek to shame him further with this vile accusation?"

"No! It *was*—"

"Silence!" Arthur roared, and heads turned in their direction. He lowered his voice, though his knuckles shone white against the armrests of his throne. "Do you think I have not divined your purpose? Whatever grudge you bear Sir Gawain is a matter for another day. On *this* day you will behave with dignity or I will have you carried to your chamber, gagged if necessary." He leaned a little closer, his eyes boring into hers. "Do you care to try me?"

"No. *Sire,*" she added grudgingly, sinking down into her seat.

Gawain's squire darted out to help him to his feet. He pulled off his helm, the sun beating down on the pale gold of his hair as he gazed up at his opponent. Lancelot sat unmoving, still holding his shield and lance, his visor concealing his expression.

Gawain bowed to him. Aislyn clenched her hands in her lap, fighting back the almost irresistible impulse to leap to her feet and shriek out the truth. When Gawain straightened, he raised a mailed hand to his lips, then flung it toward the stands with a brilliant smile.

They surged to their feet and cheered him, shouting out his name. He bowed to them, then gestured toward Lancelot and walked off, yielding him the field.

Lancelot did not remove his helm. He did not acknowledge either Gawain or the applause of the crowd. He simply sat where he was, still holding his lance and shield until his squire arrived to take them from him. Then, at last, he seemed to wake. He flipped up his visor and trotted his horse down the length of the stands toward his own pavilion. As he rode off the field, flowers fell like rain into his path.

Aislyn was already on her feet and halfway down the aisle before the crowd stood and surged toward the castle, bearing her along until she reached the bottom of the stairs. She fought against them then, cursing her frailty as she was buffeted this way and that, but at length she was free and heading toward the knights' pavilions, standing in a row beyond the tourney field.

It was quiet beyond the barrier. A few pages and squires lingered by the paddock, groaning and laughing as they settled wagers won and lost. No one spared her a glance as she hobbled between the deserted pavilions. She wished she'd brought her stick, for her legs were shaking with the aftermath of rage, and she kept her head bent as she picked her way through the shattered lances, discarded helms and buckets littering her path.

She halted when she heard harsh, rending breaths coming from between the pavilions. Her heart constricted; she turned to leave, reluctant to intrude on such a private grief. But it was wrong that Gawain should be alone now. Even her company must be better than nothing.

She rounded a corner and halted at the sight of an armored man bent almost double, his back against a post. He dragged off his helm and let it fall, then raked his fingers through his hair, the heels of his hands pressed hard against his eyes as he drew another of those terrible, sobbing breaths.

Aislyn stood motionless, the words frozen on her lips. At last the knight raised his head. Their eyes met and held for an endless moment, long enough for Aislyn to take in his pallor, the dark patches like bruises beneath his eyes, the moisture on his cheeks—

Lancelot's face twisted with rage. "What are you looking at?" he shouted, his voice hoarse and shaking. "Foul witch! Go—leave me—" He turned and buried his face in his hands.

Aislyn went.

• • •

SHE had only a glimpse of Gawain through the open flap of his pavilion. His younger brother, Agravaine, after informing her curtly that Gawain could not see her, planted himself firmly in her path.

"Look here, you," she said, poking him in the chest, "I have every right to—"

"Agravaine, what are you doing?" Gawain called from within. "Stand aside and let my lady enter." He was seated on a stool as a squire unlaced his greaves, sweat-soaked and disheveled with a streak of dirt on one cheek. But he smiled and lifted a hand in greeting. "I took no hurt," he assured her. "Do not wait for me, Dinadan can take you to the hall. I'll be up as soon as I am washed and dressed."

Dinadan obediently came forward and took her arm, guiding her back through the pavilions.

"How is he really?" she asked Dinadan.

He shrugged. "As you saw him. He's taking it a good deal better than the rest of us."

Particularly Lancelot, she thought, casting a quick glance toward the place where the knight had stood. He was gone now, and she would have been tempted to dismiss their strange encounter as imagination if she did not see his helm still lying where he had dropped it.

Well, it *was* a grand victory, and apparently Sir Lancelot's heart's desire. Yet he had not looked like a man who wept for joy.

"And what of you?" she said to Dinadan as they stepped into the courtyard. "Are you all right? What Sir Lancelot did to you was a shameful thing."

"I've had better days," he agreed dryly, "but I daresay I'll survive. And Lancelot apologized very nicely earlier. I suspect the king ordered him to do it, but what's done is done and best forgotten. But stay, I owe you thanks—forgive me, I should have said so earlier—"

"No thanks needed," Aislyn said. "So long as you are well, I am content."

"I am. And I did learn something . . ."

"No more songs, then?"

He raised a brow. "I didn't say *that*! No, next time I'll fight my own battles." His smile died. "If not for me—"

"They would still have met some time," Aislyn said, patting his arm. "It was bound to happen. But you're right. If you're going to set yourself up as a court jester, you'd best be prepared to defend yourself . . . or learn to run fast."

"A knight of Camelot does not run," he said reprovingly.

"Then you'll be spending a lot of time in the practice yard, won't you?"

He sighed. "I daresay I will."

• • •

THE feast was already in progress when Dinadan delivered Aislyn to her seat and went off to the knights' table.

King Arthur glanced at her across Gawain's empty place and nodded shortly by way of greeting. Beside him, Guinevere was still subdued, though she brightened visibly when Lancelot walked into the hall.

*Swept* into the hall, borne on a wave of applause to his seat at the high table beside the queen. He was clad in white—a magnificent silk tunic sprinkled with tiny diamonds about the neck—and wore a silver circlet round his brow. His dark hair curled around it, still damp from his bath, and his cheeks were blazing with fresh color. He smiled and waved as he took his seat, managing to look both modest and proud at the attention.

Was this really the same man she had seen behind the pavilions earlier? It seemed impossible to believe. When he met her gaze down the table, he smiled and raised his goblet to her, nodding in the friendliest fashion imaginable, as though the thought of shouting at her had never crossed his mind.

*Someone* was mad, and Aislyn was fairly sure it wasn't her. She knew what she had seen before, both behind the pavilions and earlier in the lists. Sir Lancelot was no mere knight . . . but was that any surprise, given who had raised him? He had come to Camelot from Avalon, a place shrouded in such mystery that many believed it a legend. Oh, they *said* he was the son of King Ban of Benwick, but as both his parents were dead and Benwick had fallen to invasion, how could there be any proof? He could be anyone . . . or any*thing*.

Aislyn frowned, watching him. He was a handsome lad—perhaps a bit *too* handsome? They said the men of faery were so fair that no mortal woman could resist them. It did not seem that Guinevere was even trying; she was turned toward him, laughing, her hand resting on his forearm. Nor did the king seem at all troubled by this familiarity. He was smiling, too, having obviously forgiven Lancelot for what had passed the night before. And Aislyn couldn't really blame the king for that. Sir Lancelot could be extremely charming when he put his mind to it, and she had never seen him on anything less than his best behavior when Arthur was present.

But who was he? *What* was he?

There was one way to find out.

Aislyn closed her eyes, picturing a page in her grimoire. She could see the spell now, tucked into the margin in Morgause's sprawling hand. She muttered the words beneath her breath, dipped a finger in her wine and flicked a few drops in Lancelot's direction.

Nothing happened. She tried again, careful to get the words exactly right, but the effect was just the same. The third attempt, directed at the king, yielded no better result.

*Either you've lost your touch,* she said to herself, *or . . .*

She scanned the hall. There was Sir Agravaine, Gawain's younger brother, sitting beside Dinadan, scowling up at the high table. Aislyn had never liked him. She muttered the words once more, flicked a drop of wine—and Agravaine's goblet twisted in his hand, dousing him with its contents. He leapt up, sputtering, and the knights around him laughed.

Well. So she *did* still have the knack. She looked back at Lancelot. It was not proof as such, but it was all the proof she needed.

The one puzzle was why the king was impervious to magic, too, when by all accounts he had never been before. But perhaps . . . yes, she was almost certain . . . Lancelot had not been with him at those times.

*Lancelot du Lac,* she mused, *brought by the Lady of the Lake herself to serve King Arthur. I wonder if Arthur knows the true nature of her gift? Or her purpose in bestowing it?*

Lost in her thoughts, she had not seen Gawain arrive. He had slipped into his seat without fanfare, and was cutting the meat on the trencher they shared. When he was done, he set it before Aislyn.

"Eat, lady," he said.

Arthur turned at the sound of his voice. "Gawain! How—how fare you?" he asked uncomfortably.

"Very well, sire. A bit stiff, perhaps—" He looked past the king and queen and nodded to Sir Lancelot. "I've rarely taken such blows as I was dealt today." He picked up his goblet and saluted Lancelot before drinking. A murmur ran through the hall and a few knights slapped their palms upon the tables in approval.

Lancelot flushed, and for just a moment Aislyn glimpsed the young man she had seen behind the pavilion. "I—I—" he stammered, then recovered and returned the salute, an insufferably haughty smile curving his lips. "Thank you, *Sir* Gawain."

"Please, lady, eat," Gawain said to Aislyn.

"I've no appetite. Here, you have it."

Gawain nodded and speared a slice of mutton on the end of his dagger. He made a show of eating, though in truth he consumed almost nothing, and though he lifted his goblet often, she saw that it was three-quarters full when at last the meal was over.

He sat, smiling with every appearance of enjoyment as a harper plucked his way through three songs. The last was a long ballad about a knight who wooed two sisters, one for gain and one for love. It was a sad tale, and at the end, Aislyn furtively wiped her eyes on her sleeve. She turned to Gawain, only to find his seat empty.

When the harper began a new tune, she took the opportunity to slip away.

# Chapter 17

• • •

SHE found Gawain in the chamber they shared, wearing nothing but a shirt pulled down to his waist as he dabbed at his shoulder with a cloth. A long gash sliced across his collarbone, surrounded by puffed and purple flesh, with bruises darkening his rib cage.

"That looks nasty," she said.

"It's not bad."

She snorted, coming closer to look. "And now you'll tell me it doesn't hurt, either."

He glanced up at her. "Oh, it hurts plenty. But nothing's broken."

"You sure of that?" She ran a hand across his ribs, then nodded. "I'll bind it for you. That'll help."

"Thank you."

He was quiet as she wound a strip of linen around his rib cage. She was quiet, too, wondering how to approach what she would say.

"About today . . ."

"Yes, I meant to speak of that myself. I am sorry I failed to—"

"But you didn't! Fail, that is. You won."

He smiled faintly. "I think you must have been watching a different match."

"No, I was watching the right one, and I saw what you didn't. The first time you hit him, he went down—or would have done, if something hadn't interfered." She tied the strip off and stepped back, fisting her hands on her hips. "He was falling, anyone will tell you that. They were saying it was a miracle he kept his seat. But it was magic sure enough."

"It is kind of you to say so, but—"

"There's no kindness in speaking the truth. I know what I saw." She sat down on the edge of the bed. "Tell me about Sir Lancelot du Lac."

"He is the son of King Ban—"

"And you know that for a fact?" she interrupted.

"I know what the king has said. How *he* knows, I never asked, but I'm sure Sir Lancelot has proved his claim."

"Hmph. The Lady of the Lake is a mystery, but everyone agrees she is a powerful enchantress at the least. I reckon she gave her foster son a little extra protection before sending him out into the world. That is, if he's not her *real* son. How do you know he's even human?"

Gawain looked startled. "Of course he's—"

"Have you ever seen him bleed?"

"Yes. He was wounded in his first battle—a glancing blow, but it did bleed."

"Well, that's something," she allowed. "But still—"

"I'm sure he is exactly who he says he is," Gawain said firmly. "And he won today fairly."

"He did not. I'm telling you, I saw—"

"Whatever you saw—or thought you saw—goes no farther than this chamber. You haven't said anything of this to anyone else, have you?"

"Well," Aislyn said reluctantly, "I did mention it to the king."

"Oh, God." Gawain leaned his head against the wall and closed his eyes. "What did he say?"

"To hold my tongue or he'd have me gagged. He seemed to think I was saying it to shame you—"

"As it would have done had it gone any further. Just let it be, I beg you."

"It isn't right," she protested. "He's fey, I tell you, and he beat you unfairly—"

"Fairly or unfairly, it is done. I will not complain of it, and I forbid you to do so."

"Don't you think the king should know what sort of knight he's welcoming to court?"

"Sir Lancelot has given me no reason to doubt his loyalty. He is an exceptionally skilled warrior, devoted to the king—"

"And to the queen," Aislyn muttered.

"And to the queen," Gawain repeated steadily. "He is her champion, after all, and her friend, and if the king has no complaint of that arrangement, it is not my place—or yours—to question it."

He rose stiffly, stifling a groan. The shirt fell to the floor. He bent to retrieve it, then halted, one hand moving to his bound ribs. Aislyn tried not to stare as he eased his way onto the bed.

"I could give you something for the pain," she offered, "that is, if I had my bag."

He hunched on the edge of the bed, looking miserable, but shook his head.

"Don't be a fool," she said sharply. "If you go and marry a witch, it's only sensible to let her use her magic to good purpose."

He turned his head and regarded her intently. "Are you a witch? Truly?"

She snorted. "You seemed sure enough the first time you laid eyes on me."

"I was wrong to say that. You surprised me, appearing so suddenly that day, but that does not excuse my rudeness."

"Well, my looks are against me," she conceded. "Live long enough to gain a bit of wisdom and a few warts, and most men will cry witch without thinking twice. What is a witch, really, besides a woman who's old and a bit cleverer than the men who fear her? What passes for magic with most folk is just a smattering of herb lore and telling people what they want to hear."

"For most folk, that might be true," he said quietly. "But you forget, or perhaps you do not know who my mother is."

"Oh, I know well enough. And as she's neither old nor full of warts, they call *her* an enchantress. A much nicer word, isn't it, than witch? And before you ask again, I'll answer your question. I know a bit of herb lore, and I know a bit of magic, too. The one you don't much care for—fair enough. Having the Queen of Air and Darkness for a mum could sour any man on magic. But that's no reason to keep me from using my other talents, especially when you need them."

Gawain braced his arms, making the muscles leap, and eased himself back against the bolster with a hiss of pain. "There's probably a flaw in that argument, but I hurt too much to find it now. Hand me that leather purse on the table."

• • •

GAWAIN fished inside his purse, which was stuffed full of odds and ends. "What the devil do I have in here?" he muttered irritably, and finally his fingers touched the little key. He handed it to Ragnelle, saying, "Your bag is in the trunk."

He was faintly ashamed of making such a pother over a

cracked rib or two, but there wasn't anyone to see but Ragnelle. He watched her unlock the trunk, wondering if he'd done wrong. Morgana had been insistent about the bag . . . but he did not need any woman, aunt or not, to tell him how to manage his own wife.

He made to toss his purse on the table, then changed his mind and upended it on the bed. A shower of coins fell onto the coverlet, mixed with a handful of stones he'd picked up to mark one battle or another, a twig—why was he carrying a twig? Oh, it was rosemary—he remembered now, he'd plucked a bit from his father's grave, meaning to press it, but the leaves had long since crumbled into dust. A bit of twine, tangled with a twist of red-gold . . . oh.

He picked up the braid, which had been twisted into a circle and tied with a bit of ribbon, carefully brushing the rosemary dust from the strands glistening in his palm. He hadn't looked at it in years. But he always knew it was there, a secret talisman shielding him from pride. From folly.

From love.

He should throw it in the fire. Many a time he'd started to, but something always held him back.

He closed his fingers on the braid as Ragnelle appeared beside him. "Here," she said, offering him a cup. "Drink this down." He was careful to give no sign of his revulsion as their fingers brushed; she had been kind to him and he would not offend her willingly.

"I thought it would be bitter," he said, handing back the empty cup. "My mother's potions—"

"I am *not* your mother."

He sighed, relaxing back against the pillow. "God be thanked for *that*."

"You don't like her much, do you?" Ragnelle asked as she tidied her things away. "Your own mother. Why not?"

"I have my reasons," Gawain said shortly, his fingers clenching on the braid.

"What are they?" Ragnelle asked, pulling the stool beside the bed and sitting down.

"It is a long story . . ."

"I'll stop you when I'm bored," she said, and began to gather the scattered coins from the counterpane.

"My mother has certain . . . ambitions." He stopped, wondering what he was thinking of to speak of such things to a stranger.

Even if she was his wife.

"Oh, aye," she said easily, " 'tis common knowledge your father led the rebellion against King Arthur all those years ago, and there's not a woman in Britain who didn't suspect your mother was behind it. She's the Queen of Air and Darkness, after all, and your father—well . . ."

"He was just a man," Gawain finished. "Though in truth, they were of one mind over the rebellion. But once defeated, my father accepted the king's pardon, and his terms."

*Unlike my mother.*

*"You could be king of Britain!"*

*Gawain's fingers clenched on the stem of his goblet. "I will never wear the crown."*

*"No man is immortal," his mother said, "and the king has many enemies."*

*He leaned across the small table between them, scattered with the remains of the private meal they had just shared in honor of his homecoming to Lothian. "Any enemy of my king—whomever that might be—will reach Arthur only by stepping over my corpse. So you see, I will never wear the crown of Britain. I have rendered my king my oath of fealty—as you bade me, Mother—and I will honor that oath unto death."*

Unto death. *The words seemed to echo in the little chamber. Morgause stared at him, eyes narrowed.*

*"So you would turn traitor to your family?"*

*"Arthur is my family." Gawain stood so abruptly that*

*his chair overturned. "All I know of loyalty and honor I learned from him."*

*Morgause buried her face in her hands. "Oh, Gawain, that you could say such things to me! You loved me once—do you not remember? That you should look at me like that—so coldly—and say such cruel things. I cannot bear it!"*

*Gawain regarded her suspiciously. "You mustn't talk treason, then."*

*"Is it treason for a mother to love her son? Is it treason for her to want the best for him? When I look at you—and imagine what a king you would make—" Her shoulders shook with sobs.*

*"It will never be." He bit his lip, then righted his chair and sat down again. "Don't cry, Mother."*

*"But you hate me now—do not deny it, I can see it is the truth. You were such a good child, Gawain, my little golden boy—do you remember when I used to call you that? I was only fourteen when you were born, just a child myself—"*

*"Aye, I know." Gawain sighed.*

*"Everything would have been different if my father had lived! It was so terrible when Uther came to Cornwall," she said rapidly, dabbing at her eyes. "I cannot tell you how terrible it was. He murdered my poor father, bewitched my mother, smashed up my home—"*

*Gawain patted her shoulder awkwardly. "But that was Uther, Mother. Not Arthur."*

*"I know, it's only—when I see him on the throne—and then I think of you, serving Uther's brat . . ."*

*"Arthur is not his father," Gawain said firmly. "He is a good man and a great king. You must let go of the past, Mother, before your hatred leads you to do something we will all regret."*

*Morgause drew a long, shuddering breath. "Yes. Yes, you are right. I see that now. Can you forgive me?"*

*Gawain stood, relieved, and bent to kiss her cheek. "Aye, Mother, of course I can. Why don't we both forget this conversation ever happened."*

Gawain's limbs were heavy, and it was very peaceful in his chamber as Ragnelle sorted through the pile on the bed. She dropped the coins back into his purse, then the stones, as well, and began to untangle the twine.

"And your mother?" she prompted. "Did she accept King Arthur's terms, as well?"

Gawain smiled grimly. "She merely changed her tactics."

"Really?" Ragnelle asked, her eyes bright with curiosity. Strange, but he'd never really noticed her eyes before. The lids were drooped and wrinkled, but the irises were a very clear light green. "What did the Queen of Air and Darkness do?"

"She knew I was the king's man, but she still hoped to win me to her side," Gawain said. "So she used a maiden—her apprentice—to do her work. The maiden was . . . very beautiful. I knew her only as my mother's guest, I had no idea she was . . ."

"What?"

"A sorceress." He laughed shortly. "I suppose you'd call that a pretty word for witch."

"It's all one to me." Ragnelle wound the twine around her fingers. "So what did she do, this beautiful maiden? Put a spell on you?"

"No. She was meant to, but—no."

"Botched it, did she?" Ragnelle's eyes glinted before she lowered them again to the twine. "What happened? Did she turn you into a toad? Vanish in a puff of smoke?"

Gawain managed a wan smile. "She did not even attempt it."

"Then how did you find her out?"

"Aislyn told me. That was her name," he said, running

his thumb across the soft strands in his hand. "Aislyn. She told me all. How she was meant to seduce me, then use foul sorcery to bind me to her will. Which would, of course, have been my mother's will, for Aislyn was completely in her power."

"She told you all that, did she?" Ragnelle asked. "Now why would she do that?"

"She said . . . she said it was for love of me."

Ragnelle snorted. "A likely tale!"

Gawain bristled at her tone. "Is that so impossible?"

"Did *you* believe it?"

"No."

"Well, then, there we are. I imagine she thought herself discovered. You suspected her already, didn't you?"

He shook his head. "I had no idea."

Ragnelle set his purse on the table. "Then what did she have to gain from telling you?"

"I don't know."

"Oh, come now, you're not trying! Mayhap your mother sent her—"

"No," he said decidedly. "Aislyn came on her own."

"Then it sounds as though she had turned against her mistress—but why would she do that? Did she ever say?"

"She said . . . she told me she had not really understood what she agreed to."

"Lost her nerve, eh?"

"No, she found herself," Gawain said slowly. "And she was frightened at how close to evil she had drifted."

"Weak," Ragnelle muttered, shaking her head. "I expect she wanted you to save her."

Gawain bent his head, remembering Aislyn begging him to take her with him. "Yes," he said. "She did ask—but I was too angry to think clearly. How could I trust anything she said? She was a witch. And she had *lied* to me . . . so many lies."

"That hurt you," Ragnelle murmured. "Aye, of course it did."

He nodded without speaking, ashamed that even now the memory should cause him pain.

"Did you love her?"

"Yes," he whispered. "More than— But I left her anyway."

Ragnelle was silent for a time, studying his face, then gave a harsh cackle of laughter. "Well, good for you. Why burden yourself with a foolish girl who would only make your life a misery? If she'd drifted once, she likely would again. I daresay she's gotten herself into some new mischief by this time."

*No.* Gawain's throat was oddly constricted; he stared down at his clenched fist, blinking hard.

"There, now, lie back, just put your head down," she said, her voice gentler than he had ever heard it. "You've earned your rest. It's been a hard day, hasn't it?"

"Has it?" he asked vaguely. "Oh, the tournament. That doesn't matter. Once it would have, but . . ." He closed his eyes. "It's only words. As long as I can serve the king, I am content." Her hand was gentle on his brow, soothing and relaxing. "You are very kind," he murmured.

"No, I'm not. I tricked you into marriage."

"Not a trick . . ." He forced his heavy lids open. "An honest bargain accepted freely. And it doesn't matter, truly. I never wanted to marry anyone, not after . . . But she never loved me, it was all a lie . . ."

Ragnelle's hand stilled.

"Later, I thought—I don't know what I thought, but I felt—hoped—that I had wronged her." His eyes stung and he turned his face away. "But by the time I went back to Lothian, it was too late."

"You went *back*?"

"It took so long . . . I lost my way . . ."

But he'd pressed on. Only when Gringolet shied and he realized they'd nearly ridden over the edge of a precipice did he stop and wait for the mist to clear.

"'Twas dawn before I got there. Too late. It was the millpond . . . where we found the kittens."

"What about the millpond?" Ragnelle asked, and there was something strange about her voice, something wrong . . . He tried to name it, but his thoughts were dissolving into memories of that terrible morning, Aislyn's mother weeping, saying . . .

"Aislyn drowned. That very night. They said she fell, but I always wondered if . . . whether . . ."

"*Drowned?* But—" Ragnelle was seized by a coughing fit; she hacked and sputtered, then finally gasped, "That must've been a shock to you. It is to me," she added in a mutter.

"I was . . ." But no, he could not speak of that morning. He could not think of it, he *would* not. Instead, he closed his eyes and let the darkness take him.

# Chapter 18

• • •

GAWAIN'S breathing deepened, and his hand, outstretched on the coverlet, relaxed in sleep. Aislyn took the braid from his palm and stared at it.

He had kept it, just as he had promised.

There had never been another. Only her.

She had seen only his anger that night, not the pain that lay beneath it. He had trusted her. She had made certain that he would. The sighs, the smiles, the sidelong glances—every one had been carefully planned to win his notice, and she had felt nothing but pride when he responded. Now it burned her to remember the skill with which she'd drawn him out, and her own smug satisfaction when he confided secrets he had never told another. When he confessed his loathing of all things magical, she had been sweetly sympathetic, but inside she laughed as she assured him she felt just the same before tripping off to her chamber to practice the fascinating new spell Morgause was teaching her. It was real magic, far beyond anything she had attempted in the past, a spell so potent that it could turn even the strongest warrior to soft clay in a skilled enchantress's hands.

She had not told Gawain all of this, of course, only enough to make him understand the danger.

The rest he figured out himself.

It had not taken him long. Halfway through her halting tale, the puzzled hurt faded from his expression; no sooner had she faltered to a stop than he was on his feet and reaching for his tunic. As he pulled on his boots, he asked one question only, and by the time she admitted that yes, she did indeed possess the gift of magic, he was halfway out the door.

Yet he had truly loved her. He loved her still. He might have ridden off that night, but he'd turned back.

"Wake up!" she cried. "Gawain, listen to me!"

" 'm awake," he mumbled.

*I am Aislyn. The duchess of Cornwall put a spell on me.*

"Azure dragons," she heard her own voice say. "The dish in the kitchen spills honey."

Gawain blinked and rubbed his hands across his face. "What did you say?"

"Listen," she cried, holding his eyes with hers. *Aislyn is not dead.*

"Ashes in the bed," was what came from her mouth.

"In the . . . what? I'm sorry, I didn't quite . . ."

"I am here, Gawain!" she cried "Right here beside you! Can you not see me?"

He took her hands in his. "I see you, Ragnelle. Be calm, now, and tell me what the trouble is."

She drew a breath. "I."

Gawain nodded.

"Am."

"Go on," he said.

*Aislyn.*

"Acorn."

*Aislyn.*

"Bannock."

*Aislyn!*

"Vellum!"

Gawain leapt to his feet, letting out a hiss of pain as he put a hand to his ribs. "Don't worry, all will be well," he said. His eyes were bleary, his hair awry, but his voice was crisp and sure. "Just lie down and I will bring the king's leech."

"No! I don't need a leech." She began to cry as he urged her down upon the bed. "I'm not dead! I'm snowdrop!"

"Do you have any pain?" He leaned over her, peering into her eyes as he touched first one cheek, then the other. "Can you feel that?"

Tears spilled over her lashes when she nodded.

"Lift each arm," he ordered. "Now your legs. What is your name?"

She sighed. "Ragnelle."

"And where are we?"

"In your chamber at Camelot. I'm not mad, you dolt!"

"I never said you were. Are you sure you have no pain?"

"No, none." Save for her heart, which felt as though someone had thrust a dagger through it, but if she tried to tell him that, who knew what nonsense would come out? "I was—it must've been a dream," she muttered.

"God be thanked." He smiled his relief, though his eyes were still anxious as he searched her face. He looked like . . . like a husband concerned for his wife, Aislyn thought, and fresh tears stung her eyes. *Don't look at my face, that isn't me! I'm here, inside—*

"Come to bed," she said, lifting a corner of the coverlet. "I'm sorry I woke you."

"Don't be," he said, sliding in beside her. "I don't mind. Wake me again if you need me."

When he slept, she rose, mixed the potion that would return her to her own form and drank it down. Nothing. She waited a few minutes more, knowing it was futile, then crawled back under the coverlet and wept.

# Chapter 19

• • •

GAWAIN woke in the moments before dawn. He lay awhile, watching the chamber take shape around him while he stroked the various cats curled up on the bed, listening to the soft, rhythmic snores coming from beside him as he deliberately recalled what he had tried for so many years to forget: the day of Aislyn's death.

*"Sit down," Morgause said, "and calm yourself. Yes, the girl is dead and I am sorry for it, but there is nothing to be done about it now. I know you were fond of her—I was fond of her myself—but I had meant to speak to you today in any case."*

*"You killed her. Don't lie to me, I know you did. She told me everything—"*

*"Did she? Did she tell you that when her father died, they were attacked by a neighboring knight, and—"*

*"What has that to do with this?"*

*"—and his designs were not only on the land. Did she tell you that she was his leman? Did she tell you that he*

*forced her—but no, there is no need to dwell on all that now. Aislyn survived a terrible ordeal and showed great courage in making her way to me, but I fear she was irrevocably damaged."*

*"No," Gawain said. "It isn't true—"*

*"You must ask Lady Olwyn if you do not believe me, but I assure you it is the truth. The first thing Aislyn said to me was that she would never marry, and I cannot say that I blamed her. It wasn't until later that I began to wonder if her mind was all it should be. She was prone to dark moods, and though they did seem to be lifting, I fear . . ." She leaned forward and rested her hand on Gawain's. "I fear that her fondness for you, her . . . desire . . . roused feelings too painful for her to bear. She took refuge in dangerous delusions—oh, if only she had come to me! I think I could have helped her. But she did not, until yesterday when she burst in here, accusing me of everything from pandering to regicide! I tried to reason with her, but it soon became apparent that she was quite mad. I sent her off to her chamber while Dame Olwyn and I discussed what was best to be done with her, but apparently she managed to escape. It is a pity, though I cannot help but wonder if she was not trying to spare her poor mother . . ."*

*Her voice, so sad, so sweetly reasonable, stole through Gawain's mind like a drug, soothing his pain, dulling his rage, clouding his certainty. Could it have been like that? Aislyn had been upset; had she been mad? Would he have known if she was? What did he know of madness?*

*His anger drained from him, carrying with it all his strength. He was so weary that he could barely hold his head up. "But," he said, making an enormous effort to rouse himself from the lethargy stealing over him, "last night she said—she came to my chamber and she told me you had—"*

*"Had what?" Morgause asked gently. "Sent her to your bed? Oh, Gawain, don't you see? She wanted you, but she could not admit it even to herself. And so she concocted*

*this wild fantasy—if it is indeed the same one I heard from her yesterday—that I was somehow using magic to force her to seduce you."*

*"She said we were to wed—that you wanted—"*

*"I? Allow my eldest son, heir to the throne of Orkney, to wed a girl with neither dowry nor breeding? Surely you knew then that she was raving!"*

*Gawain was conscious of dull embarrassment. No, he hadn't known, though now it seemed so obvious that he could not believe his own credulity.*

*"I know this has been a shock to you," Morgause said softly, "and you are weary, are you not? You need to sleep, and then you will feel better."*

*He nodded. Yes, sleep was what he needed. Then everything would be . . . be . . .*

*"Go to your chamber and get to bed," Morgause ordered softly. "When you wake, come straight to me."*

*Gawain rose to his feet, though he could not remember having sat down. He could not remember anything, save that he needed to sleep.*

*He was halfway to his chamber when he happened to glance out a window and saw Gringolet tethered to a tree. What was he doing there? He should be in the pasture. It didn't matter, someone would find him . . . but the horse's head was drooping, his golden flanks dark with sweat. Something moved in Gawain's sluggish mind, and he knew he could not leave his mount like that. Slowly he turned, plodding dully down the stairway and out into the courtyard. A groom was whistling as he carried two buckets toward the stable; Gawain called him over and told him to look after Gringolet.*

*He was just turning back to the hall when he noticed the boy sitting on the mounting block, whittling a stick.* Get to bed, *a voice said in his mind,* you need to sleep, *but another voice, faint but strangely urgent, said,* wait.

*He waited, leaning against the doorpost, watching the boy. And gradually he became aware that the boy was familiar, that he was . . . was . . .* Launfal *the faint voice said, and Gawain nodded. Right. Launfal. And he was—*

*Gawain straightened. He was Aislyn's brother. And Aislyn was dead. The memory of last night rushed back, and with it the grief. On leaden feet he walked over to the mounting block.*

*The boy looked up and smiled. "Good day, sir."*

*"Launfal," Gawain began. "I am so sorry."*

*"Sorry? Why?" His eyes were like Aislyn's, but a darker green, and they were filled with such innocent surprise that Gawain knew the boy had not yet been told.*

*It wasn't right that her own brother should not know, but Gawain could not be the one to tell him. Instead, he said, "May I ask you something?"*

*"Me? Oh, yes, sir."*

*"It is . . . difficult," he said, sitting down beside the boy. "But I want you to trust that I have good reason to ask."*

*Launfal nodded, and Gawain forced himself to continue. "It is about the time you lost your home. I know your sister suffered greatly."*

*Launfal still watched him, nothing in his face but curiosity, and Gawain was just wondering how he could possibly broach the question, when Launfal said, "You mean during the siege?"*

*"No, when the castle was taken."*

*"Oh, that. Well, it wasn't pleasant for any of us. But it was a good deal easier being hungry on the road than trapped indoors. At least we had plenty of water, and I could always beg . . . or steal," he added in a lower voice, avoiding Gawain's eye.*

*"I'm sure you did only what you had to," Gawain said. "But I was speaking of the time between the breaching of the last defense and your escape. Did Aislyn—"*

*"But there was no time. We didn't wait for them to break through! Once the matter was certain, we told everyone to flee—and we did, too."*

*The boy was telling him the truth, Gawain could see it in his eyes. And what reason had he to lie?*

*Unlike my mother, Gawain thought, a cold and deadly fury kindling in his heart.*

*"Launfal!"*

*A woman stood in the doorway to the hall, her eyes red with weeping and her face dragged down with worry.*

*"In a moment, Mother!" Launfal called back. "Is there anything else, sir?"*

*"No. Or—wait, Launfal, there is one thing. Tell no one what we have spoken of just now. If you are asked, say I—say I was bidding you farewell."*

*"Are you leaving?"*

*"I am."*

*"Oh." Launfal's face fell. "I wanted to ask you about that cut you showed me. When will you be back?"*

*Gawain smiled grimly. "No time soon. You'd best ask Gaheris. He can do it near as well as I can." He touched the boy's shoulder, conscious of all that remained unspoken between them. It was wrong to leave him in ignorance, but there was no time for explanations and even if there had been, Gawain would not have known what to say. He needed first to think, to sort the truth from all the lies he had been told, if such a feat was even possible.*

*And then he realized it was not.*

*He could spend a lifetime chasing after the truth, remembering every word he and Aislyn had spoken, weighing each intonation and analyzing every gesture she had made, and still he could never be certain. And he knew himself well enough to know that such an unsolvable puzzle would prey upon his mind until he was as mad as Aislyn. But no, that was another lie. She had not been mad at all, only . . .*

*In that moment, he came to his decision. He would not*

*waste his time or sanity in untangling the web of deception in which he'd been enmeshed, or in mourning a lass who had never been more than a dream. For whatever purpose, Aislyn had lied to him, not once but many times, and there was no reason to believe she had not gone on lying to the end.*

*And it was the end. The tale was told, even if he would never understand it. Whether by her own hand or his mother's or by some evil chance, Aislyn was dead. The knowledge slammed into him with such force that he wanted nothing but to fall to his knees and weep for his lost love, the lass who had kissed him beneath the cherry tree and given him a lock of her bright hair to carry into battle. But that small, cold voice in his mind warned him that he could not afford to linger. He must get away from this place while he was still in command of his own will.*

*"Launfal, I hope that you—whatever befalls—I wish you good fortune," he finished lamely, then strode from the courtyard, shouting for his horse.*

He had been right. It *was* a mistake to look back; he already knew everything that mattered. Aislyn had *used* him. Her kisses were sweet poison that robbed him of his wits; every lie a new betrayal of his trust. For whatever reason—be it the one she had given him or some secret purpose—she needed to leave Lothian; he was the means of her escape. Her words of love were as false as everything about her.

Unless . . . unless she had been honest with him that last night.

"I'll never know now," he said aloud.

Ragnelle stirred beside him. "Eh?"

"It was nothing. How do you feel this morning?"

She sat up and knuckled her eyes. "Well enough for an old woman. But what were you saying before?"

"Oh, I was remembering what we spoke about last night."

"The lass, you mean?" Her eyes were on his face, those clear, light eyes that were so incongruously beautiful. "The one they told you was drowned?"

He nodded. "I was just thinking that I'll never know why she came to me and told me all she did."

"Oh, I think you do. Listen to your heart, the truth is there."

*No.* His heart had misled him before, why should he believe it now? Aislyn had *betrayed* him.

But his heart refused to be silenced. *She loved you,* it said, *she trusted you with her life. The ultimate betrayal was not hers, but yours.*

"God forgive me," he breathed, "I left her and she—but I did not *know*—"

"'Course you didn't," Ragnelle said roughly. "How could you? It takes a wise head to sort truth from lies, and you were but a lad. She should have understood that. And you went back, didn't you?" Her gnarled fingers closed over his. "That was a fine thing, Gawain, a—a noble act, and 'twas no fault of yours you were too late."

Her words eased something in him, as though a splinter had been drawn from a festering wound he'd borne in secret, hiding it even from himself.

"Ragnelle," he asked, "do you think the dead can see us? Do you think she knows that I am sorry now?"

"Oh, she knows," Ragnelle said, and her voice was oddly choked. "And I—I reckon she is sorry, too."

• • •

EVEN Gawain's return from Lothian five years ago had not been so painful. Then he had done everything in his power to put Aislyn from his mind, but now his defenses had crumbled and the grief poured in, as unbearable as though but a moment had passed since he first learned of her death.

Everywhere he looked, he saw her: sitting at the high table in the hall, clad in green with ribbons in her hair;

walking in the courtyard, laughing beside the fountain, so beautiful it made his heart ache to remember.

Yet he did not push his memories aside. Instead, he gave himself over to them, visiting each place he had described to her, imagining what she would have said to him and he to her, constructing entire conversations in his mind that set him first to smiling and then to sighing, and finally to sink down on a bench and stare blankly at the fountain.

Five years Aislyn had been gone, and he might as well have leapt into the millpond after her for all the living he had done. It seemed now those years had been a dream, a frozen wasteland without laughter or music . . . and certainly without women. But it wasn't as though he *aspired* to celibacy, not like that young Sir Bors or some other knights he had met. Gawain had always been susceptible to a fetching lass and had thoroughly enjoyed his share of amorous adventures—until he met Aislyn and tumbled headlong into love.

It was more than the startling beauty of her face, or the deliciously soft body that had driven him half mad with desire, or even the kiss that had convinced him he must marry her or die. At eighteen, these had seemed paramount, but every lad of eighteen was a rutting fool. Now Gawain could appreciate the time they had spent talking, more precious than even that soul-searing kiss. Aislyn thought about the same things he thought about, pondered the same questions, and if their conclusions had sometimes been at odds, her ability to debate an issue only added to her fascination.

For five years he had told himself that every word she had spoken was a lie, but looking back, he could only shake his head in wonder. The falsehoods she had told him stood out in such stark contradiction to the rest of her words that only a fool could ever have muddled the two—a fool or a callow youth so deep in love that he could not see the difference between a lie born of desperation and a complete rejection of his heart, his soul, and his body, offered to her without reservation.

At eighteen, Aislyn had seemed to him a woman grown, but at twenty-three, Gawain knew she had been little more than a child. For all his adventures in the bedchamber and on the battlefield, he had been no wiser. He could blame her or he could blame himself, but the truth was that love had not been enough to keep them both from making irrevocable mistakes.

And so, at last, the tale was told in full. He knew what had happened, and why, but that knowledge did not make the pain any easier to bear. Perhaps in time it would. He even thought it might. But right now he could not even imagine an existence in which Aislyn was not foremost in his heart and mind, the memory of her laughter so clear that each breath was an effort.

"Gawain."

He looked up to find the king watching him. How long had Arthur been there? He had been so lost in his own thoughts that he had not even noticed his arrival.

"I have been waiting for you," Arthur said. "We were to meet before the council assembles."

"Yes, sire, of course," Gawain said. "Forgive me."

"Readily." Arthur sat down beside him. "How—how fare you today?"

Gawain did not know how to answer. A part of him wanted to tell Arthur the whole tale, if only for the sake of speaking Aislyn's name aloud, yet another part shied away from exposing a wound so fresh, even to a friend. Before he could decide, the king added, "That was a nasty fall you took."

"Fall?" Gawain wrenched his mind back to the present. "Oh, that. A couple of bruised ribs was the worst of it, and Ragnelle bound them. I hardly feel them today."

Arthur's face tightened at the mention of Ragnelle's name. "I cannot see how you can bear for that—that creature to touch you," he said in a low voice.

Gawain was surprised by the force of his anger. "Her looks are against her—as she would be the first to admit—but I would hardly call her a *creature*."

Arthur shook his head. "You are very brave—"

"Oh, rot, I'm nothing of the sort. Look you, sire, Ragnelle is no monster. She is an old woman with a peculiar sense of humor, but kindly for all that."

"*Kindly?* To force you into marriage—"

"I was neither forced nor tricked," Gawain said, annoyed. "You made it very clear the choice was mine and I made it with full knowledge of the consequences. If I have no complaint, I cannot see why anyone else should."

"Yes, of course," Arthur murmured. "Well, if that is the way you want it—"

"That is the way it *is*."

Arthur patted his shoulder, gazing at him with a sympathy that made Gawain long to strike his hand away. "Very well, then, we shall say no more about it."

"Thank you." Still unaccountably annoyed, Gawain stood. "We should talk about what King Aesc said before we see the others. I believe the alliance can be saved if we—"

"That will wait. Sit down, Gawain, I want a word with you about yesterday."

Gawain obediently resumed his seat, though he wasn't happy about it. If he could not be left alone in his sorrow, he didn't see why he should be forced to relive a day he would just as soon forget. These private jousts were ridiculous; a warrior fought in the service of his king, not for his own vanity, but neither had he enjoyed being beaten, and particularly by Sir Lancelot.

"Sir Lancelot's behavior toward Sir Dinadan was very wrong," Arthur said, "and I have spoken to him at length. He is truly sorry and has apologized."

*And what has that to do with me?* Gawain thought with

a fresh spurt of annoyance. Dinadan was a friend—a good friend—but he was also a knight, blooded in battle and quite capable of settling his own affairs. It was for Ragnelle's sake Gawain had thrown down the glove—surely that was obvious! But apparently it was not, at least to Arthur, for he made no mention of the apology that was owing to *her*. Gawain wondered if he even knew of Ragnelle's involvement, and thought briefly of explaining, but the effort seemed too great.

"I am glad they have settled things between them," he said neutrally.

Arthur nodded, looking unhappy. "If only you and Lancelot knew each other better, I am sure you would be friends. He might be a bit rough around the edges, but at heart he is a good lad."

Gawain barely repressed a derisive snort. How many times had he heard *that* before? Arthur had said the same about Agravaine, and though Gawain had wanted to believe it, he had never been quite able to make that leap of faith. Unlike Arthur, Gawain had known Agravaine from the cradle, and as far as he could tell, his little brother had always been a spoiled, sullen little bastard and a bully into the bargain, which was the one failing Gawain could not abide.

But that was Arthur, determined to see the good in everyone. Gawain had always tried to emulate this touching belief in the inherent decency of all humanity, but today his emotions were too raw to even attempt it.

"When you consider Lance's peculiar upbringing," Arthur persisted, "it is no wonder he is a bit wild. He doesn't really mean any harm, you know, it's only that he doesn't understand our customs."

That was one way of putting it. Another would be that Sir Lancelot, having been brought up among the fey folk, completely lacked the human qualities of humility and compassion—though to be fair, he made up for it with extra measures of pride and malice. But Gawain knew from long experience that to point out these truths would be a waste of breath.

"So long as you are satisfied with him, there is no more to be said," was the best that he could manage.

"I think there is. Lancelot is proud, but I know he values your opinion more than he lets on. If you would only—"

"Oh, for God's sake, Arthur, he detests me! Just let it be!"

He broke off, ashamed of his outburst, which had surprised him as much as it had the king, but his tongue seemed to have taken on a life of its own. "If Sir Lancelot really cared a whit for my opinion—which I wholly doubt—he knows what he must do: make a full apology to Dame Ragnelle. Should he abase himself properly to her—a sight I would pay good gold to see—I would think better of him. But he never will."

"Dame Ragnelle?" Arthur frowned. "What has she to do with this?"

"Ask Sir Lancelot. Such a good-hearted lad will be eager to tell you the whole tale. Now, shall we talk about the Saxons? That is why you came here, isn't it, to discuss King Aesc and his Wessex kin?"

"You disappoint me," Arthur said. "I had such hopes that you and Lance could finally learn to know each other. I had not realized you would be so inflexible—"

"Well, you know it now." It seemed a part of Gawain stood off, horrified by the words that kept springing from his lips, yet at the same time, it was an almost unbearable relief to finally speak the truth. "I am not like you. I cannot find good where none exists, and yon preening whelp has tried me beyond what any man should bear. *You* took him as a knight—well and good, I will say naught of your decision, though it is passing strange to me that you would accept a man who knows so little of respect or common decency into your service. But let it go. I will not speak of his monstrous pride or the intolerable insolence he has displayed—not only to me, but to every man at court, and a good many of the ladies, too. I—"

Arthur held up a hand. "For a man who means to say nothing, you are strangely garrulous. But I think your point is made."

Gawain stood a moment, then dropped onto the bench and covered his face with his hands. "Sire, forgive me. I do not know how I could have been so discourteous."

"I do. And to tell you the truth, I am not at all surprised. You are under far more strain than you will admit, and it was bound to come out some time. Since your marriage—"

"Nay, nay, it has naught to do with that."

"Then what is it?" Arthur asked, so kindly that the last of Gawain's anger melted away. He lifted his head and looked at his uncle, his king, and his closest friend, and found nothing in Arthur's eyes but affection and concern.

"It was long ago, yet—yet it seems it happened only yesterday," he began haltingly. "I never told you—"

"Sire!"

Sir Lancelot hesitated at the gate, one hand on the latch.

"Not now," Arthur said, though he softened his curt dismissal with a smile. "I'll talk to you later."

"I am sorry, sire, but the council was called for noon and they are all assembled—"

"Blast it," Arthur muttered. "We must go."

"Yes. Of course." Gawain stood. "I'm sorry, we never had the chance to talk about King Aesc."

"I'd far rather have heard what you were to tell me. I know, we'll dine tonight—or, no, we cannot. The queen has bidden us to her bower for supper. You haven't forgotten, have you? You will come?"

Gawain had indeed forgotten. Nor was it by accident, he thought wryly. An invitation to one of the queen's little suppers might be an honor, but it was one he could happily dispense with.

"And Dame Ragnelle, of course—that is, if you would like to bring her," Arthur added in such an obvious effort to be agreeable that Gawain could not refuse.

# Chapter 20

• • •

THE council meeting finished, Gawain wandered restlessly to the practice yard, where he exchanged a few words with Agravaine and Dinadan, who were lounging against the fence watching the other knights at work. At last his footsteps led him back to his chamber. He found Ragnelle there before him, sitting by the window with Star curled up in her lap.

She looked over as he came in, her wizened little face as mournful as a monkey's.

"Are you well?" he asked as he unpinned the brooch at his shoulder.

"I am old," she said. "And there's naught to be done about it. How was the council meeting?"

Gawain tossed his cloak onto the trunk and stretched out on the bed. "Long."

"Did you settle King Aesc?" she asked, surprising him.

"How do you know about that?"

She shrugged. "I hear things. They say his kinfolk are after him to break his treaty with the king."

"Aye. Aesc's been at odds with them for years. Now that there is peace, they want him to join with them, and a good many of his people think he should." He yawned. "It is a delicate situation."

"Can you not offer him something?" Ragnelle suggested.

"We have, but if we offer too much, we'll look weak. And his people are already saying they could have more than we will give if they fight us for it. They may be right. If he joins forces with King Ceredig . . ."

"What about King Ceredig, then? Have you tried winning him to your side?"

"A dozen times at least," Gawain answered. "He refuses to even meet with us; he sees no profit in an alliance with Arthur. These Saxons are all the same, they would as lief go to a battle as a feast. But this can hardly be of interest to you."

"Why not? I live here, too, you know."

He yawned again. "If we have to fight them, then so be it."

"And men will die," she said softly. "And their women will mourn them."

"Aye, I suppose . . ." He lifted himself on his elbows to look at her. "We're not dead yet, Ragnelle. There's no need to start mourning us today."

One twisted hand lifted to brush her wrinkled cheek. "Oh, don't mind me, I'm just a bit mopish."

"Well, I know something that will cheer you. We've been invited to the queen's bower for a private supper."

Ragnelle's face did not brighten; indeed, her misshapen shoulders seemed to sag a little. "I think I'll bide here."

"But these invitations are not easily come by! Ladies have been known to tear the hair from a rival who received one, and grown men to weep at having been missed out."

She did not even smile. "You go," she said. "I'm not feeling up to it."

"Not up to the most exclusive invitation to be had in all of Britain?" Gawain raised himself to look into her face, but she turned her head away. "Would you pass up the opportunity to scandalize the queen and her chosen favorites?"

He was on his feet now, ready to summon Arthur's leech no matter what Ragnelle might say, when she gave a short laugh.

"Well, if you put it like that, I suppose I'll have to go."

"Are you certain? Ragnelle, if you are unwell—"

"Is there something amiss with your hearing?" she huffed, setting Star on the floor. "Or your eyes? The only thing the matter with me is that I'm an old woman, not some hasty-witted dewberry who can dash off at a moment's notice!"

"I'm sorry," he said, "I should have told you sooner, but I forgot. Shall we go?"

"What, now? I should say not! If you expect to present yourself in that old tunic, you'd better think again! Here you are, a prince, yet you slouch about like some fly-bitten clodpole when I would wager Sir Lancelot—he'll be there, won't he?—will be trimmed out in some outlandish finery. Oh, stand aside, you're only in the way. Aha! I knew you must have *something* that didn't look as though it came from the ragpicker."

She shook out a gray robe with silver embroidery about the neck and hanging sleeves, and shot him a stern look from beneath her tangled brows. "If you *dare* tell me you don't have a silver circlet, I'll—I'll—I don't know what I'll do, but I promise you won't like it."

"I have one," he assured her. "Somewhere."

"Don't just stand there, go and find it! And the comb, as well. And you can take your hair out of that braid while you're at it. No, don't argue, we haven't time. I'd like to get there before *all* the food is gone."

• • •

THERE had never been so fine a knight—so proud a prince—so bonny a man as Gawain in his severe gray robe with its discreet silver edging. The fabric flowed with him when he moved, each step revealing a tantalizing glimpse of muscled thighs and chest and shoulders. His hair, confined by a plain silver circlet, cascaded down his back like moonlit silk, so soft and cool that any woman surely must long to run her fingers through it.

Sir Lancelot looked well, too, Aislyn thought, trying to be fair. His crimson tunic was undeniably dramatic, and its elaborate gold trimming set off his dark good looks to perfection. On any other night, he would have captured every eye. But on *this* night, she concluded with an inward laugh, he merely succeeded in looking overdressed, even a trifle garish in his finery.

Lancelot knew it, too. Aislyn could tell by the way he kept looking sideways, as though wondering how he could work the conversation round to the name of Gawain's tailor. He would have to work hard, though, for Gawain cared no more for his wardrobe than for the stir he had created by simply walking into the room.

Clearly he did not often garb himself as befitted his rank. Which was all to the good, for now that Aislyn came to think of it, she didn't particularly care for the way Guinevere's ladies were eyeing him. Her only comfort was that he seemed as oblivious to them as he was to anything he had done to attract their notice.

He was all concern as he escorted Aislyn to a seat and made sure she was provided with food and drink. But after he had exchanged a few obligatory courtesies with the king and queen and such guests as were assembled, he turned his gaze out the open doors leading to the gardens and there let it remain as the conversation flowed on around him.

Not that he had missed much. This was a very private gathering, indeed: Sir Lancelot, the elderly King Bagdemagus and three of Guinevere's ladies were the only guests besides themselves. The evening was overcast and oppressively warm; the sky above the garden was an odd yellowish color and not a breath of air stirred the hangings on the walls. Once the initial greetings were over, no one seemed to have much to say, and apart from King Bagdemagus, no one had an appetite for the delicacies Guinevere had ordered. "Excellent, my lady," he said when he had finished, and leaning back in his seat, promptly fell asleep.

Still, Aislyn wasn't sorry she had come. What good was it to sit alone and brood on the injustice of her situation? At least she was with Gawain when he could have easily left her behind. He had been very sweet before, offering this invitation like a boy carrying a handful of blossoms, torn up by the roots, to his ailing granddame.

One day they would laugh about that.

He loved her—or at least he had, enough that he had never thought to marry anyone else. Once Morgana knew the truth, surely she would take pity on them. She must!

"Shall we have a game of hazards?" Guinevere suggested.

Arthur yawned. "It's too hot to think."

"Hoodman's blind? Or . . ." Guinevere's voice died away.

"Riddles?" Lancelot said.

Guinevere looked at him expectantly. "Yes, tell us one."

"Me? I—I don't know any," Lancelot said. "Do you, sire?"

Arthur yawned again, slumping in his seat. "I can't recall any at the moment."

Guinevere's eyes flashed. "If you would rather be abed, my lord—"

"No, no." Arthur straightened, blinking. "This is very pleasant, my lady. Very . . . relaxing."

Lancelot looked from the Guinevere's angry face to the king. "I trust the council meeting went well?" he said. "What did you decide about King—?"

"Not now, Lance," Arthur said, and silence filled the chamber once again until King Bagdemagus snorted and sat up, staring about him wide-eyed. "Catch it by the ears, that's the way," he said clearly, then his eyes fell shut and he began to snore again.

Lancelot picked up a small harp and plucked a few strings. "Lance," the queen said, looking at him hopefully, "will you sing for us?"

"Not I!" he answered, laughing. "I couldn't carry a tune if it was strapped to my back."

He made to hand the harp to Guinevere, but she refused it. "I never learned," she said. "The sisters did not consider it proper."

"Then perhaps . . ." Guinevere's ladies all shook their heads, blushing like the gooses they were. Lancelot did not even seem to notice their confusion as he turned to the king. "I won't offer it to *you*," he said, "for fear that you might sing."

His gaze strayed back to the queen—it never left her long, Aislyn noted, and was far more anxious than seemed warranted by the occasion. Was he in love with her? If so, he was pressing his suit in a very peculiar manner, for he seemed more interested in bringing her and Arthur into accord than in winning her notice for himself.

"One morning—it was last year, when we were encamped by the river Usk," he went on, "I woke to the most fearful din. We all sprang from our bedrolls, thinking ourselves under attack—" He ducked as Arthur aimed a good-natured cuff at his head. "But it was only the king bathing in the river."

"What, a man cannot even greet the dawn with a bit of a tune?" Arthur said, pretending great affront.

"A king can do whatever he likes, of course," Lancelot

said, then added in an undertone to Guinevere, "We thought for sure he had taken a cramp—"

"It wasn't *that* bad."

"No, sire, of course it wasn't," Lancelot said, but he rolled his eyes and added in an audible whisper, "Like an ox mired in the mud."

"Rogue," Arthur said, "you exaggerate. Come, Gawain, defend me! You've heard me sing many a time!"

Gawain, who had been gazing through the open doorway, turned, blinking as though he had been woken from a dream. "I'm sorry," he said. "What did you ask me?"

"It doesn't bear repeating," Arthur said, his voice gentle as he gazed at his nephew with a small frown between his brows.

"I've never heard you sing," Guinevere said to her husband, her voice wistful and a little sad.

"Apparently you should be thankful," Arthur replied, and though he laughed, it only underscored the almost palpable gloom that had once again fallen over the company.

Lancelot turned back to the harp, trying vainly to pick out a tune. After he had hit a series of particularly sour notes, Guinevere snapped, "For pity's sake, stop torturing that instrument!"

"Right. Sorry." He turned to set it back on the table.

"Sir Gawain can play it," Aislyn said, surprising even herself.

"Can you?" Guinevere said.

"What? Oh, the harp." Gawain took it from Lancelot. "Not well." He ran his fingers across the strings. "We all learned when I was younger, but it has been years . . ."

He plucked a few chords, wincing when he struck a wrong note. "No, I am afraid I—"

"Try," Aislyn said. Leaning close, she whispered, "It'd be a kindness to the queen."

Gawain nodded and sat back, settling the instrument on

his knee. "Well, there has been one song in my mind to-day . . ."

He cleared his throat in the self-conscious manner of one unaccustomed to performing publicly and began to play, not one of the merry soldier's songs she had expected, but a delicately haunting melody. He played it through once, and then, surprising Aislyn, he began to sing. His voice was deep and tunable, and though it was untrained, its very roughness added poignancy to the melancholy air.

*I dreamed I walked beside you as the sun set on the barley,*
*Then I wakened to lie in my cold bed alone,*
*You have left my heart shaken with a hopeless desolation*
*And your beauty will haunt me wherever I go.*

Guinevere's ladies sighed in chorus, leaning forward in their seats.

*The white moon above the pale sands, the pale stars above the thorn tree*
*Are cold beside my lady, but no purer than she.*
*I gaze upon the cold moon until the stars drown in the warm sea*
*And the bright eyes of my darling are never on me.*

*My days are so weary, my days they are all gray now,*
*My heart it is a cold thing, my heart is a stone.*
*All joy is fled from me, my life has gone away now*
*Since cruel death has taken my love for his own.*

Aislyn wanted to weep for the aching sorrow in his voice, to laugh aloud for joy, to leap to her feet and shout out that it was *she* he sang for, *her* beauty that haunted him, but she knew the words could never leave her lips.

*The day it is long past now when we were to be*
*married,*
*And it's rather I would die than live only to grieve.*
*Oh, wait for me, my darling, where the sun sets on the*
*barley*
*And I'll meet you there on the road to the sea.*

His fingers drew forth a muted echo of the last line before he laid his palm across the strings, stilling them abruptly. The king stared at his nephew, astonishment writ plain upon his open face. The queen lifted one hand to brush her cheek and one or two of her ladies sniffed audibly. Even Lancelot was silent, wide-eyed with surprise.

Gawain glanced up at them, then back down at the harp. Aislyn, with an almost painful awareness, knew exactly how he felt, as if he had stripped himself naked before them all.

"Ah, well," she said brightly, "at least you still have me."

They all went rigid, faces tightening as though they'd caught a whiff of something rank. The silence was shattered by the last sound Aislyn expected: Gawain's laughter. He looked to Aislyn, his shoulders shaking with mirth he struggled vainly to suppress, but when she winked at him, he lost his composure altogether. It had been a very long time since she had heard him laugh so freely, and judging from the shock on the others' faces, the sound was strange to them, as well. At last he drew a shaking breath. "Forgive me," he began, "I was—that is—"

"There's no need to be sorry," Aislyn said. "I like to hear you laugh. You should do it more."

"Aye, you're right," he said, handing the harp back to Lancelot with an nod of thanks.

"Gawain—" Arthur began, but before he could finish his thought a knock came on the door. One of the waiting women answered it, then stepped back to allow a young man to enter. Aislyn scarce had time to wonder where she had seen him before Gawain was on his feet. "Gaheris!" he cried and went forward to embrace his younger brother.

Of course. Aislyn remembered Gaheris well from her time in Lothian, a quiet boy with laughing eyes. Brown-haired and of but average stature, he was often overlooked among his golden brothers, but he had always been Aislyn's favorite of the younger boys, for he would often make her laugh with a shrewd observation on the doings of the court of Lothian. Morgause, as she recalled, had not cared for either Gaheris or his observations. The queen much preferred her next son, Gareth, who she often likened to a young Gawain.

"Oh, yes, my mother is here," Gaheris said in answer to the king's question. "She will be along presently."

Morgause? Here? Tonight? Aislyn did not stop to think. She slipped from the open door into the garden, and keeping to the shadows, made her way to Gawain's chamber. Once inside, she bolted the door and leaned her back against the wood, drawing in deep gulps of air, shaken by the force of her heart pounding painfully against her ribs.

At last she tottered to the chair and half fell upon it, her heart thudding out a terrible refrain. *Morgause. Morgause is here.* Oh, why did she have to come tonight? Why could she not have waited a few days more? Then Aislyn would have been glad to face her, but now . . .

*I have to go,* she thought, jumping up. *I cannot risk a meeting, not as I am now.* With shaking hands, she flung up the lid to the trunk and pawed through its contents, all the while straining to hear a footstep in the corridor. After she had twice dropped what she held to whirl toward the door at some imagined sound, she abandoned her attempts to pack.

Taking her bag from its hook on the wall, she hobbled to the door, stopping only long enough to cast one last look at the place where she had known the heights of joy and sorrow. The cats were absent save for Sooty, curled up on Gawain's pillow.

"Look after him," Aislyn said, then braced her shoulders and added, "until I come back again."

Sooty blinked once, regarding Aislyn with feline contempt. "Don't look at me like that, I will be back," Aislyn said. "I *will*. You wait and see."

# Chapter 21

• • •

THE last time Gawain had spoken to his mother was on the morning of Aislyn's death. Now here she was, strolling into the queen's bower with an insouciance that stunned him. How dared she come here? How dared she face him after what she had done to Aislyn? It mattered not whether she had done the deed herself, she was responsible for Aislyn's death. He could never prove it, but he knew. And she *knew* he knew. Yet still she smiled at him—for one horrified moment he thought she actually meant to embrace him, but after a keen look at his face she swept by and bowed before the king.

"Sire, forgive me for not sending word, but I daresay my arrival is not *entirely* unexpected."

"Madam, you are welcome," Arthur said coolly.

"I see you've already met my son, Gaheris," she went on. "It is my hope that you will accept him into your service."

"Is that your hope, as well?" Arthur said to Gaheris. "To become a Knight of the Round Table?"

Before he could answer, Morgause laughed lightly. "What lad doesn't dream of such an honor?" She leaned a bit closer to Arthur and lowered her voice, though not so much that Gawain, standing across the room, could not hear her plainly. "I fear Gaheris will never achieve the same stature as his brothers. Oh, he tries, but . . ." She glanced sideways at her son, adding in a piercing whisper, "I would consider it a great kindness, Arthur, if you would make a place for him."

"Gaheris," the king said, "what is your wish?"

Gaheris dropped gracefully to one knee and bowed his head. "My one wish is to serve you, sire, in whatever fashion you deem fit." Though somewhat red about the ears, he was quite composed—remarkably so, given the circumstances. Arthur caught Gawain's eye and raised his brows, signaling both approval and surprise. Gawain nodded once. *Yes, sire, you are not mistaken. He is all that he seems.*

"I am sure you will serve me right well," Arthur said kindly.

Gaheris lifted his chin, his eyes flashing. "I ask no favors, sire, only the chance to prove myself."

"That you shall have." Arthur laid a hand briefly on his shoulder. "Welcome to Camelot, nephew."

"Thank you," Morgause said before Gaheris could reply. "That is *very* kind of you, Arthur, and I hope—that is, I am sure you will not regret it."

Having made the point—though perhaps not quite the one she had intended—Morgause glanced brightly about the chamber. "And whom do we have here?"

"Queen Guinevere, allow me to present my sister Morgause, the queen of Orkney," Arthur said, and as the two women greeted each other with wary eyes and courteous words, Gawain drew Gaheris into a corner.

"What the devil was *that* about?"

Gaheris shrugged. "I'm in her bad graces at the moment."

"I never would have guessed. What did you do?"

"Helped her latest . . . admirer on his way out the door." Gaheris's grin faltered. "That was a bad business, Gawain—I'll tell you about it, but not here. At any rate, she's—oh, God's mercy, not now."

". . . and Sir Lancelot du Lac," Arthur was saying. "Lancelot, the queen of Orkney."

Morgause smiled and extended her hand. Sir Lancelot went beet red and choked out an incoherent greeting.

"Poor gudgeon," Gaheris said. "He doesn't have the first idea, does he?"

Gawain had never seen Sir Lancelot at such a loss. He was blushing like a squire, his polished manners quite forgotten. Morgause had clearly not yet lost her power to attract, but if she thought to add Sir Lancelot to her long list of besotted young followers, she would have to think again.

"I was only the excuse for her to come," Gaheris said, nodding toward his mother. "You're the real reason. Is it true you are married?"

"Yes."

Where *was* Ragnelle? Strange she was so silent. Gawain would have expected her to be the first to welcome his mother, pushing herself forward with some outlandish remark that would infuriate Morgause. The resulting skirmish would no doubt be deplorable, but for some odd reason he couldn't help but smile to imagine it.

"Is she here?" Gaheris said.

Gawain quickly scanned the room. "She *was* . . ."

"Gawain!" Morgause called, loudly enough so heads turned in his direction. "What are you doing skulking in the corner?"

Gawain stiffened. How dare she even speak to him, let alone in such a tone? But when he came to think of it, the real wonder was that he was surprised.

"Come see me when you're done," he said to Gaheris,

"and I'll introduce you to my wife." He sketched Morgause a brief bow before turning toward the door.

"Oh, dear, I must have frightened him!" she said to Arthur, her voice lightly mocking. "Come, Gawain, there is no need to flee! Whatever mischief you've been up to, 'tis best to confess it and have done."

Having reduced him to the status of a six-year-old, she held out her hand, her eyes hard above her gently smiling lips.

He stepped across the room and took her by the wrist, drawing her away from the others and speaking so she alone could hear. "I have nothing to say to you, madam."

She pulled her wrist from his grasp. "Well, I have plenty to say to you! How dare you wed without my leave?"

"And how dare you speak one word to me upon the subject of marriage? After what you did to—" He drew a swift breath. "No. I will not speak of it. Now, if you will excuse me—"

"Do not tell me you are still nursing a grudge over that foolish girl! I had not thought that even you could be so stubborn."

"And I," Gawain replied, tight-lipped, "would not have thought you would have the effrontery to speak to me of her."

"Not speak to my own son? Have you taken leave of your senses? Look here, my lad—"

"No, you look, Mother. I *know* what happened to Aislyn."

"You—" She drew back and studied him intently. "Explain yourself."

"She did not lie to me, but you did, and whether she took her own life or was—was—"

"I did not murder the chit, or order her death, or any of the things you seem to be imagining," Morgause retorted, her composure restored. "Why would I have bothered? She was nothing—"

"She was the woman I loved, and while that may seem nothing to you—" He broke off. "This is not a conversation I wish to have with you, not now or at any other time. What's done is done. But do not ever attempt to meddle in my affairs again. You will say nothing of my marriage to me or anyone, and if you speak to my lady at all, it will be with the respect to which she is entitled."

Morgause's eyes shone with tears. "You are very hard, Gawain."

"I am what you have made me, Mother," he spat, and turning his back on her, he walked from the chamber without another word.

# Chapter 22

• • •

"IS Sir Gawain quite well?" Queen Guinevere said when Morgause rejoined her. "He has not been himself of late."

"Really?" Morgause sat down beside her. "In what way?"

"Oh, 'tis difficult to explain," Guinevere said, "but since his marriage . . ." She broke off, casting a guilty look in Arthur's direction, but he was chatting with Gaheris and did not seem to have heard.

Morgause drew a bit closer. "Of course I was surprised to learn of it and disappointed to have been left out of the festivities, but I know how impulsive boys can be!"

Guinevere bit her lip to hide her smile. Only a mother could describe the formidable Sir Gawain in such terms!

"Of course I cannot condone his unseemly haste, but I was right willing to forgive him if he was happy in his choice," Morgause went on. "Yet it seems that there is something wrong about the marriage. He refused to speak of it just now and grew so upset when I questioned him that

I lacked the heart to press him. But, madam—may I call you Guinevere? And you must call me by my name, for we *are* family now. Please, I beg you to tell me if my son is in some sort of trouble."

"Well," Guinevere said confidentially, "I hardly know myself how it all came to pass. Sir Gawain arrived here with Dame Ragnelle and announced that the two of them were to be wed that very day!"

"And when was that?" Morgause said.

"Eight days ago. I remember it particularly, because it was the same day he and my lord rode out to meet Somer Gromer Jour. I do not know if word has reached you of my lord's adventure—"

"Yes, it has, and God be thanked *that* danger was averted."

"Know you of some other danger?" Guinevere asked uneasily.

"Indeed, but we will come to that in time. You were saying that Gawain brought this woman to court—and what sort of woman is she?"

"Oh, madam—Morgause—I hardly know how to tell you. She is much older than Sir Gawain—"

"But still of childbearing age?" Morgause interrupted.

"Far, far past it. And she is quite . . ."

Morgause pressed her hand. "Go on, my dear."

"She is—they call her the loathly lady," Guinevere said in a rush. "For that she is so foul to look upon. And her manners are so gross that she cannot be of gentle birth!"

Morgause drew a sharp breath. "But—but this is infamous! How *could* Arthur—forgive me, I will speak no word against my brother, but I cannot understand why he allowed this!"

"Nor can I," Guinevere said, dropping her voice to a whisper. "He will say nothing of the matter save that it must be as Sir Gawain wishes. We have all wondered, of course, if she has some dreadful hold over him—" She broke off, blushing, but Morgause only nodded.

"It is natural to wonder, though knowing Gawain, I would think it is more likely a matter of honor. You say he rode out with the king to meet Somer Gromer Jour, and when he returned, this . . . woman was with him?"

"Yes. Do you think there is some connection?"

"I cannot see what it would be," Morgause said, frowning. "But you can be sure I will have the truth of it before long! I must say, you are not at all what I expected! What a comfort it is to find you so sensible and well-informed."

"Thank you," Guinevere said, touched and flattered by the praise, which was of a sort she did not often hear. "But you were going to tell me something about another danger, were you not?"

Morgause regarded her a moment, then nodded decisively. "I meant to give Arthur this news privately, but now that I have met you, I would like to ask your counsel first."

"Oh, yes," Guinevere breathed. "Do tell me! Lately I have felt so uneasy—as if something threatens my lord—"

Morgause's reddish brows lifted. "Do you have the Sight?"

"Me? Oh, no, I do not meddle in sorcery!" Guinevere exclaimed, then was stricken with embarrassment when she remembered to whom she spoke.

But Morgause did not seem offended. "I forgot that you were convent-bred. Oh, what a pity, for I really do believe—but no, I'll say no more, dear Arthur might not like it. Only . . . do pay heed to your intuitions, Guinevere. They may be more important than you know."

"I shall," Guinevere promised earnestly. "But do tell me of this danger!"

Morgause sighed. "It begins with a lady who served me before her marriage. When she came to me some five or six years ago, a widow in the most desperate straits, I took her and her children in."

Guinevere nodded. Of course Morgause had. She would have done the same herself for any loyal servant.

"The elder proved to be a sad trial," Morgause continued. "She was quite lovely, and not without intelligence, but she drowned herself over a broken love affair. The younger, Launfal, seemed more promising, though always somewhat heavy of spirit, for he could not be reconciled to the loss of lands and riches that were once his family's. It seemed to me he fixed upon Arthur as the culprit, and blamed him, as well, for the sister's death. It was all nonsense, as I told him more than once, but he brooded upon his imagined wrongs until I feared for his reason."

"What did you do?" Guinevere asked.

"I put him under restraint, still hoping he could be saved, but with the cunning of his kind, he managed to escape."

Guinevere shivered and peered into the shadowed garden. "So he—he could be anywhere!"

"That is the reason I came in such haste, to warn the king against him. Arthur must be brought to understand that Launfal, for all his youth and charm . . . My greatest fear is that my brother . . ."

She put her hand on Guinevere's. "Forgive me if I speak bluntly. You must have noticed that your lord does not keep such state as was common in his father's day. Arthur walks freely among his subjects and opens his hall to every sort of churl on feast days. It is all very admirable, of course, but I would not have his kindness be his undoing."

"We must tell him," Guinevere said. "Warn him of this danger. He will know what is to be done."

"Yes, of course, but . . ." Morgause cast her eyes down and sighed. "It cannot have escaped you that men—even the best of them—tend to shrug off warnings from a sister or a wife. They pat us on the head and tell us not to fear and then go off and do exactly as they meant to all along. They are all boys at heart, the dears, always so anxious to prove their courage! I fear it sometimes falls to us women to take the sensible view. To protect them from themselves."

Guinevere had never thought of it thus before. Arthur was both good and wise—so good and so wise, in fact, that she was often driven to reflect unhappily upon the many flaws in her own nature. The thought that she, by virtue of her sex, possessed a wisdom he could not was too thrilling to resist.

"Yes, indeed," she said to Morgause. "Tell me what *you* think should be done."

"Perhaps if Arthur's knights—or perhaps your knights, those who came with you from Cameliard, whom I am sure can be trusted with your confidence—were to be made aware of this danger to their king . . ."

"Yes, I see your point, and I agree completely. Can you describe this man—this Launfal—to me?"

Morgause smiled slowly. "I would be happy to."

# Chapter 23

• • •

ONCE Aislyn crept through the castle gates, she had to feel her way along the road, helped only by the occasional flash of lightning to the east and a faint, far-off glow from the market square at the foot of the hill. She went through the stalls carefully, keeping away from the lanterns hung by the merchants readying their wares for the morrow.

Once she was through the market, though, the darkness was a living thing, pressing round her like a muffling cloak. If not for the white stones marking the edges of the road, she would have given up entirely, though even so her progress was agonizingly slow. *At this rate, I won't make it a mile,* she thought, but kept on walking, one careful step after another, until her breath came short and her legs began to ache.

*Don't think about that. Think about Gawain and what he'll do and say when he discovers I am gone. He'll be a bit sad, but likely he'll be relieved, as well, though for form's sake, he'll send someone out to look for me. Or no, I'm wronging him,* she thought. *He'll come himself.*

That spurred her on, and when the clouds began to break, she took new heart. There was no moon tonight, but even the faint starlight seemed a gift, for it was enough to make out the whitewashed stones lining the broad road.

*Aye, he will be sad,* she thought, *though not nearly so sad as I am to leave him. And at least Gaheris is there to cheer him.*

She thought of the first day of Gawain's visit home five years ago, when Gaheris had been chided by the queen for some imagined want of courtesy to his brother. Gaheris, who usually bore the queen's rebukes in silence, suddenly announced to the entire hall that Gawain was not a deity, and he, for one, refused to worship at his shrine. Morgause was livid, but Gawain only laughed and said Gaheris was obviously a sensible lad and he looked forward to knowing him better.

His words had not sprung from any deep affection—he and Gaheris were all but strangers—but only an instinctive desire to help his brother out of a scrape. At the time, Aislyn had been faintly amused, and then annoyed when for the rest of Gawain's visit, Gaheris hardly left his side.

One careless comment. One kind word. And look how warmly they had greeted each other earlier. She thought of her own brother Launfal and tried to imagine how he would greet her in the unlikely event of their meeting again. But the two cases were hardly comparable. She and Launfal had never been close. Or rather, she thought, she had not allowed him to get close to her. She had always been too busy, too wrapped up in her own concerns, to regard her sickly younger brother as anything but a nuisance.

The last time she had seen him was in the practice yard at Lothian. Launfal had been smiling when he disarmed a boy who overtopped him by a foot. Had she ever told him how proud she was that day? She didn't think so. For Gawain had been there, too, and when he looked at her, all else had been forgotten.

She should have said something to Launfal. There was no one else to do it. Their mother never cared for him; he'd been conceived when Aislyn was still an infant, and the pregnancy had been difficult from the first. At seven months, he'd come into the world, and Mother nearly died of it. Aislyn knew that everyone assumed it was a late miscarriage, for she'd heard the story often from Nurse, who liked to tell it every time she'd had a drop too much of ale: how the child was forgotten in the worry over the mother until Nurse realized that the faint mewing sound coming from the corner was a living babe, though such a puny one that no one expected him to live.

Mother found the entire experience revolting, including the child that had come of it. It was an aversion that deepened over the years when it became clear that her sickly son was to be the last child she would bear.

Their father was no better. Always disgusted by any form of illness, Sir Rogier ignored Launfal's existence completely, while Aislyn simply thought her brother tedious. He spent most of his time hovering between life and death, and by the time he finally spoke, the family had already dismissed him as an imbecile. Even when he began to resemble a human, he was so fragile that he was no good for any sort of game.

But on that day in the practice yard Launfal had not looked fragile. He'd looked strong and healthy and happier than Aislyn had ever seen him.

She wished she had spoken to him. There were so many things she should have said, but only one that really mattered: don't trust the queen. Four words, that's all, and she'd had plenty of opportunity to speak them between the time she'd fully understood the extent of Morgause's wickedness and her disastrous meeting with Gawain. But she hadn't. She hadn't even thought of it. And now it was too late.

Aislyn doubted anything remained of the sweet-tempered

little brother who had trailed after her for so many years, waiting vainly for her notice. He'd been so patient—annoyingly persistent, she'd thought then—and on the few occasions she had been bored enough to play with him, so grateful. Her heart burned with an emotion she did not at first recognize, but then she realized it was shame.

Of course he had turned to Morgause—who else did he have? A father who'd spoken to him perhaps a dozen times before expiring, a mother who actively disliked him, a sister who had not even cared enough to say the four words that might have saved him.

The long years she had spent alone, nursing her solitary grudge against the world, no longer seemed a punishment undeserved, but the inevitable result of her own self-absorption. Had she but an ounce of Gawain's generosity, Launfal would have gone with her into exile. He would have followed her to the ends of the earth if she had only showed him some small kindness.

"Watch over him. He's not a bad lad, he's only fallen into evil ways," she muttered as she walked along, and smiled wryly, thinking she could as easily be speaking of herself. Speaking *to* herself, as well, for much as she longed to believe someone listened to her prayers, she could not force her mind into obedience.

These reflections carried her into the utter darkness of the forest. When she could no longer trust her ability to find the path, she sank down on a boulder and eased off her shoes, groaning as she massaged her swollen ankles and throbbing toes.

Time to think. On the night of the king's Midsummer feast she must be back in Camelot to find Morgana. Between now and then, the only sensible thing to do was to go back to her hut and wait.

But tonight she had gone as far as she could manage. Her heart was doing an odd little hitch and skip, and it was some time before she managed to rouse herself long enough to crawl off the boulder into a patch of ferns, where she fell asleep to the night call of an owl above her head.

# Chapter 24

• • •

GAHERIS perched on the edge of Gawain's bed and watched his older brother exchange his fine robe for a leather tunic and leggings. He had not said a word as Gawain told him the story of the king's meeting with Somer Gromer Jour, though he had thought many things, and wondered even more, and liked neither his questions nor his suspicions. When Gawain explained about Dame Ragnelle and how he had come to marry her, Gaheris was hard put to hide his shock.

Was this really Gawain talking? Gaheris had never subscribed to the common wisdom that put Gawain only slightly below God's own son, but he had always thought his eldest brother too sensible to land himself in such a humiliating mess. Of course, it wasn't Gawain's fault, not really—what else could he have done but marry her? Gaheris even understood why Gawain had kept the reason for his marriage hidden from the court. He wasn't sure that he agreed with that decision, though he might well have done the same in his brother's place. It was all perfectly understandable—even noble—but God in heaven, what a mess! And the oddest part was that Gawain seemed completely unaware of the gravity of the situation.

Gaheris drew one knee up and rested his chin upon it. "Is she as ugly as I've heard?"

"I don't know what you've heard," Gawain answered, tossing his robe into the trunk. "But I'd wager it falls far short of the mark."

"She's that bad?"

"Worse," Gawain assured him, laughing.

It was one thing to bear up bravely under what could only be considered a disaster, but laughter seemed to be taking things a bit too far. In fact, Gawain was behaving very oddly altogether.

"Have you considered," Gaheris said, "that this Dame Ragnelle could well be a witch?"

"Oh, she is," Gawain answered, pulling the tunic over his head. "She told me so herself. But there's no harm in her."

"And what," Gaheris asked carefully, "leads you to that conclusion? Exactly?"

Gawain frowned, then shrugged. "There just isn't."

"She forced you to marry her—"

"She did *not*. I wish people would stop saying that!"

"Who else has said it?"

"Arthur. He's taking all this very badly, and just between the two of us, I'm getting a wee bit tired of his moaning."

Gaheris blinked. That was the closest he had ever heard Gawain come to a criticism of the king, and it made him uneasy. So did the fact that Arthur, too, was clearly troubled about Gawain.

"Let me be sure I understand," he said. "You married a woman you had never laid eyes upon—one who appeared out of nowhere and offered you a choice you could not possibly refuse—a hideous crone who is, moreover, a self-confessed witch. She has now vanished back into thin air—and you are going to *look* for her?"

"Aye." Gawain slung his sword over his shoulder and began to buckle the straps across his chest.

"Gawain, sit down a moment, and give me one reason—one *good* reason—why you are not on your knees thanking God for your escape."

Gawain sat down on the bed and raked a hand through his hair. "It is my duty to find her."

"Be damned to that! I'm sure Arthur can have this farce annulled, particularly as she has now deserted you. I mean to say, it isn't a *real* marriage." He felt his cheeks burn. "That is, you didn't . . . did you?"

"Nay, nay, there was nothing of that sort between us. Although," he added with a grin, "Ragnelle did her best to give the impression that there was."

Gaheris stared at him. "And that is *amusing*?"

"You can be sure I did not find it so at the time. But—if you had seen their faces—ach, never mind, 'tis impossible to explain."

He began to rise, but Gaheris put a hand on his shoulder. "Try."

Gawain sighed. "Camelot is a fine place, Gaheris, but we are none of us quite so noble as we like to think ourselves. That is not a pleasant truth to have flung in one's face, but it is a thing worth knowing."

"Yes, I daresay it is," Gaheris said slowly. "But if you want my opinion—"

"Oh, I have a choice? Well, then—"

"*Will* you be quiet and listen!" Gaheris could hardly believe he was speaking to Gawain in such a tone, but he was more than uneasy now: he was frightened. "Don't you understand what you've been telling me? This witch has deliberately deceived the court about your marriage—and that is no joke, Gawain, it is a trap. Not only that, but now she is attempting to turn you against your friends and kin.

No, hear me out," he urged as Gawain began to protest. "You take her side in everything, even when she is clearly in the wrong, and dismiss the king's concerns as moaning. Gawain, that isn't like you! Can you not see how you've changed? Think back on everything you've said, and then tell me again there is no harm in her!"

Gawain shook off his hand and stood. "You don't understand."

"I think I do."

Gawain shot him an exasperated look. "Look you, Gaheris, this is all much simpler than you would have it. I married Dame Ragnelle. You can dispute my reasons or hers, but in the end they make no matter. We are wed. I vowed to honor and protect her and what I have sworn to do, I *do*."

That, at least, sounded like Gawain, proud and stubborn as the devil. "But if your oath was given under—"

"*Enough.*" Gawain swung the cloak over his shoulders, settling it so his sword hilt poked through the split in the fabric. "I don't want to brangle with you, Gaheris, particularly not on your first night at court. Believe it or not, I *am* glad you are here."

"So am I. Lothian is a bad place these days."

"Ach, that's right, you were going to tell me about your quarrel with our mother. As soon as I return we'll have a good, long talk."

Gaheris sat for some time after his brother had left him, a worried frown creasing his brow. At last he went through the door and down the passageway. He was almost to his chamber when he turned back, and finding a page, asked him to run and see if the king would grant him an audience.

# Chapter 25

• • •

*DAMN Morgana. Damn her coming and going, sleeping and waking, damn her eyes and her hands and her feet and . . . and everything else,* Aislyn thought as she stopped yet again to detach a clinging branch from her skirt. Beneath the shelter of the trees, the air was warm and still, and the underbrush a mass of blossoms. *Very pretty,* she thought, though she would rather have kept to the road—if only she didn't think Gawain might be on it, too. Not that she didn't want to see him—she missed him sorely, another misery for which she had Morgana to thank—but she could not afford for him to find her yet.

She reached her hut at dusk and slipped inside. Her supper was a handful of nuts and a mug of water from the stream, and by the time she had finished, full dark had fallen. Too weary to kindle a fire, she lay down on her pallet and waited for sleep. It was long in coming, giving her plenty of time to reflect on how she had gotten into this pathetic mess and the unlikelihood of ever getting out of it again.

She had never stopped to measure the crone's years, but now she found herself counting each beat of her heart and cataloging every ache and pain. How much time was left to her? What if Morgana did not return as promised? What if Gawain was called to battle? He could be gone for months or even years. What if some other lady caught his heart?

She twisted on the thin pallet, feeling the dampness of the earth beneath creep into her bones. Strange that she had never noticed before how uncomfortable it was. She had always cast herself down thoughtlessly and closed her eyes, drifting into sleep without a backward glance. But then, she had been young and strong—what adventures she might have had, what great deeds she might have accomplished had she not hidden herself away here! What was it Gawain had said? *In destinies sad or merry, true men can but try.*

*Coward,* she thought, *that's what you are, skulking here for years while the world went on without you.* Had she but faced Gawain that first day in the forest and spoken her heart honestly, she would have known that his was hers and always had been. But he had never really known her—and she had never really known herself. Only Morgana had seen the truth. She *had* been selfish and irresponsible, and she had no one but herself to blame for her predicament.

*If only I could go back, I would do it all so differently.* But there was no going back. She must go on and not fall into despair. Gawain was likely lost to her, but even if she could never have his love, she could live in such a way as to earn his respect—and more importantly, her own.

The next few days passed slowly. She saw no one but an elderly woman who lived high up on the hillside; the woman's son, a shepherd, had begged Aislyn for a potion to cure his mother's ague some winters back. Now when Aislyn puffed up the hill and introduced herself, she was greeted as an old friend. Sitting among drifts of wool, she learned that Sir Gawain had passed through the village on the day after Aislyn had left Camelot.

"He was seeking an old woman," the shepherd's mother said. "I thought it might be you."

"What would Sir Gawain be wanting with me?" Aislyn asked. "Are you sure it wasn't you he was after?"

They laughed together, and Aislyn obligingly put a charm upon the woman's loom in return for half a loaf.

*So Gawain had been here,* she thought, making her way carefully down the hillside to the forest. She wondered if he had given up or whether he would be back.

The next morning she woke to the sound of fists hammering on her door. For a moment she was entirely disoriented, then she remembered where she was and why, and thought with a sinking heart that Gawain had found her. "A bit of patience, if you would!" she called. "I'll be there as soon as I can manage!"

Grunting, she raised herself to hands and knees, and using the wall for a handhold, slowly pulled herself upright.

"All right, you found—" she said as she flung open the door, then halted, speechless when she saw four warriors upon the doorstep.

*Saxon* warriors. They towered over her, blocking the sunlight, barbaric, fierce, and terrifying. Their backs were to the sun, their faces shadowed. Light hair was oiled and twisted into complicated plaits that hung over broad shoulders. One carried an enormous bow, another a battle-ax, and all were armed with sword and dagger. Every instinct screamed for her to run, but even if she could have forced her legs to move, the warriors filled the only exit.

They seemed equally surprised at the sight of her. As one, they stepped back, and all at once, when the sun shone on their faces, Aislyn realized they were not merely Saxons, but men. The one who carried the battle-ax—who Aislyn now saw was little more than a boy with curling reddish hair—flung up his hands, fumbling his grip on the ax as his fingers twisted in what Aislyn imagined was a sign against the evil eye. The tallest, who wore a circlet of beaten bronze round his brow, bent to retrieve the fallen ax, lips curving in a sardonic smile as he handed it back to the lad.

If they'd come to kill her, they were going about it very oddly, she reflected, and straightened her back. "What do you want?" she demanded boldly.

The redheaded lad, his cheeks flushed with embarrassment, stepped forward. "We need a woman," he said.

Aislyn leaned against the doorway and grinned. "Bit early in the day for that sort of thing, isn't it?"

The boy's face reddened, and the tall man beside him—who seemed to be their leader—laughed. "I am Torquil. We are escorts for my lady Elga, bound for Winchester. The lady—" He frowned, then sketched an arc before his belly. "It is—before her time. Yet she is . . ."

He clutched his stomach and groaned in such a lifelike imitation of a woman in labor that Aislyn couldn't help but laugh. That he took it without insult impressed her. Any man prepared to set aside his dignity for the sake of accomplishing a mission so clearly foreign to his nature was a man to be reckoned with. For a moment she was reminded of Gawain and thought that the two of them could be friends.

If only they weren't enemies. He *was* a Saxon, after all.

"Where are her women?" Aislyn asked suspiciously.

"There is but one." Torquil sighed, clearly mastering his impatience with an effort. "The one knows nothing of . . . birthings. There is time, the lady said when we set out, much time. But now there is no time. We tried the vill, they slam the doors and send us here. You come."

It wasn't a question, but Aislyn pretended to consider it and Torquil did her the courtesy of pretending to allow her to do so. Another surprise, as the Saxons were said to be barbarous folk who knew naught of gentle manners.

"Aye," she said, "I'll come. Just let me fetch my bag."

• • •

THEY found the lady in a small clearing. Like most Saxons, she seemed uncouthly tall, though Aislyn noted her broad shoulders and wide hips with approval, for strength would be needed to survive such a rude birthing as this was like to be. Her hair, caught back in a single plait as thick as Aislyn's wrist, was not the butter-yellow of the men's, but a soft honey-brown. She paced slowly round the clearing's perimeter, pausing now and then to lean a hand against a tree, her expression one of deep concentration.

A serving girl sat on a fallen log, munching a hunk of bread and looking bored. A few men hovered about uncertainly, and greeted Aislyn with such relief that they scarcely seemed to take note of her appearance. Nor did it matter that she did not understand a word they said. When they bowed and touched their brows, their gratitude was plain enough.

The lady dismissed the men with a wave of her hand and a smile. The moment they had vanished, her smile did, as well, and the eyes she turned to Aislyn were wide and frightened.

"Good day, lady," Aislyn said. "I'm Dame Ragnelle. Now, if you don't mind . . ."

Aislyn had seen many births before, in her own home and at Morgause's castle, but there had always been a midwife in attendance to take charge of things. During the short ride to the clearing, she'd cast her mind back over everything the midwives had said and done. She felt the girl's swelling belly, and as far as she could tell, the baby seemed to be head down. "That's all in order. Why don't you take another turn about the clearing while I get things ready here?"

When the lady had gone out of earshot, Aislyn turned to the serving girl. "Get the fire going," she ordered sharply, "and heat some water. And have those men dig me a good deep hole by yonder oak." She pointed to a towering tree some distance from the clearing.

The maid looked up at her, uncomprehending, jaws working as she chewed her bread.

"Go on, get moving!"

"Bah, bah," the maid said, and giggling at her own wit, she made a flicking motion with one hand.

Her laughter turned to a shriek as Aislyn seized her by the ear and dragged her from the log. "Heat. Water." She twisted her fingers until the girl screamed. "You'll mind me now, I'll warrant! Hi, there!" she cried. "Who can understand what I say?"

"What is it?" The boy who had borne the battle-ax appeared between the trees, his gaze fixed on the lady, who had stopped on the other side of the clearing and was watching Aislyn with a small smile.

"I need hot water," Aislyn said. "This lazy slut doesn't seem to understand."

The lad barked a harsh order to the serving girl, who slipped from the clearing, her expression sullen.

"Have someone dig by that tree," Aislyn went on, pointing to the oak. "A good hole, mind you, not a scrape."

"A—a hole? For what?"

"That's my business," Aislyn retorted sharply. "Just do as I say."

She hobbled over to the lady and took her by the elbow. "Now, that's better. Why don't we keep walking and you can tell me when the babe was meant to come."

Elga looked at her blankly, and with a sigh, Aislyn held her outstretched arms before her belly. "The babe," she said slowly. "When did it—" She lowered her arms. "Drop?"

"Ah! Two—three days. My—my man's mother says—" Elga drew in a sharp breath. "She says there is time. She says, go and come back and still many days—" Another pain gripped her, and when it passed, she said fiercely, "She hopes I die. But I will *not*."

"That's the spirit. But I'm sure it was just an honest mistake," she added, though she could hardly keep the doubt from her voice. Anyone looking at this girl must have known that she was due in the straw at any moment.

"She lied. She hates me. I am peaceweaver, you see."

"Piece weaver?" Aislyn repeated. "You mean with a loom?"

The girl laughed, revealing strong white teeth, and Aislyn could see that she was really quite attractive in her own way. "No, no, I bring the peace. Between our people. I marry the thane's brother—he who was our enemy—and we have no more war between us."

"Ah, a *peace*weaver."

"We had much war," Elga said between clenched teeth. "Many men died. There is much . . . bad feeling. The women—they do not—do not—forgive—"

"Go with it," Aislyn said, "don't fight it, keep breathing."

"That was very bad," the girl said at last, wiping the sweat from her upper lip.

"Very *good,*" Aislyn corrected her. "Why, you'll be holding your babe before you know it. Let's see if we can get around the clearing once more."

"I wish my mother was here," she said, and her dark blue eyes filled with tears. "We go to meet her, she is promised to be with me for the birthing."

"She'll be here soon, and won't she be surprised to have it all over and done? Give her more time with her grandbaby, that will, and she'll likely spoil the two of you rotten."

Lady Elga looked puzzled, then laughed. "You know not my mother. She bears many babes and never does she complain. Two daughters, eight sons, and all of us still living."

"You come from good stock, then," Aislyn said, guiding her onward. "But I'll wager she never bore a one of you in the middle of a forest! Oh, she'll be rare pleased to hear how brave you've been."

"I—I hope so," was all Lady Elga had time for before another pain had her in its grip.

"Good! Aye, I know it hurts," Aislyn said as the girl stared at her in terrified disbelief, "but that just means you're nearly done. A few more like that and you'll be a mother. It isn't pleasant," she went on, leading the girl around the clearing once again, "but 'tis all exactly as it should be, just as it was for your mother and hers before her. There, now, that's enough walking. Lie you down here—they've made a good job of this bedding, haven't they? Just like in a palace, with a canopy and all. Off with your gown, now, and let's have a look here."

She reached into her bag for her ointment. "Just relax your legs. Good, that's the way. Do you have a name for the babe?" she asked.

"No," the girl replied, tight-lipped.

"You'd best start thinking of one. There, that will ease the passage nicely," Aislyn said, blinking hard as sweat dripped into her eyes. "Let's see how far this babe has come—good, lady, that's done, and oh, you're doing fine, this won't be a long job. Now, we'll just undo that braid, we don't want anything bound about you. My, what nice hair you have!" she gabbled on, hardly knowing what she said. "Like—like wheat before the threshing."

The lady gave a choked laugh. "Threshing. Aye."

"Here we go," Aislyn said as the huge mound of the girl's belly drew together into a tight knot. "Lean against me, that's the way, and when you feel the need, you give a good, hard push. That's it. Now. Go on, push! Don't hold back, yell if it helps—good! There, that's past and it was a good one. Lie back . . . that's right, hinny, that's the way. I know it's hard," she said, stroking the sweat-darkened hair back from her brow, "but you're a strong lass, a brave lass, and it will soon be done. All is well, you did just fine, you've earned a rest . . ."

A rest was what she needed, too, but that was impossible

with the girl's weight in her arms. She eased herself back until her spine was against a tree trunk and cradled the girl's head against her breast, while the birds chattered and scolded in the branches above. Seen thus closely, Aislyn could appreciate the beauty of the girl's pure, high brow and the bold planes of her face.

Before the afternoon was gone, she had come to have a deep appreciation for her courage, as well.

It wasn't a particularly hard birth, but it seemed terrible to Aislyn. The pains grew longer and harder, and when the girl began to shake as though in the grip of a high fever, Aislyn was sure something had gone terribly awry. But even if it had, there was naught that she could do save the small things women have always done for one another: wipe the girl's brow, hold her hands, assure her—with a creeping shame at her own duplicity—that all was well. From time to time, she would see one of the men—usually the youngest—peering through the trees, but they never stayed long. Aislyn wished that she could leave, as well.

*I could never do this,* she thought, as another piercing scream ripped through the clearing. Never. What could possibly be worth this agony? But then, as the sun was sinking over the topmost trees, the babe was born at last. Aislyn cradled the tiny scrap of flesh that had been the cause of all this pain and worry, too relieved that it was over to even check its limbs or ascertain its sex.

She glanced down into its face. Two eyes stared back at her, slate blue and very serious. This wasn't just a burden for its mother to be rid of. It was a living thing—or more, it was a person, utterly unique and completely individual. *We come into the world, we play our part, and then we leave. But where do we come from? Where do we go?*

Looking into those gravely knowing eyes, Aislyn had the feeling that this tiny being, so newly arrived from that other place, had the answer. "A pity you can't talk," she croaked, and the babe's almost invisible brows drew together in a tiny frown.

But of one thing Aislyn was certain: there *was* an answer. There was another place, a world beyond this world, one from which every living thing had come and to which they would one day return. A place as real as this one, though very different. And she herself had been there—not once, but many times, and had been born just as this child had been today, had lived and died and been born again . . .

A piercing memory came back to her: herself, a child of two or three, standing naked in a shaft of morning sunlight in her chamber. "Here I am again," she had thought, and laughed aloud. "Oh, I'm so glad that this time I am a girl!" She had *known*. How *could* she have forgotten?

"Is it sound?" Elga gasped. "Does it live?"

"Oh, aye," Aislyn said, smiling down at the baby in her arms. "You have a . . . a bonny daughter!"

"Let me have her!"

Aislyn laid the child in her mother's arms, and with eyes half blinded by tears witnessed a second miracle. Lady Elga's pallid face was suffused with color; the lines of suffering etched about her eyes and mouth melted into a soft smile that transformed her.

Aislyn's arms were strangely empty, almost as empty as her heart.

But there was still work to be done, and no one to do it but herself. First the afterbirth to be delivered, then mother and child washed and wrapped. Her legs were shaking with exhaustion by the time she'd buried the afterbirth in the hole she'd ordered dug, then washed her face and hands in the remainder of the warm water. When she returned to the clearing, both mother and child were sleeping, so she made her way to the group of men crouched around the fire.

"Well?" the leader demanded.

"It's done," Aislyn said. "They're resting."

"The babe—it is whole?"

"*She* is beautiful. And the mother came through it just fine," she added, seeing from the corner of her eye that the redheaded lad dropped his face into his hands with a shuddering breath of relief.

The leader, Torquil, smiled and poured mead into a wooden bowl. "To wet the baby's head," he said, handing it to Aislyn.

"Now, don't you even think to go a-pouring mead on—oh!" The man raised his own bowl, and all the others followed suit.

"To the babe," they said, and drank, looking as pleased with themselves as if they'd all delivered the child. Aislyn sat down among them and accepted bread and cheese, thinking that they weren't so different from any other men she'd known.

"To my lady Elga," the youngest cried, his eyes aglow. "She is well? You are sure of it?"

*You'd best learn to hide your feelings a bit better than that, my lad,* Aislyn thought. Apparently the leader thought so, too. He turned and snapped a few words that Aislyn didn't catch, and the young man set down his bowl and went off toward the horses.

Torquil caught her eye. "He is young."

*He is in love,* Aislyn thought, but she only said, "Where's her husband? He should be here."

"Soon. I sent to him. Swift horse, strong rider. Soon he comes."

"The lady told me she's a peaceweaver," Aislyn said, leaning her back against a tree trunk and holding out her empty bowl. The men exchanged looks.

"Aye," the leader said, refilling her bowl. "Peaceweaver. It is—not easy. Many battles have we fought. Much death have we seen. We men—" He shrugged. "We are—what is your word? We fight—"

"Warriors," Aislyn supplied.

"Warriors," he repeated, nodding. "Our enemies, too,

are warriors. They fight well, we fight—better," he said, which provoked a burst of laughter from the men. "Now it is done. We meet, we talk, we drink, we give honor to the fallen. Not so for the women. The peace—for them, it is not here." He touched his heart. "They are—unkind—to the lady."

Aislyn nodded her understanding. "That's a heavy burden for a lass to bear."

"She is strong. Now she is a mother, it will be better."

There was some muttering at that, but the leader cut it off with a glare. "You stay," he said to Aislyn, "until the women come." He turned his head, and a moment later, all the men followed suit. "They come now," he said, and only then did Aislyn heard the sound of hoofbeats in the forest. "Good. Soon we bring you home."

# Chapter 26

• • •

GAWAIN spotted the smoke first, a thin tendril threading through the branches of the trees. He dismounted some distance away and approached on foot, drawn sword in his hand.

The villagers had said a band of Saxons was on the loose, but this did not seem to be a warrior's encampment. He did not even meet a guard until he was almost upon them, and then it was hardly more than a boy who he took completely unaware.

Gawain sheathed his sword and raised a hand, palm up. "I seek an old woman," he said, "and I was told—" He broke off, turning toward a stand of trees, where a shrill voice was shouting.

"You thrice-cursed son of a goat, you—you craven bully!"

Gawain met the boy's eyes. "I think I've found her."

The lad nodded and gestured Gawain ahead, not even bothering to relieve him of his weapon. Shaking his head at this laxness, Gawain passed through a clearing where a fire still smoldered, a grin tugging at his mouth as Ragnelle's voice became clearer. If the Saxons had taken her prisoner, they must be regretting it by now.

"You oaf, you lout, you—you festering carbuncle! If you knew what she suffered bearing *your* babe, you'd be on your knees right now begging her pardon!"

"Be quiet, old woman!"

Gawain could see Ragnelle now, arms akimbo as she faced a Saxon twice her size. Half a dozen warriors stood about, faces so carefully expressionless that Gawain suspected they were struggling against laughter.

His own smile died when he recognized the man Aislyn faced. Gudrun. The Saxon thane's own brother and Aesc's envoy to King Arthur's court. He was scowling, rage twisting his features as Ragnelle went on. "But did she complain? She did *not*! She gave you a fine daughter, and what do you say but—"

"Hold your tongue!" Gudrun cried, and raised his hand as though to strike her.

"I wouldn't do that if I were you," Gawain said, stepping into the clearing.

"'Tis Sir Gawain," the men murmured, "the Hawk of May."

He walked past them without speaking, his eyes fixed on Gudrun's face.

"Ah, Sir Gawain," Gudrun said, struggling to compose himself. "Good."

Gawain kept walking until he and Gudrun were eye to eye. "If you have aught to say to my lady, 'tis better said to me."

"His lady?" he heard the men around him murmur. "Is she his mother? Granddame?"

"This old woman does not know when to shut her foul mouth," Gudrun spat. "She needs a beating."

"That," Gawain replied, "is not for you to say." He turned to Ragnelle. "Lady, have you been mishandled in any way?"

"Nay, but an apology is owing. Not to me," she added quickly. " 'Tis his own lady's pardon he should beg."

"That is between him and his lady," Gawain replied. "You are my concern. If you have no complaint, let us depart this place forthwith."

"I won't leave her," Ragnelle declared, her voice rising shrilly. "Not until I'm sure she will be cared for."

Gawain sighed. "Who must be cared for? And why is it your concern?"

"I delivered the baby, didn't I? And I won't go until I have his word"—she jerked her head toward Gudrun—"that she'll be looked after properly."

"Sir Gudrun," Gawain said, "if you would be so kind as to explain—"

"I owe you no explanations, Hawk of May. Take your bitch and begone."

Gawain eyed the Saxon narrowly. "I can only believe you spoke without thinking. Do you reflect and try again."

"I said what I meant," Gudrun spat.

"I beg you to reconsider."

Gudrun broke into a loud laugh. "Hark you all to that? Sir Gawain *begs* me!"

A hard-faced warrior stepped from the shadow of the tree against which he had been leaning. "Sir Gudrun," he said, low-voiced, "I believe you mistake him."

"I? Nay, 'tis *you* who mistake *me*—just as you have ever done—but I am in command here. Now stand back and hold your tongue."

The man met Gawain's eye and gave the slightest of shrugs before he resumed his place against the tree, arms folded across his chest and an ironic smile curling his lip.

"Sir Gawain, you were saying?" Gudrun went on. "Ah, no, you were *begging*! Pray do contin—"

He reeled back as Gawain's glove struck him smartly across the cheek.

"You shall meet me in the lists, Sir Gudrun."

"The lists! Oh, no, I'll meet you here and now, man to man—" Gudrun cried, reaching for his sword.

"With fists." The man who had spoken earlier once again detached himself from his tree and stepped forward. "*Fists.* No weapons. That is custom."

Gawain relaxed his grip on his own sword. "Very well."

"Don't do it," Ragnelle said in an undertone as he removed his cloak and unbuckled his scabbard. "This is all my fault—"

"Probably," Gawain agreed, handing her his sword. "What happened?"

"His wife was delivered of a babe this afternoon—the others brought me here to help her. She's a good lass—far too good for *him*—and bore a fine daughter. Well, he comes riding up and what does he say but that she's worthless for not giving him a son, shouting at the poor girl until she was in tears. So I lit into him. I was that angry that I didn't mind what I said."

He regarded her a moment, then nodded briefly. "I see."

"It had naught to do with you," she said. "I don't know why you had to go butting in."

"Would you rather I had let him go on abusing you?"

"Well, no, but this is my fight, not yours."

"Your fights *are* mine," he replied. "Now, if you will stand aside—"

"I shan't! The king won't like this," she said quickly, "you know he won't. I suppose it wouldn't kill me to beg Gudrun's pardon—"

"You shall do no such thing."

"But what if—"

Gawain took her by the elbows, lifted her, and set her down on the far side of the path. "Stand here. Keep silent."

She opened her mouth to argue, then seemed to reconsider. "Aye, Gawain. Just as you say."

"And no magic."

"Magic?" She widened her eyes. "Me?"

"Aye, you. Promise me you won't interfere."

"But—"

"Your word on it."

She scowled fiercely. "Oh, very well, you have my word."

• • •

GUDRUN was a big man. He was not quite so tall as Gawain, but far heavier, with the thickly muscled arms of a blacksmith. The Saxons ringed them round, shouting out encouragement as the two stepped into the clearing and circled each other warily.

Gudrun landed the first blow, and Aislyn winced as his fist connected to Gawain's jaw. Gawain rocked back, but did not fall, and he easily sidestepped Gudrun's second attempt, which sent the Saxon staggering off balance, though he recovered himself quickly and scrambled out of reach. Gawain nodded thoughtfully as they went back to circling, and Aislyn—to the great amusement of the warriors—began to dance with impatience.

"Hit him!" she cried, demonstrating. "Knock him down!"

At that moment, Gudrun rushed forward. Gawain took one step to the side, easily evading the Saxon's fist, and brought his own up. Gudrun rocked back with a grunt, tripped over his own feet and sprawled upon the forest floor.

Gawain glanced over to Aislyn with a grin. "Like that?" he called, and Aislyn's answer was lost amid a burst of laughter.

"Sir Gudrun, shall we call it—" Gawain began, but Gudrun was already on his feet again, charging forward with his fists up and his head lowered. Without seeming to make the slightest effort, Gawain knocked him down again.

And again.

And once more, until the Saxon Torquil stepped forward and held up his hands. "It is decided," he said. "Sir Gawain is the victor."

Gawain was not even breathing hard as he buckled the sword harness across his chest, giving his shoulders a shake to settle the hilt. Gudrun was sitting up, spitting out a mouthful of blood and angrily refusing all offers of assistance. As she and Gawain turned to leave, Torquil stepped before them.

"Thank you," he said to Aislyn and touched his brow. "*He* did not say it," he added, jerking his chin toward Gudrun, "so I do."

"You are quite welcome," Aislyn answered, and led Gawain into the clearing where Lady Elga still lay, her baby in her arms. Several of the Saxon women were there, as well, standing about uncertainly. One, Gudrun's mother, tried to stop them, but fell back at a sharp word from the girl, who gestured them closer. She looked up at Aislyn through reddened eyes and smiled wanly.

"Lady," Aislyn said. "This is Sir Gawain. My—my husband," she added. "He's come to fetch me home."

Elga's eyes widened, but she only nodded and shifting the babe, held out her free hand. "Sir Gawain," she said, "your name is known to me. Thank you for the—the gift of your lady's help. I know not how we would have lived without her."

She spoke with a simple dignity that touched Aislyn, and apparently Gawain, as well. He went down upon one knee and smiled. "May I see your daughter?"

Elga's face lightened as she lifted the babe.

Gawain peered into the tiny, wrinkled face and said with every appearance of sincerity, "She is lovely."

Tears shone in the girl's eyes. "Thank you."

"You rest now," Aislyn said. She turned to Gudrun's mother. "Rest," she repeated. "You ken the word? She's not to be moved, not for another day or two."

The woman made a harsh sound and flapped her hands. "Go."

"I'm going," Aislyn said, "but you mind what I say. No moving. Not today, not tomorrow. Stay here." She pointed to the earth.

"Go!" the woman repeated.

Aislyn hobbled off, but before they reached the horse, she saw the young redheaded Saxon hovering between the trees as though he could not quite make up his mind to approach them.

"Hi, there, you!" Aislyn called, gesturing him over. "Lady Elga mustn't be moved for another day—two would be better," she said, holding up two fingers. "She stays here and rests."

The young man nodded. "Two days. Yes."

"Gudrun might not want to wait," Aislyn began.

"Gudrun." The young man turned his head and spat.

"Right then, we understand each other well," Aislyn said.

The boy looked at Gawain. "Hawk of May," he said, "I thank you." He touched his chest with a clenched fist, then turned and ran into the forest.

"What—?" Gawain began.

"He's in love with her, poor wight," Aislyn said. "But mayhap he'll see she isn't moved. I wouldn't put it past that old bitch to have them rig a litter today—and drag it over every rut and hillock betwixt here and wherever it is they come from."

Gawain said nothing more as he helped her mount, then swung himself into the saddle. They rode on for a time, and then he said, "What does the old woman have against her?"

"She's Gudrun's mother," Aislyn explained, "and the girl is a peaceweaver. That means—"

"I know what a peaceweaver is," Gawain said. "It is a role the Saxons honor highly."

"The men do. The women see it a bit differently. Yon

Saxon laddie explained it—you know, the one that said it must be fists. He likes Lady Elga," Aislyn said drowsily. "All the men like her. So far as they're concerned, the fighting's over and that's the end of it. But it seems the women have a harder time accepting changed conditions. The peace is not in their hearts—that's how he put it. Bit of a poet, or so he seemed to me, for all he barely speaks our tongue."

"A poet?" Gawain snorted. "Those Saxons know naught of poetry. They are savages—"

"No, they're not. They're men like any others—fierce in battle but all knees and elbows when it comes to women's matters. Yet nice enough for all that," she added on a yawn. "When we were wetting the babe's head, they were all mannerly enough—more so than some other knights I've met."

"You drank with them?" he asked, surprised.

"Aye, and good mead they had, too. I'd like to know the trick of brewing it . . ." She leaned her cheek against his back, then drew away. "I wish you wouldn't wear your sword like that. Why don't you get a hip scabbard?"

"A *hip* scabbard?"

"Half the knights at court are wearing them, and they look right handsome, too."

"Oh, aye—right up until the moment they need to draw their sword and find it tangled in their cloaks! Then they just look dead."

"Well, it makes a cruel hard pillow," Aislyn grumbled, "and those Saxons had me up just after dawn. Can we not stop a bit?"

"We'll be late enough already—"

*Not late enough for me,* she thought, wondering how to best convince him to return her to her hut. " 'Tis a pretty wood," she said, "and the evening is fine. We can get an early start tomorrow. Oh, go on, you're not in all that much of a hurry to get back, are you?"

"No, I suppose not." He looked around the glade as though seeing it for the first time, and his eyes lit in the way they used to do so long ago as he took in the running brook, its surface glittering beneath the westering sun, and the deep violet shadows beneath the hanging branches. "Aye, you are right, this is a bonny spot . . . but unless yon Saxon laddie gave you provisions, we've naught to eat."

"A night's fast won't hurt us. Unless," she added, struck by a sudden inspiration, "d'you think there are any fish in that stream?"

That caught his interest as she had known it would. He dismounted and helped Aislyn down, then hung Gringolet's saddle on a branch and looped the reins over it. The stallion bent his head and began to pull at the thick grass as Gawain walked to the bank and crouched to peer into a pool. "Look at them all! If only I had a line . . ."

"We could use my shawl as a net," Aislyn suggested. She hiked up her skirts, tucking them into her girdle, and chose a spot upstream from the pool where the water ran shallow, enjoying the feeling of it on her feet, cool enough to soothe but not so cold as to make her bones ache. "I'll stand here and you can drive them toward me," she said, spreading her shawl before her.

Gawain regarded her for a moment, no doubt reflecting on the improbability of catching anything by that method, but then he shrugged and snapped two leafy branches from the tree above his head. "Move to your left a bit," he said, pulling off his boots.

Aislyn was pleased to see him grin as he waded barefoot into the brook. "Ready?"

She grasped the edges of her shawl. "Go on."

His face was intent as he peered into the water, and slowly he began to move in her direction, sweeping the branches to either side. "There!" he cried, surprising her, and she pulled the shawl tight, lifting it into the air. The unexpected weight of it sent her reeling, but he ran to her and caught her before she fell.

"Are you all right?"

"Aye, I'm fine—and look!" She held the wriggling shawl aloft. "I got one!"

"So you did! Two, in fact." He laughed as he took it from her. She laughed, as well, feeling a rush of pride when he said, "Well done!"

"Shall we try for another?"

"Are you up to it?"

"Oh, aye."

By the time dusk gathered beneath the tree trunks, the fish were cleaned and Aislyn was washing her hands in the water. Up on the bank, Gawain was adding dry grass to the tiny blaze he'd kindled. His cheek was a bit red and his lip had begun to swell, but for all that, he looked happier than she had seen him since she arrived at court. She stood a moment, watching him plant two forked branches beside the fire, which would hold another branch upon which their three trout were impaled.

By the time she made her way up the slope, Gawain was stretched full length beside the fire, his expression pensive. "What are you thinking?" she asked, sitting down upon a boulder.

"About the bairn," he said, surprising her. "Such a wee small thing . . ."

"Big enough," Aislyn said, shuddering as she remembered the hours it had taken to bring her forth. "And sturdy, too. I think she'll do well enough."

"Aye." Gawain smiled a little, but his gaze was wistful as he stared into the flames. "Gudrun is a fool."

"That he is, but he's a sorry fool tonight," Aislyn said, but Gawain's expression did not lighten.

"Do you have any faith, Ragnelle?" he asked after a moment, his eyes flicking up to her face.

"Yes," she said, the answer slipping out before she

stopped to think. "At least—well, for a long time I did not. I was brought up to believe one way, you see, and I kept all the rules as I was bidden. I felt I'd lived up to my side of the bargain, so when I needed help and it didn't come for the asking, I gave up the whole business as a bad job. But now . . . well, now I think I didn't quite understand. I still don't," she said honestly, "but I believe there is something . . . not a stern judge to fear, or a huckster who trades favors for obedience, but . . . something too beautiful to bear, just beyond our sight. I can feel it here," she added, gesturing around the dusky clearing toward the stream, where a pearly mist hung over the singing water.

"Aye." Gawain nodded. "Aye, I can, as well." He sighed deeply, then smiled and sat up to hang the trout over the fire.

The fish were excellent. Only when the last morsel had been finished did Aislyn notice that her skirts were still clinging damply to her legs. She lowered herself from the rock where she'd been sitting with a groan.

"Are you all right?" he asked, putting out a hand to help her down.

"Just a bit creaky in the joints." She leaned against a tree and rubbed her shoulder. "I hate being old," she burst out, surprising both of them.

"You did too much," he said. "I'm sorry—"

"No, no, it isn't that. A few more aches don't matter."

"Then what is it?" he asked, stretching out on his side and propping his head on his hand. "Go on, I want to know."

"You look at me and see a hideous old woman, but inside, in here—" She touched her heart. "—I'm still a lass."

Gawain stirred the fire with a twig. "What were you like . . ."

"When I was young?" She laughed without humor. "You won't believe it, but I was a beauty."

"Oh, I believe it," he said quietly. "I can see it in your eyes."

She looked away, blinking hard.

"And I don't think you're hideous." He touched her hand. "Truly."

She let out a sound, half a sob and half a snort of disbelief. "You're a good man, Gawain."

His lips twisted in a smile. "Is that why you left me?"

Hope flared in her, so bright and sharp that it was close to pain. It wasn't love he felt—not the sort that a man feels for a woman he desires—but it was something. Could it be enough to break Morgana's spell?

"I wasn't leaving you for good," she said gently. "Just for a bit. I did not want to meet your mother."

"Are you afraid of her?" he asked, surprised.

"I'd be a rare fool if I wasn't! I thought that if I could meet her at the Midsummer Feast, it would be easier. So why don't I go back to my little hut tomorrow, and—"

Gawain shook his head. "She'll mind her tongue, I've seen to that. And you needn't meet her if you'd rather not."

"That's kind of you to say, but I think it would be best if I just stayed away for a few days."

"No," he said decidedly, "I want you where I can keep an eye on you. And you must promise not to run off again without so much as a farewell."

"It was wrong of me to do that," she admitted. "But when I learned your mother had come to court I didn't stop to think."

"And that," he said, "is why *I* should do the thinking for us both. You are coming back with me tomorrow. Now, don't let's quarrel," he added, smiling and holding out his hand. "Come and see the nice bed I made for you."

Aislyn knew when she was being managed, but when she saw Gawain's cloak laid upon a thick mound of soft greenery, her resentment collapsed into a muddle of confusion.

"Where will you sleep?" she asked, lying down on the pallet, which smelled deliciously of fresh-cut grass.

"I'll be fine here," he said, sitting cross-legged by the fire and laying his sword within reach.

She wanted to protest, or at least offer to share the watch with him in turn, but she was asleep before she formed the words.

# Chapter 27

• • •

GAWAIN wasn't looking forward to telling Arthur what had happened with Sir Gudrun, but in the event, he never had the chance.

"What," Arthur said by way of greeting, "were you thinking?"

The king sat behind the long table in his presence chamber, doing what he hated most. Parchments were piled all around him, his hair was awry, and the finger he tapped impatiently upon the table was stained with ink.

"You are speaking of Sir Gudrun, I presume?"

"None other. This—" Arthur plucked a parchment from the pile and waved it in the air. "—is from King Aesc. He wonders why my nephew—my *heir*—seems determined to wreck an alliance we have worked so long and hard to build—one that is in danger, as well you know, of imminent collapse. An alliance," he went on, his voice rising to a shout, "purchased at the cost of many brave men whose lives I believed—perhaps mistakenly—you valued as much as did their widows and their orphans. For their sakes, perhaps you would be so kind as to give me an answer I might pass on to our ally, and that he, in turn, might relate to those of his council who are demanding your head. Because I tell you, Gawain, I tell you in all honesty, I have no idea what to say to him."

"Sir Gudrun was impertinent," Gawain began.

Arthur drew in a sharp breath. "*Impertinent?* He had better have been a good deal more than that."

"I didn't kill the man!"

"No, you did worse. You *shamed* him. You know how these Saxons think, you're not a fool. Gudrun is now your sworn enemy—you have all but driven him into the arms of his Wessex kin! He was one of the few voices on Aesc's council we could trust to speak for us, and now—"

"Is he really such a half man that he would bring all his people to war simply because he cannot endure a beating? One he all but begged for, I might add, and one I was right pleased to give him."

Arthur began to speak, checked himself, then bent his head, raking his ink-stained fingers through his hair. "Tell me what happened."

"Sir Gudrun's lady was on the way to meet her mother when her birth pangs overcame her. Her escort went in search of a woman to help her, and they came upon Dame Ragnelle. She delivered Sir Gudrun's daughter—single-handed, in the depths of the forest—and when Sir Gudrun arrived on the scene, he began to abuse his lady for not giving him the son he had hoped for."

Arthur nodded briefly. "Go on."

"Ragnelle took him to task for it. You can say that it was foolish and I will not disagree, but she felt herself bound to defend the lady. Gudrun, being what he is, decided to vent his spleen on Ragnelle, and so I came upon them. I tried to withdraw peacefully, sire. On my word, I did all I could to take Ragnelle and leave. But Gudrun spoke such insults as could not in honor be ignored."

"In short, Dame Ragnelle interfered in a private quarrel between a man and his wife, and you, for reasons known only to yourself, upheld her."

"Had she been at fault, I would have been the first to chide her. But the Saxon lady, Gudrun's bride—who is little more than a child, sire, and had just endured a terrible ordeal—did not merit such treatment at his hands."

"I find it passing strange, Gawain, that you would concern yourself with a lady hitherto unknown to you—a Saxon lady, at that!"

"What has that to do with it? Is not the protection of all women the duty of all knights?"

"Of course it is, but—damn it, the lady is Gudrun's wife! 'Tis only natural he would be disappointed, and at such a time any man might say things he would later regret."

"*Any* man? Would you, sire?"

Arthur frowned. "What I would say is not the issue."

"Gudrun drew back his hand to strike Ragnelle—he told me to take my bitch and begone. What would you have had me do?"

"I had not heard that," Arthur admitted, "but from all you've said, he was sorely tried. Gawain, Dame Ragnelle is simply unendurable, and she has brought you naught but misfortune and unhappiness."

"I thought you don't approve of interfering between a man and his wife," Gawain said evenly.

"I don't. But when she endangers Britain, it becomes my concern. I am sorry, Gawain, but Dame Ragnelle must go. Send her to Lothian or Orkney—or if you do not want her so far, find a convent where she can live. But she cannot remain at court."

"So all the blame is to fall on her?" Gawain demanded. "Is that what you mean to tell King Aesc? That Ragnelle is at fault, and has perforce been *banished*?"

"Yes," Arthur said. "That is precisely what I mean to tell him."

"But I—"

"You would oblige me very much, Gawain, if you would accept my decision without argument."

Outside the long window, the sun was setting behind a heavy bank of clouds. Only a few shafts of golden light pierced the mist-laden air, lending the garden an unearthly beauty. Gawain remembered the eve of his knighting, when he and Arthur sat together on the low stone wall planning the future. He had agreed with Arthur then that the Saxon settlers were here to stay; the only way to a united Britain was to ally with them. What battles must be fought should be swift and decisive; not an end in themselves but a preface to the real work that would begin once Britain was at peace. He had lost sight of that goal when he allowed his personal feelings to intrude, but to break his word to Ragnelle and allow her to be punished for his fault would only compound his failure.

"Very well, sire," he said. "Dame Ragnelle shall leave court for a time, while I go to King Aesc and apologize. And to Sir Gudrun, as well," he added with an effort he hoped did not show, "formally, before all his kin."

Arthur shook his head. "I have given this a good deal of thought, and I believe any apologies would only worsen matters."

"But I must say something to King Aesc," Gawain protested. "We are meant to meet in ten day's time and discuss—"

"You will not be meeting with him. In fact," Arthur said, rearranging the parchments before him, "I think it would be best if you stayed clear of the Saxon matter for a time."

"I do not understand—"

"You've been under a good deal of strain of late, Gawain, even if you will not admit it. I don't want you to concern yourself with anything; just leave it all to me."

Not *concern* himself? This was Gawain's work—more, it was his life. Did they count for nothing, then, all the nights lying on cold earth, the battles he had fought, the weeks—sometimes months—he had spent sweating over each clause of the treaties he negotiated once the battles had been won? He had ridden from one end of Britain to the other a dozen times at least, either in warfare or as the king's emissary, and now, after one misstep, he was to be dismissed like an erring squire? And someone else was to—

*Oh, no,* he thought, *I am wrong. Arthur would not—*

"Who is to carry your message, then?" His voice seemed to come from very far away. "Who is to treat with them in your name?"

"Sir Lancelot."

Gawain felt as though he had been dealt a solid blow between the eyes; numb, but with the certainty of pain to follow.

"He and Sir Gudrun have always been on good terms," Arthur went on, "and I believe, given his reputation and his—well, his standing at court, that King Aesc will accept him."

Gawain was on his feet with no memory of having risen from his seat, and once standing, he had no idea of where he meant to go. He had just reached the door when Arthur spoke again. "About Dame Ragnelle—"

"I shall see to it."

"I only wanted to say that I am sorry."

"Yes, sire. So am I," Gawain said politely, and stepping into the corridor, he shut the door silently behind him.

# Chapter 28

• • •

GAWAIN walked through the courtyard to the practice yard below. Not bothering to go round to the gate, he vaulted the fence around the enclosure where he had spent so many hours, first in learning and then in teaching the lads who flocked to court.

The yard was empty now. The boys Gawain had taught were long gone—some dead in battle, others to their own lands, a few up in the hall, which spilled light and laughter into the dusk. All that was left was the quintain, standing to attention like a forgotten soldier on a deserted battlefield.

A few wooden swords lay in the dusty patch of earth. Gawain picked them up and set them neatly in the rack before passing on, giving the quintain an absent push as he walked by, instinctively leaning to one side as the arm with its dented shield swung round with a squeak. *I'll have to see to that.* He cut the thought off before he could pursue it.

He reached the back of the yard and climbed the fence again, grasped the bough of an overhanging chestnut tree and pulled himself aloft, until he was sitting with his back against the trunk and his legs drawn up before him.

A warm breeze ruffled the leaves around him; the quintain squeaked in the practice yard below. The sound was comforting, as familiar as the scents of horses and honeysuckle and new-turned earth drifting on the evening air. He inhaled deeply, his eyes stinging. He could travel the whole world and never find a place he loved as he loved Camelot. It was his home.

The sun was gone now, the battlements a shadow against a star-strewn sky, the Pendragon pennant invisible in the darkness. But he could see it in his mind's eye—splendid, invincible, the proud banner of a new Britain. Arthur's Britain.

But no longer his.

• • •

AISLYN jumped up from her seat when the door opened.

"Well?" she said. "How was it with the king? Was he sore angry?"

"Yes." Gawain removed his cloak and hung it on its hook, then unbuckled his sword harness and hung that, as well.

"Did you tell him—"

"There was no need," Gawain answered, smoothing the folds of his cloak. "Sir Gudrun apparently ran off to his brother, and King Aesc lost no time in complaining to the king of me."

"And of me, I'll be bound," Aislyn said. "I am sorry, I know how important this alliance is, and now I've gone and put my foot in it. Will you have to beg Sir Gudrun's pardon?"

"No. I am relieved of my duties as envoy to the Saxons."

Gawain turned to her at last, but there was something

off about his smile. Even in the reddish glow of the candles burning on the table, his face looked pale and drawn as he sat down on the edge of the bed. "I have been thinking . . . what say you we go to Orkney for a time?"

"Orkney?"

"It has been long years since I visited my demesne. That was wrong of me," he added in a lower voice, passing the tip of his finger through the candle's flame. "I have neglected my obligations."

"Orkney?" she said again.

"It is very beautiful," Gawain said, watching the candle flicker. "The sound of the waves against the shore . . . the terns swooping from the cliffs . . . I spent a year there as a boy—just before I was sent here—and have often longed to see it again."

*"Orkney?"* Aislyn gave herself a shake. "But you have duties here—"

Gawain smiled, his eyes still fixed on the flame. "Sir Lancelot can take my place."

"He could never take your place! He isn't fit to wipe your boots!"

Gawain stood abruptly. "We shall travel slowly—you can have a litter if you like—"

"A journey like that could take months," she protested. "It would hardly be worth it if you were to . . . just how long were you thinking to stay?"

"Some time. A long time."

"Forever?"

He looked away without answering.

"Leave Camelot?" she demanded shrilly. "*You?* Does the king know of this?"

"Not yet."

"He won't just let you go off to Orkney!"

"He cannot stop me. I am his liege man, not his prisoner." He turned to gaze out the window, adding in a lower voice. "Not anymore."

"I reckon the king's not the only one in a temper, but it's not like you to run away. You *are* his liege man, you've given him your oath, and what you've sworn to do, you *do*. What are you not telling me?"

"Nothing—it does not matter—"

"If the king isn't going to make you beg Gudrun's pardon, then . . ." She sat down hard. "It's me, isn't it? What did he say to you?"

"You are banished from court," Gawain said.

"And you?"

He shook his head.

Aislyn's throat tightened. "You'd do that? Leave court for me?"

"I would indeed, for so I promised. But as it happens, I would like to go anyway."

"Why?" Aislyn said. "Because the king was angry?"

"Because he does not need me now. As I said, I am relieved of my duties, so there is no need for me to stay."

Aislyn stood before him. The crone was so short that with Gawain seated, they were almost eye to eye.

"There is a need, and what's more you know it," she said. "You cannot just ride off and let that Sir Lancelot step into your shoes. What would become of Camelot then? Why, look at how he treated Dinadan, a brother knight! He doesn't understand, not as you do! You have to stay."

"I cannot," Gawain said. "I promised—"

"You don't have to tell me what you promised. I'm the one you promised it to. And I'm the one who's saying you mustn't keep that promise." He wavered before her eyes, but she went on fiercely, "I won't have it. It isn't right. I'll go back to where I came from—"

*What then?* A small voice asked in her mind. *How will you ever find Morgana? And if you do, why should she care what happens to you now that you've been banished?*

She pushed those thoughts aside. "I managed well enough before you came along—"

*But you were young then, not an old woman with an ailing heart.*

"—And I can go on managing just fine. You have work to do here, and I've been keeping you from it, but once I'm gone, things will go back to the way they were before."

"No." Gawain shook his head, a faint smile touching his lips. "They won't. Having known you, I doubt I will ever be the same."

"I'll take that as a compliment." Aislyn sniffed. "And you'll know where I am. You can come visit me from time to time, if—if you've a mind to."

Oh, this was hard, the hardest thing she'd ever done, but she refused to spoil it by weeping. But when he laid his hands upon her shoulders, the tenderness of the gesture nearly undid her. "I cannot ask it of you."

She had never loved him as she did now, and though she could not speak of it, it was in her eyes and in her voice when she declared, "You don't have to ask."

His expression altered to one of understanding and pity. "Oh, Ragnelle," he said helplessly. "I—"

And leaning forward, his hands still resting lightly on her shoulders, he kissed her.

Pain speared through her, driving her to her knees. Gawain was beside her in a moment.

"What is it? Are you—"

She dropped onto her side and drew her knees to her chest. Oh, it had never been this bad before, she must be . . . must be . . .

• • •

"RAGNELLE!" Gawain reached for her, but drew his hand back with a disgusted cry when her flesh moved sickeningly beneath his palm. She—it—dear God, what *was* the thing beside him? He scrambled awkwardly across the floor until his back was to the wall and drew his dagger.

Ragnelle—but no, it was not Ragnelle, it was—it seemed to be—a maiden, sat up, her features obscured by a wealth of tangled copper hair. Half laughing, half weeping, she shook her hair back to reveal—no, he was mad or dreaming, it was impossible that she could be— His dagger clattered to the floor.

"Aislyn?" he whispered hoarsely, then signed himself with the cross. "St. Michael and all his angels protect me—"

"I'm not a ghost!" she cried. "I'm not dead, I never was! That was a lie! I've been under a spell—I could not tell you, but it is me, Gawain, really—"

His head struck the wall when she flung herself into his arms, pressing kisses on his jaw.

"Aislyn?" He touched her cheeks, her hair, hardly daring to believe that she was real. "But—but where is Dame Ragnelle?"

"I *am* Dame Ragnelle! At least, I was, but you've broken the enchantment—well, half of it—"

*"What?"* She felt real enough, warm and soft and trembling beneath his hands. "You are—but you—I do not understand—"

"I know and I am sorry." She took his hand, holding it between both of hers. "Oh, my love, I wanted to tell you—I tried—but it was part of the enchantment—"

He held her at arm's length, his eyes searching her face. "You are Aislyn," he said, the words not quite a question.

"Yes. Yes, I swear I am. Dame Ragnelle was a seeming, but she was always me—and I was her, only . . . only . . ."

"Don't weep," he said, though his own eyes were far from dry. "Don't weep, Aislyn, all will be well."

"Will it?" she said, her sea-green eyes shining between tear-spiked lashes. She had been a lovely lass five years ago, but now—oh, now she was infinitely more beautiful, almost unreal—

"And—are you are certain I am not dreaming?"

She wound her arms around his neck and drew him down to her. "Quite, quite certain," she whispered against his lips. "Oh, Gawain, I love you—I always have, but now—now I love you so much more—"

His mouth closed over hers. At last he pulled away to gaze down into her eyes. "Aislyn," he said, drawing a fingertip across her lips. "Aislyn—it *is* you. You've come back to me."

And those were the last words spoken between them for many hours.

• • •

GAWAIN shifted Aislyn's head from his chest to the hollow of his shoulder and stroked the hair back from her brow.

"You were Dame Ragnelle," he said, as though he could not quite believe it, and traced her cheeks and nose and brow as though to assure himself of her reality. "You said I broke the enchantment. How?"

She turned her head and lightly kissed his mouth. "Like that."

"That was all? Why did you not ask—? Oh, you did, that day in the garden. Then why—"

"Not just any kiss. One given with love," she said, "like this." After a very pleasant interval, she settled back into the crook of his arm, lazily trailing her hand over his chest.

"But you said it was only half broken."

Aislyn sighed. "Yes. For half each day I shall be as you see me now. For the rest . . ." She turned her face into his shoulder. "I don't know how I can bear it."

"But there must be some way to free you. I will go to the king, have him—"

"No!" She pulled away. "No one can know."

"Not *know*? But—"

"If your mother learns that I am here—oh, Gawain, she mustn't. We must keep quiet until the duchess of Cornwall returns. She can break the spell."

Gawain nodded thoughtfully. "But we can trust the king."

"He cannot help me, and if he were to say the wrong thing—even without meaning to— Please, promise me you won't say anything. Please."

He wrapped his arms around her. "I mislike deceiving the king, but Morgana should be back in a day or two. I suppose it cannot do too much harm to wait for her."

"And in the meanwhile, I can go back to my cottage as we planned."

"No," he said decidedly.

"Have you forgotten I am banished?"

He shrugged. "The king will grant me a few day's grace, I'm sure."

"But I would feel safer away from here. If I were to—"

"No," he said again. "I want you with me. You are far too apt to get into trouble on your own."

Stung, she drew back to look into his face. "I have been getting myself into—and out of—trouble for some time."

"I daresay you have," he answered, "but things are different now. You wanted to marry me—or was that part of the enchantment, too?"

"No," she admitted, "it was not."

"Well, then," he said, seeking to draw her down again as though the matter had been settled.

"Then what? I don't see what you being my husband has to do with me going back to my cottage."

He sighed. "I don't want to quarrel with you, Aislyn. Just do as I say."

"But why should it be as *you* say?"

"Because I am your husband. Look you, sweeting, you cannot have two leaders of a battalion, no more than you can have two kings. I have sworn to obey my liege lord, just as you have promised to obey me. And that is as it should be. Men are fitted by nature to command. We are trained to weigh the risks of any course of action, and not be influenced by . . ." He waved a hand. "By whims and fancies."

"You think me *fanciful*?" she demanded, remembering some of the decisions she had been forced to make. What about the day, soon after she'd left Lothian, when she woke to find a ruffian bending over her, his stinking breath in her face and his hand halfway up her skirt? Or the time she had been snowed into her hut for a solid fortnight, with the ice so thick she could not force the door to open? She'd gotten through those times, and she hadn't done it by wringing her hands and waiting for Gawain—or any man—to tell her what to do!

"I have never met a woman so prone to mad fancies," Gawain said, and laughed. "Do you forget that I have lived with you these past weeks? There is no knowing what you might do next, or what trouble it will lead to." He kissed her shoulder, then the place where it joined her neck, his teeth moving lightly over her skin.

"But—"

"Let me be a husband to you," he said, his breath soft and warm in her ear. "Is that not what you wanted?"

"Yes, but—"

He moved to lie atop her, his weight supported on his elbows, his eyes inches from hers. "Is it what you want now?"

"Yes." She wound her arms around his neck. "But—"

He mouth covered hers, cutting off her words. She began to protest, but his knee glided between hers and she arched to meet him. By the time she could speak again, she had forgotten what she meant to say.

# Chapter 29

• • •

"GOOD morning, sire," Gaheris said, walking into Arthur's presence chamber. "How was it with Gawain yesterday? Did he agree to send the witch away?"

"Yes," Arthur said, frowning. "Yes, he did."

"God be thanked." Gaheris took a seat. "And to a rest, as well?"

"Yes. But . . ."

"But what?"

"I think perhaps I should have waited."

"She has to go," Gaheris said decidedly. "And you will never have a better chance. Come, sire, he must have understood the damage she has done. You did put the case strongly to him, did you not?"

"As strongly as I could." Arthur rubbed absently at his jaw. "But he pled his—or should I say her—case with equal strength. What Dame Ragnelle did was unwise, and certainly inopportune, but worth banishment? I think not."

"What she has done to my brother merits that," Gaheris argued. "She has obviously enspelled him."

"We have no proof of that. Even his defense of her to Sir Gudrun was understandable."

"In any other man, perhaps, but in Gawain? After the effort he put into this treaty, would he really toss it all aside so lightly? And you know as well as I how he feels about sorcery, yet he admitted she is a witch as though 'twere naught."

"True, but . . . the more I reflect on it, the more I doubt my judgment. It is only that I am so very fond of Gawain—" He sighed. "But I fear I mishandled this badly."

"No, sire!" Gaheris protested. "You *could* not!"

Arthur laughed shortly. "Of course I could! And it would not be the first time, either. I should have been honest with him, Gaheris. Even if he has been enspelled, it was wrong to deceive him."

"You meant it for his good. Once she is gone, he will understand that. When is she leaving?"

"I saw him this morning," Arthur said, "and he asked for a day or two to make a suitable arrangement for her."

Gaheris frowned. "I do not like this."

"Nor do I. But I can hardly deny him such a reasonable request. I have given him two days, and I shall take care to keep him from her. Today, he will attend me and tonight, I have bidden all my companions to keep watch with me in the chapel in honor of St. John's feast."

"And tomorrow?" Gaheris asked.

Arthur sighed. "The guests will be arriving; it should be no trouble to keep him busy until nightfall and then there is the feast. God send that Morgana will be here by that time, but whether or no, Dame Ragnelle will be gone the next morning."

# Chapter 30

• • •

LAUNFAL stopped dead in the road when he saw the spires of Camelot rising above the treetops, scarcely aware of the people jostling him as they pushed by on their way to market. There was the Pendragon banner, gold and crimson against the blazingly blue sky. It was real, all real, and he was nearly there. He laughed aloud, drawing a few suspicious glances from the crowd, but the tradesmen streaming down the road were far too intent upon their own concerns to pay such a ragged stranger any mind.

And he was far too happy to care what they made of him. Nearly there, he thought, unconsciously flexing the fingers of his left hand. The skin across his palm was still very tender, but the pain which had been nearly unendurable for the first few days had subsided to a dull ache, easily ignored as he strode quickly toward the distant castle. The road grew more crowded as he climbed the hill, and when he reached the crest, he saw the market spread below. The scent of roasting meat hit him like a blow; his empty belly collapsed in upon itself and his mouth filled with water, but his gaze was riveted to the road beyond, rising on a gentle slope to the open gates of Camelot.

A laden donkey nudged him in the back, sending him staggering into a woman with a basket balanced on one brawny shoulder. "Geroff!" she shouted, fetching him a clout, and he barely stopped himself from measuring his length upon the dusty path.

Impatient with the crowd, he turned off the road and into the wood, enjoying the cool shadows cast by slender birches. The way was easy here, the ground carpeted in springing moss and starred with bluebells. He began to whistle as he leapt lightly over a merry little brook, matching his steps to the rhythm of the tune, keeping an eye out for roots and rocks that might trip him up.

He did not notice he was not alone until he nearly collided with the warhorse in his path.

"Good day, sir!" he cried, springing back and touching his brow in an instinctive gesture of respect.

"Good day," the knight replied. He wore no mail, but a hauberk of leather, and a round cap studded with iron sat upon his graying hair. "Where are you bound in such a hurry?"

"To Camelot."

Launfal grinned, relishing the musical sound of the word upon his lips.

"What is your business there?"

"To see the king."

"The king?" The knight laughed. "And do you think the king receives every chance-come beggar to his door?"

Launfal's smile was not so easy now, but he held on to it with all his might. "Indeed I do not," he said with such courtesy as he could muster. "But I dare to hope he will see me."

"Why should he? What is your name?"

"My name is my own, good sir," he answered, lifting his

chin and shaking his tangled hair back from his face. "Though I will render it gladly to any man who gives me his."

"What's this?" The knight nudged his steed closer, leaning down from his saddle to peer closely into Launfal's face. "You are insolent, boy."

Launfal held his ground. "I am no boy, sir, but a man, and what I ask of you is no more than my right."

"Your *what*?" The knight laid a mailed fist upon the hilt of his sword.

"My right," Launfal answered stoutly. "Courtesy demands that—"

"Who are you?" the knight cut in. "From whence do you come? Speak out, boy, and smartly."

"I have told you once I am no boy," Launfal replied evenly. "My father was a noble knight, and I his only son. For that, if nothing else, I will thank you to address me as befits—"

"Let me see your hand."

"My—?"

"Your *hand*. No, not that one, the left. Hold it up—palm toward me, if you please."

Caught between bewilderment and affront, Launfal obeyed. The knight drew his sword.

"What—?" Launfal began, but before he could say more, he was flat on his belly with the knight's blade whistling over his head. "Stop! Sir, what are you doing? You have no cause—"

But apparently the knight did not need a cause. *He must be mad,* Launfal thought, rolling as a spear buried itself in the moss beside him.

"Wait!" he cried, leaping to his feet. He glanced wildly about the wood, hoping against hope that someone—anyone—would appear and call a halt to this insanity. But the wood stretched empty to either side, and a moment later, he was diving behind a boulder as the knight's sword sparked against the stone.

"Sir, wait!" he cried again. "We have no quarrel, there is no reason—"

The knight halted, notched blade lifted. "Your name," he cried. "What is it?"

Dear God, is that all the man wanted? He must be mad in truth. "Launfal!" he cried. "I am Launfal, son of Rogier of Penhelm, lately of—"

"I know where you come from," the knight snarled, and Launfal sprang back as the blade swept by, bare inches from his belly. "Just as I know where you are bound—and why, you scurrilous dog!"

"You—you mistake—" Launfal gasped, but the knight was done with conversation. Launfal was twisting, stumbling, dodging behind trees, and though half of him was tempted to burst out laughing at the ridiculous sight they must make, a mounted knight chasing an unarmed man through the wood, the other half was grimly intent upon survival.

Had they been in the open, Launfal would have had no chance at all. It was the trees that saved him, the thin silver trunks and whipping branches that he kept between him and the warhorse, his desperation driving him to unimagined feats of agility. At first he continued to cry out, but soon he had no breath to spare for questions and no desire left to ask them. When he fell, his cheek against a jagged stone, he blinked the tears of pain from his eyes and, looking up, saw the knight towering above him, one arm drawn back to throw the dagger glinting in his fist. Launfal seized the stone, wrested it from the earth, and flung it with all his strength.

It struck the knight on the brow, and though the blow was glancing, the surprise of it sent him reeling back so sharply that his mount, startled by the sudden shift of weight, reared, iron-shod hoofs beating the air. The knight went over backward and landed with a thud upon the moss. His mount pranced nervously, then halted, trembling, beside the prone form of his master.

Launfal scrambled to his feet, breathing hard, a second stone ready in his hand, but the knight lay unmoving. After an age had passed, Launfal forced himself to approach the fallen man.

"Sir?"

The sound of his own voice startled him so much that he jumped, and something between a sob and a laugh burst from his lips. "Sir?" he said again, not knowing why he bothered. The man obviously could not hear him. *If you had any sense, you would take to your heels,* Launfal told himself . . . and yet he could not leave this poor madman lying unconscious in the forest, prey to any sort of beast.

*I'll get him on his horse,* he thought and went down on his knees, slipping his hands beneath the man's arms and lifting—and it was then he saw the dagger's hilt protruding from the knight's back. With a low cry, Launfal laid him carefully on his side and drew the dagger forth, staring in dismay at the blood seeping from the wound.

And it was thus that the knight's companions found him.

# Chapter 31

• • •

GAHERIS arrived rather breathless in the hall, where Arthur and his queen were breaking their fast.

"Sire, have you seen Gawain?" Gaheris asked.

"He left me a quarter of an hour since," Arthur replied. "To meet you in the practice yard."

"He did not come," Gaheris said.

The two exchanged a glance, and Arthur half rose from his seat. Guinevere looked at him questioningly. "Sir Gawain must have been delayed," she said. "My lord, do sit down, you have not finished, and I did want to talk to you—"

"No, I—I have no appetite," Arthur said and when Guinevere's puzzled frown deepened, he remembered that he had only just declared himself half famished after his vigil in the chapel. "That is, I—I will eat this as I walk," he said, seizing a slice of bread. "I shall attend you and the queen of Orkney later this morning," he promised, noticing her hurt expression with only a small part of his mind as he hurried from the hall.

• • •

"COME out," Gawain said.

"No, I don't think so. Why don't you go off and do whatever it is you do," Aislyn said from behind the screen. "Come back at sunset."

"Don't be ridiculous," Gawain said, smothering a laugh. "It's not as though I've never seen Dame Ragnelle before!"

"But it's different now."

"No, it's not. I want to talk to you."

"Talk then," she retorted. "I can hear you fine from here."

• • •

ARTHUR and Gaheris hesitated outside the door to Gawain's chamber. "Perhaps it would have been better to send a page to him," Arthur said. "I do not want to alarm the witch."

Gaheris gnawed his lower lip. "Aye, you are right. Let us—"

The sound of Gawain's laughter came from within. "Sire," Gaheris said, "it is not my habit to listen at doors . . ."

"Nor mine," Arthur said.

Their eyes met briefly, then broke away to peruse the hallway.

"But this once . . ." Gaheris began.

"Do it," Arthur ordered tersely, and Gaheris put his ear to the door.

"Well?" Arthur said after a moment, alarmed at the expression on Gaheris's face. "What do you hear?"

"Oh, sire—"

Arthur leaned forward and laid his head against the wood, where a voice that sounded like Gawain's was clearly audible.

"Now, stop being foolish and come sit on my knee.

That's better. It seems an age since I have seen you. I thought about you all last night."

"Did you?"

That was Dame Ragnelle; her harsh croak was unmistakable, even when lowered to a sickening coo.

"I could scarce keep my mind on anything I did." It was definitely Gawain, much as Arthur longed to deny it. "Come, love, don't turn away—"

Gaheris and Arthur exchanged looks of horror.

"Oh, God," Gawain groaned, half laughing, "I don't know how I can wait until tonight."

Arthur leapt back, his stomach heaving. Gaheris followed suit, his face a shade of delicate green as he pressed the back of one hand against his mouth. But when Arthur raised a fist to pound upon the door, Gaheris caught him by the wrist.

"No," he mouthed, jerking his head down the passageway. "Wait."

Arthur followed him some distance down the corridor.

"This is far worse than I suspected," Gaheris whispered. "I fear for Gawain if we confront her in his presence."

"You are right." Arthur looked toward the door. "Oh, Gaheris, don't think badly of your brother. The fault is mine. I should never have allowed—"

"You did not know what she was, no more than Gawain did. But all will be well once he is free of her. You must send again to the duchess of Cornwall—"

"I have already done so."

"Then we *must* keep them apart until she arrives. Sire, do you keep Gawain by you, and we shall post a guard outside the door."

---

# Chapter 32

• • •

LAUNFAL half fell into the windowless chamber, propelled by a hard shove at the small of his back.

"But I told you—it was an accident."

"You can tell the king himself—when he has time for you," one of the knights replied.

"At least unbind me. For pity's sake—"

"Pity? You dare—" Mailed hands pushed him against the wall. He hit it awkwardly with his shoulder and went down hard upon his knees. "I'll give you pity—the same pity you showed Marrek!" the knight shouted, drawing back his foot.

"Peace, Kay," a cool voice cut in. "He's just a lad, and he hasn't even been tried yet, let alone condemned."

Launfal knew that voice—it was the one that had stopped the others from slaying him out of hand back in the forest. Now its owner drew off his helm and went down upon one knee, taking the dagger from his belt. "Relax, lad, I'm not going to slit your weasand. Just turn so I can get to these—"

"Dinadan, don't!" the other—Sir Kay, Launfal thought—protested.

"Why not?" Sir Dinadan stood and sheathed his dagger. "He's no danger here to anyone save himself."

"At least put him in the cell," Sir Kay said, gesturing toward an iron cage, barely visible among the shadows.

"Oh, for God's sake, Kay, what do you think he'll do, dig through solid rock with his bare hands? We'll bolt the door and post a guard."

Launfal stood, rubbing his wrists where the ropes had cut into them. "Thank you, sir," he said with a bow. "I shall never forget your courtesy."

Sir Dinadan nodded, his eyes cool and watchful. "Let us hope you have a long life in which to remember it. But if you are guilty, I'll be the first in line to watch you die."

Die? Was he to die? No, it was impossible—and yet Launfal knew that it was not. He had as little control over his life as a piece upon a game board, moved hither and yon by some unseen hand. He had known that since he was a child, when his life was a frail thread like to snap at any moment, and as a child, he had accepted it. Later, he had pushed the knowledge aside, but now he knew how foolish he had been.

But to die like this—for nothing! It was unendurable . . . and yet, was it not somehow fitting that his death would be as futile as his entire life had been?

"Don't look like that," Sir Dinadan said. "The king is a fair man, he will hear you out."

Launfal nodded, but he did not allow himself to hope. He had hoped too often in the past. Better not to think at all, to simply accept whatever happened next without complaint.

He slid down the wall, wrapped his arms around his

shins and laid his brow on his bent knees. He heard the knights departing and thought himself alone until a voice broke the heavy silence.

"Lad." Launfal lifted his head to see Sir Dinadan leaning against the doorpost, arms folded across his chest. "Do you have a name?"

"It is Launfal."

"Launfal, then. Why did you do it? Really? Were you hungry?"

"I told you," Launfal said wearily. "He attacked me; I attempted to defend myself. His horse threw him and he fell on his dagger."

Sir Dinadan made a low sound of disbelief. "Marrek? He hasn't attacked anyone since Uther Pendragon's day. You'd do better to leave that part out when you tell your tale to the king."

"I cannot say other than the truth."

Dinadan raised one brow. "Why did you stay, then? Why did you not run once he was down?"

"Leave him insensible in the forest with the wolves and vermin? Would *you* have done that?"

"No. I would not leave any knight—even an enemy—in such a case."

"Well, then—"

"But I am a knight of Camelot."

Launfal's face flamed. "While I am nobody, and perforce a stranger to all honor?"

"I meant," Dinadan said coolly, "that I would have no need to run from the outcome of any challenge. Were I in your situation—" He shrugged. "I daresay I would have taken to my heels."

Launfal shook his head. "You wouldn't have."

"Lad, any boyish dreams of chivalry I might have cherished were beaten out of me long before they could do me any harm. If you want to survive, you'll have to learn to—" He broke off with a curt laugh. "I'll save the lecture; you have enough to bear. Is there anyone who should know where you are? Family? Friends?"

Launfal shook his head. "No. There is no one. Only—is Sir Gawain at court?"

"You know Gawain? Why did you not say so at once?"

"I don't. Not really. But we did meet, long ago—not that I expect him to remember, but . . ."

"A slim chance is better than none. I'll see if I can find him. Good fortune to you."

"And to you," Launfal answered, but Sir Dinadan was already gone.

# Chapter 33

• • •

GAWAIN mastered his instinctive shudder as the crone sat down upon his knee. This was Aislyn. His Aislyn, who had lain in his arms just two nights past, trapped in a form that seemed far more revolting now that he knew it was a magical creation. It was that, more than her wrinkled skin or misshapen body that disgusted him.

*Poor lass,* he thought, his stomach twisting as he forced himself to stroke her lank hair and speak cheerfully until at last she smiled. *My poor little love. This must be infinitely worse for her than it is for me.*

"Sweeting, this is folly," he said gently. "Hiding like this, keeping all a secret. I know you fear my mother, but we cannot wait for Morgana to return. I will go to the king—no, hear me out—and explain all. Even my mother daren't disobey a direct order from him; she will be forced to lift this vile enchantment."

"She cannot," Ragnelle—Aislyn—said.

"Isn't there always a counterspell—or whatever it is called?"

"It was not your mother who put the enchantment on me."

"Not my—? Then who?"

"Your aunt," she said, not looking at him. "The duchess of Cornwall."

"Morgana?" Gawain laughed aloud from pure relief. "But why? What did you do to get in her bad graces?"

Aislyn slid from his knee. "It makes no matter now. But if you were to ask her to lift it, then she might."

"You can be sure I shall. I'll send her a message at once, explaining . . ." But there was no need to explain. Morgana had been here, she had seen how matters stood with him. And she had done nothing.

"I cannot believe it was her," he said, his amusement dying. "Oh, we have sometimes been at odds of late, but still—" He stared unseeing out the window. "She knew we were wed, and yet she told me nothing. Why? Why would she do such a thing to me?"

"It was me she did it to," Aislyn pointed out.

"Aye, it was. And I never would have thought her capable of such cruelty. What *did* you do?"

"Naught so bad as to deserve this," she replied, her back to him as she smoothed the coverlet over the bed.

"But what was it?" he insisted. "Aislyn, you must tell me."

"Yes, I suppose I must." She turned to face him. "Now, Gawain, I don't want you to get angry. You see, that day when you and the king came riding into the forest to meet Somer Gromer Jour, I always meant to give the king the answer."

"And you did," he said.

"Yes, but—well, when I saw it was you with him, I decided to—You have to remember that I didn't know you'd gone back for me that night in Lothian. I thought you just rode off and forgot all about me, never caring if I'd lived or died. I was wrong, I know that now, but when I saw you riding down that path with the king, I was still a bit—well, more than a bit angry. So I changed myself into this form—"

"*You* changed?" he repeated, bewildered. "But you said Morgana—"

"Yes, but that was after, when she came to court that time. She knew what I'd done, you see, and she didn't like it—you being her favorite nephew and all—so she put a spell on me so I couldn't turn myself back, not until you'd kissed me. A kiss given with love and received in kind, that's what she said, and she made it so I wasn't able to tell you anything. But it all worked out, you've broken the enchantment—well, half of it, anyway, and I think if you were to ask her, she might lift it altogether."

Aislyn had been speaking more rapidly as she went along, and it took him a moment to sort out all she'd told him. "After?" he repeated slowly. "You mean to say that when we first met—and when we married—you did that yourself?"

"Well, yes, I did," she said, "it was—well, a joke."

"A *joke*? You—the wedding, and—and—when you—for a *jest*?"

"Not only for that," she said quickly. "I had to get away from your mother—she's the one who was behind that whole Somer Gromer Jour business—"

*"What?"* He took a step away from her. "You and my mother are still—"

"No! I haven't seen her since that night you left Lothian! I've been hiding from her ever since, but when I heard about Somer Gromer Jour, I knew it was her plan. And I knew she'd guess 'twas I who gave the king the answer. So I thought I'd be safer here than anywhere, and—I never meant for you to be wed to Dame Ragnelle forever! I just meant to hide here for a time, and to teach you a bit of a . . . I'm sorry for it now," she added quickly. "I know it was . . ."

Gawain stopped listening. He stared at the bent old

woman before him, remembering the first moment he had laid eyes upon her in the forest and all that happened after. Morgana had not arrived on the scene until two—or was it three?—days after they were wed. She'd come early, and he was still abed, reluctant to wake because . . .

"Wait," he said, cutting off Aislyn's voice. "Wait. That night. Not our wedding night, the one after, I dreamed . . . or did I? Aislyn, was that—was it a dream?"

The crone seemed to contract upon herself, but her eyes did not waver from his face. "No," she whispered. "It was not a dream."

"It was *you*?"

"I thought you didn't love me," she cried. "I thought there was another, and—and—"

"You touched me here"—He put a hand to his brow—"and said it was a dream. You *enspelled* me, didn't you? And then you—we—"

He sat down hard upon the trunk, feeling as though he might be sick. She had lied to him. Again. And this had been no lie borne of desperation, but one chosen of her own free will.

Aislyn was not the victim of enchantment, but its mistress.

She had tricked him, humiliated him, played him for a fool.

She had robbed him of his reason and stolen his will.

She was a *witch*.

Oh, she might say she loved him—she might even believe it—but she did not know the meaning of the word. Witches loved nothing but themselves and their own power. They asked no man's leave to work their will, and no man could stop them from doing it.

"Gawain, don't look at me like that!" Aislyn cried, laying her clawlike hands on his shoulders. "I was wrong, I'm sorry—but you were not the only one to suffer. Please, you must believe me—say you do, say that you forgive me—"

Her eyes were brilliant with tears—Aislyn's eyes, the very eyes he had gazed into the night that vile spell was broken—and five years ago, in Lothian. She had not changed—and, God help him, nor had he. Even knowing what she was, he could not give her up.

"If you love me—" he began.

"I do!" she said, her voice breaking.

"Then renounce magic forever."

She drew away, looking so stricken that he wanted to call back his words. The only thing that stopped him was the knowledge that she could never be a wife to him. Not as she was now. He could love her with all his heart until it ceased to beat, but that would not prevent her from using her arts upon him whenever she desired.

"Renounce—" She faltered.

"—Magic," he said implacably. "Forever."

"But—but that is impossible," she cried. "You might as well ask me to tear off my arm."

He forced himself to speak calmly, hoping against hope she could be reached by reason. "It is not the same at all. Your arm is a part of you—"

"*Magic* is a part of me."

"Perhaps, but it is a part you need not use. Don't you see, this is what destroyed our love before! Please, I beg you, give it up. For my sake."

"No! I cannot!"

"You mean you *will* not," he said bitterly. "But that is no more than I expected."

"Expected?" she shot back. "Or *wanted*? Why else would you set impossible barriers around your heart, knowing full well that I must fail to breach them? I am as I am—either you love me for myself or you do not love me at all!"

"You speak to me of love?" he demanded, leaping to his feet. "You know *nothing* of how I love you—how I have always loved you, even when I believed you to be dead—"

"*Especially* then! It is easy to love a dead girl, isn't it? A memory never argues, she never speaks her mind—"

"Have I *ever* stopped you from speaking, even when it was to insult me before the entire court? Have I treated you unkindly?"

"No, but—"

"I have risked my life and reputation to protect you—all I have is yours—and the one thing I ask in return is that you give up these unnatural powers that have brought us naught but misery!"

"No, don't you see?" she said, holding out her hands imploringly. "You are asking me to give up a part of myself, a gift I have been given for a purpose and one I have worked hard to master. Oh, I don't deny I've misused it in the past, but that doesn't mean I won't do better in the future. I've learned from my mistakes—"

"So have I. I've learned that for all your years, you are still a thoughtless, selfish child. I am the laughingstock of the court because *you* wanted vengeance for an imagined slight. You ran off without a fare-thee-well—and now the Saxon treaty is in shambles and the king holds me to blame."

"But I never asked you to fight Gudrun. I told you it was none of your concern! I said—"

"You are my wife!" he shouted over her. "*Everything* you do is my concern. How can you possibly expect me to trust you with any sort of power, let alone something as dangerous as magic?"

"I know I have not always acted wisely, but I would never use any sort of enchantment on you again. Gawain, I love you—"

"Then do as I ask," he snapped. "A wife owes—"

"You don't want a wife," she cried, "you want a mindless servant—"

"I want a woman who can share all my life, not just a part of it! A wife who will be always at my side—not a whore by night and a crone who makes me sick to look upon by day."

They faced each other across the room, Gawain's breath rasping in his throat as the red mist of rage faded from his sight.

"Then go to the king and ask him to have our marriage annulled," she said. "You know he will do it."

"Aislyn—" he began, then broke off with a curse as a knock sounded on the door.

"What?" he demanded, wrenching it open.

"Sir Gawain," a page said, gulping as he stepped back. "The king sent me to say you are needed at once."

"Thank you, I shall come anon." He shut the door and leaned his brow against it, then turned back to Aislyn. "I spoke in anger and I am sorry for it."

"I was angry, too," she said.

"I do not want to have our marriage annulled. I love you."

"Oh, Gawain—"

He held up his hand. "But I cannot be married to a—witch, enchantress, use whatever word you like. Anything else I could bear—even this—" he said, gesturing toward her crone's form. "But not magic."

"But—"

"I don't want to quarrel any more. That is my decision, and it is final."

Without waiting for her answer, he walked out.

# Chapter 34

• • •

AISLYN sank down on the bed and put her face in her hands. She wished she could weep, but only a few slow tears wound down her cheeks, the best the crone could manage. Well, she could cry all she wanted to tonight, and for every night after. What else would she have to do?

Unless . . . unless she stayed. Then she could lie in Gawain's arms and know the same joy she had experienced the other night. All she would have to do was renounce her powers forever.

No! She could not—*would* not do it. No matter what Gawain might think, this decision wasn't selfishness on her part, or even the desire for control. How much easier life would be if Gawain made all the decisions, and she had naught to do but enjoy his love and bask in his approval! But it would be a betrayal of the gift she had been given—by whom, she hadn't yet decided, though she was sure it was Someone, just as she was certain she had been given it for a purpose. To deny it was to deny not only herself, but that greater power she had glimpsed after the Saxon baby's birth. She had known then that she was but a tiny part of something greater than she could ever comprehend, and yet even a speck like her had a part to play, and the duty to play it to the best of her ability, using every talent she had been given to the utmost.

If only Gawain wasn't so stubborn about magic! But perhaps there was a way. If she could prove to him that it could do as much good as ill . . .

She took Morgause's grimoire from her bag and set it on the table, where it fell open to a spell to wither a man's potency. Well, yes, that was bad, but here was another that would restore the luster to a woman's skin and the brightness to her hair. Not terribly useful, she thought, turning the page, but still, not harmful, not like . . . ugh. That would have to hurt. Flipping quickly past, she paused briefly at a page, grimacing as she wondered what it would be like to lose all one's teeth in a single night.

Now, here was something . . . or no, it was a spell to cause cramping of the legs, not to ease it—but this next one would turn the speaker invisible, and that could come in very handy for the king. She scanned the ingredients and cast a guilty glance at Sooty, deciding it would be better not to mention this one to Gawain. Turning each page, she found spells she had learned and used to good advantage, though for every one that brought ease and healing there were five to cause harm or even death.

She slammed the grimoire shut.

Perhaps Gawain did have some reason for his prejudice. This was his mother's book of spells after all, and what else did he know of magic but what he'd learned from her?

*Well,* she thought, resting her chin in her palm, *and what he learned from me. What I showed him was no better than any of this.*

But still, there was far more to magic than this book of spells, or the terrible mistakes Aislyn had made. In itself, magic wasn't good or evil, no more than a sword was good or evil. Both could kill or maim, but wielded wisely, both could save lives, too.

And neither should be given to a person who was not in complete control of their emotions.

*Her* emotions.

Shame flooded her at the memory of Gawain's face when he realized his erotic dream had been no dream at all. It had been unforgivable of her to make him think he was still sleeping . . . though he hadn't seemed to mind it at the time. In fact, as she remembered, he had enjoyed himself right well, and it wasn't as if she had forced him or taken him unwilling. She'd merely convinced him he was dreaming, and everything after that had been entirely up to him.

But that, she told herself sternly, was not the point.

He should have known it was really her, and what was happening was actually happening. It had been wrong of her to deny him that knowledge. And yet, when he *had* known, he had done just the same and enjoyed it just as much.

But that wasn't the point, either.

Was it?

Come to think of it, she wasn't quite sure what the point was, or what she'd done that was so terrible, which either proved Gawain was right and she was lost to common decency or that he was making a great deal of pother over nothing. At least in that one instance. His other grievances could not be so easily dismissed.

She had lied to him. She had humiliated him before his friends—and more importantly, his enemies. Through her own spite, she had forced him into a marriage he would never have chosen for himself. Those were genuine complaints, and against them she had no defense.

Sighing, she went to the window and gazed out upon the courtyard. Ambrose leapt up upon the window frame and she stroked him absently as he turned and twisted beneath her hand, purring loudly.

She summoned her memories of their night together, the joy of being one with Gawain, the utter certainty that all was completely as it should be. In that moment, her entire life had made perfect sense, for every step had led her to the one place she belonged.

If only it could always be like that. If only Gawain wasn't so damned dictatorial, with his "I should do the thinking for us both," and his "you cannot have two leaders of a battalion" speeches, as though she were some witless squire who could not be trusted to pull up her own hose. *Oh, he is insufferable,* she thought, anger rising in her again. *He is an arrogant bully, and I hate him.*

*But what if he is right?*

She had always taken pride in her own cleverness, but what if that pride had been entirely misplaced? Looking back, what did she have to show for her life but a series of failures? Was there one single person in all the world who was the better for having known her? She had no friends, no family—and whose fault was that but hers? And then look at Gawain, so strong and honorable and—yes, she must admit it—kind. The wonder wasn't that he wanted to bring order to her life—it was that he cared enough to try. And when he did try, what did he get from her but arguments and complaints?

"He *is* right," she whispered, horrified. "I *can't* be trusted."

Slowly she walked back to the table. One by one, she tore the pages from the grimoire and held them to the candle's flame. It took a long time, and the chamber was thick with smoke by the time the last page had crumbled into ash.

She walked to the window and breathed in the fresh air. Now she did not only want to weep, she needed to. But even at that she failed. She could only stare dry-eyed into the courtyard, her throat aching with the tears she could not shed.

# Chapter 35

• • •

GAWAIN told himself he had every right to be angry. And he *was* angry. Surely it was rage that made his heart pound jerkily, fury that stopped the breath in his throat.

*If Aislyn truly loved me, she would do as I ask.*

He did not expect her always to obey him without question, at least not all at once. But in time she would understand that he was a rational man, a fair man, one who was prepared to indulge her in most things.

But not this one.

Why could she not see that? Why must she insist on doing what she knew would bring him pain? She did not love him. Not as he loved her. He leaned against the wall of Arthur's antechamber, trying to convince himself that he was wrong and she would renounce her powers altogether. Because he did not know how he could bear it if she did not.

"Sir Gawain?"

A page touched his arm, looking up at him with worried eyes. "Shall I announce you?"

"Yes. Thank you." Gawain straightened and passed a hand quickly across his face, composing his features with an effort as the boy threw open the door to the king's presence chamber.

Arthur was seated behind the long table. Dinadan leaned against its edge, arms folded across his chest. Sir Kay sat rigidly in one seat; Sir Sagramore slouched in the other. A young man stood just before the window, sunlight catching the edges of his reddish hair and leaving his face in shadow. "Ah, at last," Arthur said.

"I am sorry to have kept you waiting, sire."

"No matter, you are here now. Do you know this lad?"

The lad in question came forward and went down upon one knee, looking up at Gawain with desperate hope in his eyes. Very green eyes, they were, an unusual shade, rather like Aislyn's—and why must he think of her now?—but darker, even as his hair was more chestnut than Aislyn's ruddy gold. God help him, could he think of nothing but—? And suddenly he realized why this lad brought Aislyn so sharply to his mind.

*"Launfal?"*

"Sir Gawain," the lad said, releasing a long breath that was half a sob.

"You remember him, then?" Arthur said. "He seemed to think you might not."

"Of course I remember him. How came you here, Launfal?"

"I—oh, Sir Gawain, I—"

"He came here in chains," Kay said. "And he'll be going to the gallows in the same fashion."

*"What?"*

"He murdered poor old Marrek," Sagramore said. "We were there, all of us—me and Kay and Dinadan, that is."

"Launfal," Gawain said, "is this true?"

"No!"

"We caught him in the act," Kay said.

"But why?" Gawain demanded, looking from Launfal to Arthur, who had resumed his seat and assumed his most noncommittal expression, the one that usually meant he was about to do something he disliked intensely, but deemed unavoidable.

"Sire, I don't see what purpose is served by dragging Gawain into this," Kay said, annoyed. "What difference does it make if they have met before? The lad will hang whatever," he declared with perfect confidence and Sagramore nodded his vigorous agreement. Arthur sighed but spoke no word, and Gawain, though his heart was wrung with pity for the boy, could think of nothing pertinent to add.

"Oh, must it be a hanging?" Dinadan drawled into the silence. "Beheading is so much more amusing for the common folk, and I cannot remember the last one we had. What say you I arrange an entertainment—nothing too elaborate, of course, just a few jugglers, mayhap a tumbler or two . . . ?"

The king rounded on him. "By the Rood, Dinadan, you go too fast! The lad hasn't been convicted yet!"

"Oh? I rather thought—my mistake, sire," Dinadan replied with a courteous bow. "Do carry on."

As he straightened, he caught Gawain's eye. It was only a fleeting glance, but enough to convince Gawain that Dinadan, at least, did not consider the matter to be cut-and-dried.

"Now that I *have* been dragged into it," Gawain said. "I would like to hear Launfal's side of the story."

Launfal drew a deep breath. "It happened like this . . ."

• • •

WHEN Launfal had finished and been led from the chamber, those remaining sat in silence for a moment.

"He seems an honest lad," Arthur began.

Kay sat up. "Honest? Sire, we came upon him kneeling

over Sir Marrek's corpse with the dripping dagger in his hand! The lad's story is utterly fantastical from start to end. Anyone who knew Marrek would agree."

"It *is* fantastical," Dinadan said. "So very fantastical that I, for one, am inclined to believe it is the truth."

"You have no proof!" Sagramore said. "I saw with my own eyes—"

"I have eyes, too," Dinadan snapped, "and I saw just what you did. And I still say—"

"Thank you," Arthur said, holding up a hand to still them. "I believe I understand the situation. I shall think on this carefully, and—"

The door burst open. When Gawain saw his mother stride into the room, he stepped back into a shadowed corner. "Sire, I must—oh! Forgive me, I did not realize you were not alone."

Guinevere came in after Morgause, her expression half guilty and half defiant. "My lord," she said, "you promised to attend us this morning."

"I know," Arthur said, looking harassed. "But this matter could not wait, and—"

"There is always some matter that cannot wait," Morgause retorted. "But you *promised*."

"Yes, you are right, I did. And I shall, as soon as I am finished here. If you would excuse me—"

Guinevere began to make him a courtesy, but Morgause put out a hand to stop her. "Arthur," she said severely, "you are being deplorably rude."

"Kay, Sagramore, Dinadan," Arthur said, "I thank you for your assistance. Should I think of any further questions, I shall call upon you."

The three knights bowed and retreated.

"Yes, my lady?" Arthur smiled at his queen, though Gawain could tell he was annoyed. "What is it you wanted of me?"

"Well, it was Mor—the queen of Orkney, really,"

Guinevere said. "She—that is, we—wanted to speak to you about Sir Gawain."

"Then let me make haste to depart," Gawain said, stepping forward. "So you can speak more freely."

Guinevere reddened. "Sir Gawain," she said. "Forgive me. I did not see you—"

"Don't apologize to him," Morgause said. "He's only trying to put you in the wrong when you are nothing of the sort. See here, Gawain, I've had more than enough of your impudence. I demand to meet this woman you married, and—"

"Sire?" A guard stood at the door, holding Launfal by the arm. "Will you be wanting the prisoner again?"

"No," Arthur said. "Not just now. Return him to the dungeon."

Gawain nodded encouragingly at Launfal, but the young man did not seem to notice. His face was blanched of all color as he stared past Gawain before the guard pulled the door shut.

"The dungeon!" Guinevere exclaimed, her voice warm with pity. "Oh, but he's so *young*! What did he do?"

"He is accused of murdering Sir Marrek." Arthur raked a hand through his hair. "His only excuse is that Marrek attacked him first, which seems unlikely, to say the least."

"What—what is his name?"

"Launfal. Now, lady, you can see that I have pressing business to attend to."

*"Laurfal?"* Guinevere turned to Morgause. "Oh! Is that—"

"Arthur, forgive me," Morgause declared, taking Guinevere by the arm. "We shall wait until you are at leisure to attend us. I had not realized you were so occupied."

"But, Morgause—" Guinevere began.

"Come, my dear, let your lord be about his work.

These matters," she added deliberately, "are no concern of ours."

"No *concern*—? But—"

"Good day, Arthur," Morgause said, drawing Guinevere from the chamber. "Gawain, I shall speak to *you* anon."

# Chapter 36

• • •

"MORGAUSE!" Guinevere exclaimed once they had reached the privacy of the deserted corridor. "Why did you not tell the king—?"

"Tell him what?"

"That this Launfal is known to you!" Guinevere said, astonished.

"I fail to see how that information would shed any light upon the business. If Launfal has committed murder, 'tis naught to do with me—or you. I suggest you put it from your mind."

"But—no, wait—" Guinevere cried, hurrying after her. "You said the lad was a danger—a madman—"

"I believe Arthur has already deduced that for himself."

"But my lord must know the truth!"

"The truth?" Morgause halted. "What truth is that?"

"You—you told me—" Guinevere stammered. "You said Launfal was coming here to murder my lord—"

*"I?"* Morgause raised her brows.

" 'Twas the night you first arrived. You said he blamed my lord for his misfortunes. You had him confined, but he escaped, and you feared . . ." What *had* Morgause feared? Thinking back, Guinevere could not remember Morgause ever saying, but the implication had been clear. "You said my lord's knights should be warned," she went on a little desperately.

"Yes," Morgause said, frowning. "I *did* advise you to have the knights look out for Launfal, lest he accost poor Arthur and make some sort of unpleasant scene."

Guinevere blanched. "A *scene*?"

"Alas," Morgause said, "apparently the poor lad's wits were more disordered than I knew. To have attacked one of your lord's knights without provocation . . ." She shook her head, sighing. "But there is naught to be done about it now."

"But it was not without provocation!" Guinevere cried, seizing Morgause by the arm. She had never realized how imposing Morgause could be, but now, as the older woman drew herself up, Guinevere felt almost frightened.

"You are distraught," Morgause said coldly.

"But 'twas I who told Sir Marrek to detain him—to stop him at all costs—that he was coming hither to assassinate my lord—"

Morgause gazed at her in astonishment, then her expression changed to one of deepest pity and concern. "My dear, is *that* what you thought? Oh, no, you completely misunderstood me! And now—what a terrible tragedy! But still, had Launfal gone peacefully, all would have worked out well. He did very wrong to resist a knight."

"Yes," Guinevere said doubtfully. "That is true."

"Of course, Arthur might not see it quite that way. In fact, I am certain he would not. I daresay he would be very angry if he learned that you had gone behind his back, and now that the poor knight is dead, I hardly like to think *what* he would say!" She patted Guinevere's shoulder, her eyes gleaming like a cat's in the dim light of the passageway. "But do not worry, dearest Guinevere. You can trust me to keep your secret."

Smiling, she turned and walked away.

# Chapter 37

• • •

AISLYN rested her elbows on the windowsill, watching dully as grooms and servants hurried through the courtyard. Sir Kay strode by, red-faced and shouting. A poor little kitchen wench went before him, a basket of onions perched upon one bony shoulder, while a varlet followed, his hands full of chickens for the plucking.

*That's right,* she thought, *tonight is the feast. I wonder if Morgana is here yet?* But even this thought could not rouse her from her lethargy.

Sir Kay vanished through the doorway leading to the kitchens and silence descended on the courtyard. Aislyn leaned her chin on her palm and reminded herself of all the reasons she had to be happy. Gawain loved her. That was the first and best of them. He did not respect her—indeed, she wondered if he even liked her—but he said he loved her and Gawain was incapable of lying. In time, he would learn to think better of her judgment, she told herself. So long as she did all he asked and never questioned his decisions, no doubt he would come to think her very wise indeed.

Two men walked by; one, a guard by his attire, and the second with his hands bound behind his back. He looked full young to be guilty of any serious crime, she thought, and then straightened, her gaze sharpening as he turned to look over his shoulder and she saw his face.

Standing on tiptoe, she leaned far out the window to get a better look, but she knew already who he was.

"Launfal!"

It was not Aislyn who cried his name, but Sir Dinadan, who hurried across the courtyard and stood talking to him a moment. *Launfal,* she thought, raising a shaking hand to her lips. She would have known him anywhere, though he looked nothing like the stripling lad she had last seen in Lothian. He was the image of their father. Their hair was the same shade of chestnut, their features very like, and what Launfal lacked in breadth of chest and shoulder would come to him in time.

As he stood listening to Dinadan, Aislyn could see that he was terrified, yet he nodded from time to time, and when they parted, even managed a smile.

Then, he was again her little brother. His smile hadn't changed at all; it was as sweetly melancholy as it had ever been, and as he turned away, straightening his shoulders, he wore an expression she had hoped to never see in him again—that of suffering patiently endured. But then, she thought, her eyes filling, Launfal had never been one to complain.

In that moment she knew him to be innocent. Whatever they said he had done, they were wrong.

She went briskly to the door, but it did not open to her touch. She pulled and pushed, and finally beat upon it with her fists. "Help!" she cried. "Let me out! The door is stuck!"

"Quiet, there," a deep voice said, startling her with its nearness. "You are to bide where you are."

"And who says so?" she returned.

" 'Tis by the king's order."

The *king*? She stared nonplussed at the door, then turned and went back to the window. She set her palms on the sill and attempted to lift herself, but fell back with a curse.

By the time she'd dragged the stool over to the window and clambered up on it, Launfal and the guard were gone. She carefully eased her legs over the windowsill, looking doubtfully at the earth five feet below.

The drop would have been as nothing to a woman of twenty-one. To the crone, it was enough to shatter bones.

"Oh, damn you, Morgana!" she muttered, carefully twisting herself so she could grasp the windowsill and lower herself. "Damn you, why don't you—"

She broke off with a choked gasp, her heart giving such a tremendous thud that it seemed like to break through her rib cage. Half in, half out of the window, she watched in terror as Morgause glided into the courtyard. After a terrible moment during which she was sure she was about to tumble headfirst into Morgause's path, she scrambled back the way she'd come, falling through the window to land hard upon her hands and knees. She crouched beneath the sill, fighting to draw breath, one fist pressed to her breastbone as she strained to listen for Morgause's voice above the thundering of her own heartbeat.

At last she dared to peer over the windowsill to find the courtyard once again deserted.

Relief flooded her, weakening her knees. She tottered to the chair and sat down, her head falling back limply as she waited for her heartbeat to subside.

"Coward," she muttered as soon as she had breath. "Look at you, halfway to a faint just from a little glimpse of her! And here you were always *so* proud of your spirit. Well, you showed precious little of that just now, cowering on the floor! What's happened to you?"

*I am old,* she thought. *I don't have the strength to fight her.*

"Well, you'd better find it," she said aloud. "Because that's your *brother* she's after. Whatever she's done to him, she's not going to go on doing it. Not while I'm here to stop her."

She stood, staggering a little, and clutched the back of the chair. *I can't,* a small voice wailed, but she cut it off.

"Bugger that," she muttered, going to the window and climbing up on the stool. Even that small effort exhausted her and she sat a moment, legs dangling over the sill. The drop looked even farther now, and she was just steeling herself when she caught sight of a man on the edge of the courtyard.

"Hi, there!" she called. "Sir Dinadan!"

He came over to the window. "Dame Ragnelle," he said, glancing up at her quizzically. "How do you today?"

"Not well," she answered bluntly. "The king has gone and set a guard at my door."

Dinadan's brows rose. "Why did he do that?"

"I don't know and I don't care. I need to get out of here."

"Dame Ragnelle, if the king himself has ordered—"

"That lad you were talking to," she interrupted. "Launfal, isn't that his name?"

Dinadan frowned. "And how do you know that?"

"Never you mind. What's he a prisoner for?"

"He killed a knight—"

"Nonsense," she said sharply. "He *wouldn't*—well, not unless he had good cause."

"You know him, then?"

"I've known him since he was breeched. He's in trouble—worse trouble than you know—and I need to talk with him *now*. Will you help me or not?"

Dinadan tipped back his head and considered her. "I cannot find a single reason why I should," he said. "And a dozen why I should not. But do you let yourself down and I will catch you."

Once safely on the ground, she took his arm. "You are not looking very well," he said, gazing at her with concern. "Are you sure you should be—"

"Oh, aye, very sure. Just get me to the place where Launfal is held, and then you go on your way. Now, don't argue with me, I won't have you dragged any further into trouble than you've already been."

"As you wish," Dinadan said doubtfully, and led her toward the dungeon gate.

# Chapter 38

• • •

"GAWAIN," King Arthur said, "please sit down. When we spoke yesterday—"

"I understand why you were angry," Gawain interrupted. "But there is something I must tell you. About Ragnelle—"

Arthur held up a hand. "I know about Dame Ragnelle."

"You do? But—how could you?"

"Never mind that," Arthur said, flushing slightly. "The point is that I know, and I have taken steps to remedy the situation. I am expecting Morgana shortly—indeed, I had hoped she would be here before today. In the meantime, I have placed Dame Ragnelle under guard."

"Thank you," Gawain said, his voice warm with relief.

Arthur slumped in his seat. "I was afraid you would be—well, never mind. Now, about this young man, Launfal. I could see that you were surprised to find him in such trouble. You knew him well?"

"No, not well. But—"

He started as the door flew open and banged against the

wall. The queen stood upon the threshold, and after one look at her face, Arthur was on his feet.

"Guinevere! My lady, what is it?"

"Arthur—oh, Arthur, I must speak to you at once."

"Gawain," Arthur said, "wait for me, would you?"

Gawain paced the antechamber, wondering what could have upset the queen so deeply. She had gone out in the company of his mother, and when she returned she looked entirely overset.

*"What?"* Even through the thick door, the king's voice was audible. "But *why*?"

Gawain's jaw tightened. *What now, Mother?* he thought. *What did you say to the queen?*

The door opened and Arthur beckoned him inside. The queen stood by the window, her back to him.

"Take this to the dungeon," Arthur ordered, holding out a square of parchment with a few lines penned upon it and the royal seal at the bottom, impressed in wax that was still warm. Gawain glanced down at it, then to the king.

"He is pardoned? But—"

"The lad was attacked," Arthur said curtly. "As for what happened next, we have only his word—but I must give him the benefit of any small doubt that remains."

"Sire," Gawain said carefully, "may I know why Sir Marrek set upon the young man?"

"No," Arthur replied. "I have pardoned him. That is all anyone need know."

"But I would like to know—I *must* know— My lady," he said to Guinevere, "if my mother's hand was in this—"

"The fault was mine," Guinevere said thickly. "Please, Sir Gawain, let us not speak of it again."

"As you will, lady," he said, bowing. At the door, he hesitated, then turned back. "Sire, whatever has befallen, I cannot believe the queen is to blame."

Guinevere did not turn. "That is very kind," she said, her voice choked, "but—"

"It's all right, Gawain," Arthur said with a strained smile, "there is no need for you to defend the queen to me. You may trust me to sort it out."

Gawain bowed without speaking and set out for the dungeon.

# Chapter 39

• • •

LAUNFAL paced his tiny cell, his mind whirling. He had known Morgause would be here before him, but he had not counted upon meeting her before he had the chance to tell his own tale to the king. Of course, he had not counted on arriving at Camelot bound hand and foot, or that he would be lodged in the dungeon. Indeed, now that he came to think on it, there were many things he had failed to anticipate about this journey.

But he was in no doubt of what would happen next.

Morgause would be here soon. He knew too much for her to let him live. *Fool,* he thought, striking his fist against the wall. *I should have told the king straight-out about Somer Gromer Jour. I could hardly be in worse trouble than I am right now, and at least he would know about—*

He stiffened as the door creaked open behind him. Turning, he saw Morgause walk into the chamber.

"Madam." He bowed and, leaning casually against the wall, remarked, "You cannot keep away from me, I see."

She laughed. "What a pity I never really got to know you, Launfal. You would have amused me."

"I thought I did."

"Yes, well, you did have your charms . . ." All the amusement vanished from her face as she dropped her gaze to the flower she held between her long white fingers. "We parted badly, and I am sorry for it. My temper . . ." She looked at him from beneath her lashes. "I am glad I did not mar you," she said softly.

He shrugged, watching her warily.

"We were happy once, were we not?" Her red lips curved in a wistful smile. He had once thought her the most beautiful woman in the world, and now, for a moment, the old admiration stirred in him again.

"Yes. Once."

"I was wrong to keep you as I did," she went on, "I should have allowed you more freedom. 'Tis only . . . you were so much younger, and so fair . . . I feared you would grow weary of me, and I . . . But I should have remembered that you are the son of a noble knight."

What was this? Apologies from *her*? She could not possibly mean what she said, though he could find no reason for her to lie to him now, when he was completely at her mercy.

"Madam," he said, "if you are sincere, you would speak for me to the king."

"Do you think I have not already done so?"

Yes, that was precisely what he thought. Or . . . at least, he *had*. But her voice was so sweetly reproachful that he wondered if he had wronged her, and her eyes . . . he felt a little dizzy looking into their emerald depths. With an effort, he lowered his gaze to the blossom she turned between her slender fingers. It was gillyflower, usually the gift of a lady to her lover before he rode forth to battle, and white for purity of love. Its spicy scent filled the little chamber.

"But against such a grave charge as murder," she went on, "my words availed me nothing. But I am sure you did not do it!"

"It was an accident," Launfal said, lifting his gaze to hers. "I only sought to defend myself, and he fell on his own dagger."

Her eyes shimmered. "I knew it could not be as the king said! If only Arthur—but his mind is set." A tear spilled over her lashes and sparkled on her cheek. Launfal stared at it, transfixed, as she went on. "You are to hang. Oh, my poor boy, I am sorry, I should not have blurted it out like that! Sit down, I beg you—let me help—"

"No," he said numbly. "I—I am well."

"So brave," she murmured, and he shivered as her hand caressed his cheek. "But what else did I expect from the son of such a noble house? Of such a father! He was a proud man, was he not, your father? Oh, what would he have said if he knew how his line would end! That forevermore, when anyone speaks of him—or his father or his before him—their brave deeds will be cast into shadow by your fate—"

Launfal leaned weakly against the cold stone wall as the full impact of the sentence hit him. To die was every man's fate, but to hang! That was a churl's death. There could be no greater disgrace. Morgause turned away to lay the flower on a small table, then took both his hands in hers, looking deeply into his eyes.

"That such a man as you should be cut down in his youth is bad enough," she said, her voice trembling with emotion. "But to die in such a fashion—the son of Sir Rogier of Penhelm, strung up before a crowd of jeering peasants—"

*"No!"* He looked wildly around the chamber, and his eyes fell upon the small table. Beside the gillyflower, half hidden by its petals, lay a silver dagger.

He reached out and took it in his hand, testing its point

against one thumb and staring at the drop of blood that formed upon his fingertip. "Sharp," he murmured. "Madam, I thank you. Now, if you would leave me . . ."

She gazed at him through tear-filled eyes. "No, please—let me stay with you until . . . the end."

His heart swelled with gratitude for her kindness. "As you will."

He set the dagger's point against his heart. One thrust and it would be ended. He drew a long breath, his fingers tensing on the hilt—

"Here, now, what's this?" a shrill voice demanded. "Put that dagger down, you fool!"

Launfal looked up, wondering for one confused moment if he was already dead and gone to hell. A ghastly apparition stood inside the open door, arms akimbo as it glared into his face.

"Get out," Morgause said distinctly, and the little goblin-woman staggered back a step and sat down hard. "Go on, dear boy," Morgause crooned, stroking his cheek and gazing deep into his eyes. "Ignore the old woman, she is not important, she does not matter in the least."

"Don't you listen to her, Launfal!" the little woman wheezed, struggling to pull herself upright.

Morgause rounded on her, eyes flashing, magnificent in her rage. "I told you to get out!"

"And I'm telling you to keep your poisonous tongue between your teeth!"

"Grandmother," Launfal said, frowning, "you are as ill-mannered as you are unwelcome. Pray leave us now."

"I'm not going anywhere! I—"

"Launfal?" Sir Gawain stepped through the open door. "Mother," he said. "What do you—"

"Silence!" Morgause commanded, one hand extended stiffly toward her son. Sir Gawain stopped short, the words dying on his lips.

"Don't you dare do that to him!" the old woman shrieked.

*"You,"* Morgause said, her eyes narrowing. "I *knew* it!" Her laughter rang from the stone walls. "Begone!"

Again the old woman staggered, and this time when she fell, she did not rise. Morgause's face was livid, her lips drawn back in a snarl as she turned back to Launfal. He blinked, staring down at the dagger in his hand. How had it come to be there? He could not quite remember . . .

Morgause seized him by the shoulders, her eyes burning into his. "Finish it!" she cried. "Unless you would rather hang. Can you not see that I want only to help you?"

"Stop that!" The old woman struggled to her feet. "Morgause, *be still*!"

Morgause lifted a hand to her throat. "Can you not see—" she whispered hoarsely. Her face worked strangely as she tried to speak—her nose began to lengthen, sharpen, and blue-black feathers sprouted from her temples. Her eyes, shrunken to black beads, sparked red with fury, and she screamed like a crow in an autumn field. Long fingers, scaled and sharp, clawed the feathers at her throat, and Launfal sprang away with a cry of horror.

"Launfal, don't you look at her," the crone gasped. "You mind me now and *drop that dagger*!"

It fell from his nerveless fingers to clatter on the floor. Morgause screamed again, throwing back her head, auburn hair shot through with raven feathers cascading down her back. She shrieked a word in a language Launfal did not know, and the crone gave a short bark of laughter. "Can you do no better than *that*? You aren't really trying!"

Morgause seemed to shrink in upon herself—or no, Launfal realized, she *was* shrinking, her cloak billowing about her.

"I should do it," the crone muttered. "It'd be a kindness, really." She glanced at Sir Gawain, who still stood in the doorway, apparently as frozen with horror as Launfal was himself. "But I don't suppose I can," she added on a sigh, then raising her voice, said, "Morgause of Orkney, come back."

As suddenly as that, Morgause was herself again, an expression of mingled fury and terror contorting her features. She bent to retrieve the silver dagger from the floor, tucking it into her girdle, and when she straightened, she had recovered her composure. "Farewell," she said to Launfal. "I tried to help you, but . . ." With a shrug, she walked away. Gawain's hand shot out and grasped her arm.

"Leave," he rasped. "Go back to Lothian and stay there."

Morgause pulled free of him. "I had already decided to do so," she said loftily. She glanced down at the old woman, leaning weakly against the wall. "Oh, and felicitations on your marriage, Gawain. I trust you will be as happy as you deserve."

• • •

AISLYN slid down the wall and closed her eyes. As though from a great distance, she heard Gawain say, "Are you all right?"

"I've been better. But I'll do. I just need to catch my breath, is all." She opened her eyes to find him kneeling beside her, looking even worse than she felt. His face was dead white and his pupils so dilated that only a thin rim of gray showed around the edges. She reached out her hand—

But he was already on his feet. "Sunset is nearly upon us," he said stiffly. "I trust you will be restored then."

She nodded. "Aye. Gawain, I'm sorry. I had no choice."

"We always have a choice," he said, and when she would have said more, he shook his head. "Not now."

He held out the parchment to Launfal. "The king's pardon."

"Pardon? Oh, Sir Gawain, I thank you."

"I had nothing to do with it," he answered. "The king ascertained the facts and you are free. Good fortune to you."

His gaze swept over Aislyn once more as he walked out the door.

"Grandmother," Launfal said. "I believe I owe you my thanks."

"You owe me your *life*, and stop calling me Grandmother. I'm your sister."

"My—?" Launfal laughed a little wildly. "Have I gone mad?"

"You tell me. Trying to do away with yourself—what were you thinking?"

"I—I hardly know now."

"Silly nit. Come and give me your hand."

Launfal stopped, his hand extended. "What did you call me?"

"I called you a silly nit, and so you are, standing there like a moonstruck calf when you—ah! Oh, Lord, turn away," she groaned. "Hurry! You don't want to see—"

Morgana's spell was superior to hers in one respect, she reflected as she sat up. It worked much more quickly. But it was still damnably unpleasant.

Launfal stood with his back to the wall, an expression of revulsion on his face.

"All right, all right, I know it isn't pretty, but you only have yourself to blame. I *told* you to turn away, didn't I?"

"Aislyn?" he whispered hoarsely.

"Do you have another sister?" She laughed at his expression. "You're not mad, Launfal. I was enchanted, that's all."

"That's *all*?"

"Well, no, not quite—in fact there is a good deal more to it than that. But first come here and let me kiss you."

• • •

"SO Sir Gawain . . ." Launfal halted her outside her chamber door, his hands on her shoulders. "You and he . . ."

"It is over," Aislyn said brusquely. She tapped on the

chamber door, and when there was no answer, opened it and stepped inside.

"But—you did that—for *me*?"

"Of course I did. Let's not talk of it now," she added, biting her lip. "I just want to get through this and begone."

"Where will we go?" Launfal asked as she went to the trunk and began collecting her belongings.

"I thought—for a time—I have a cottage where I was living before . . . before . . ."

Launfal sat down on the stool. "That will suit me well. But I think I should speak to Sir Gawain before we leave."

"Save your breath. His mind is made up and there is nothing to be done for it."

"But if you promised to renounce magic now—"

"I won't. Oh, I could say it, but I wouldn't really mean it, and Gawain would know that. He cannot abide magic—"

"I have a certain sympathy with him there," Launfal said.

"Aye, and you have every right to feel that way—as does he. He's a good man, Launfal, he's just not—that is, I'm not—" Aislyn dragged her sleeve across her cheek. "But I mean to make things right for him before I go."

Aislyn had nothing but her old green gown to wear and no ornament with which to adorn it. But she combed out her hair until it glowed like new-minted copper in the candlelight, and arranged it so it streamed over her shoulders like a cloak, falling in shimmering waves to her knees.

"Well?" she said to Launfal.

He nodded. "You'll do."

"Good," she answered tersely. "Keep close. This will be bad enough, I don't want to have to look for you when it is done."

"As my lady commands." He made her a mocking bow.

She reached out, and his warm, strong fingers closed around hers. "I'm a wretched sister, aren't I?"

"The worst. But as you're the only one I have, I'll just have to make do."

"Nit."

"Witch."

She squeezed his hand tightly. "I never should have left you in Lothian."

"You made up for it before."

"I can never make up for it."

"Hmm." He frowned, staring into space as though considering the matter. "Yes, most likely you are right. But I will allow you to beg for my forgiveness. I can't promise you will win it, but you have my leave to try."

She laughed through her tears. "I can't imagine why I missed you so much!"

"Did you? No, never mind, you can tell me later. Let's get this over and get out of here."

She looked around the chamber. It was exactly as she had seen it that first night; stark and plain, with the four cats stretched out upon the bed, Sooty in the place of honor on Gawain's pillow.

"Yes," she said. "It's time to go."

# Chapter 40

• • •

GAWAIN walked from the dungeon into the gathering twilight. He instinctively avoided the courtyard, where crowds were gathered for the feast. He should be there. All the king's companions were expected to be with him, but he could not bring himself to face anyone just yet. Instead he walked into the gardens and stood watching the water splash into the fountain.

He swallowed convulsively, his stomach churning as he remembered his mother's hand rising, choking off his words. Just so had he felt after his adventure with the Green Knight, sickened and ashamed. Nothing to do with magic had ever gone well for him. No earthly danger had ever made him feel so weak and helpless. Magic was a weapon against which he had no defense.

There had been nothing he could do before in the dungeon. He had simply stood there, mute and motionless as a stone while Aislyn challenged the Queen of Air and Darkness—and defeated her.

Aislyn was no mere hedge-witch. She was an enchantress

of enormous power, the sort that did not come for the wishing. She had worked hard for it—just as she had tried to tell him earlier. He could no more stop her wielding it than she could prevent him picking up a sword in defense of those he cared for.

It had nothing to do with obedience. Aislyn was as she was, and to demand that she be something else was not only cruel, but futile. The question was whether he could live with what she was and keep his sanity.

How could he ever feel safe, knowing the sort of power she had at her command? She was everything he feared—yet she was Aislyn, too, the only woman he had ever loved.

He would always love her. He was a simple man, really, and having once given her his heart, had lost it for all time. But he could live without love. He had already proved that he could live without Aislyn. Or, no; what he had proved was that he could *exist* without her. But could he really go back to merely existing when he knew now what it was to live? Could he bear to even try?

She was proud and headstrong, with a temper that could lead her into folly. These were faults Gawain did not take lightly, for they were his own. The most he could say in his own defense was that he knew his weaknesses and fought them every day. He could ask no more of Aislyn—nor could he accept any less from the woman who would share his life. Better to live alone than bind himself to a woman he could not respect—or one who did not respect him.

*Did* Aislyn respect him?

His head bent in thought, he paced through the crowded courtyard and back to his chamber. Standing in the open doorway, he realized he could not ask Aislyn these difficult and painful questions, for she and her belongings were already gone.

• • •

ANY doubts Aislyn might have harbored about her appearance were allayed once she stepped into the hall. The varlets at the lower trestles nudged each other, whispering, as she passed by. Squires stared openmouthed, the contents of their trays sliding unheeded to the floor, where the hounds snapped and snarled as they fought over the unexpected bounty.

Head held high, Aislyn passed beyond them to the knights' trestles.

Silence descended like a thunderclap. Sir Sagramore choked on a mouthful of mutton and no one even thought to pound him on the back. Sir Kay dropped his goblet with a clatter. Sir Griflet leaned so far back to catch a better glimpse of her that he tumbled off his seat.

Still Aislyn went on until she stood before the high table. The king gaped, his goblet frozen halfway to his lips. Guinevere looked from her lord to Aislyn, her eyes narrowed.

"My lord king," Aislyn said. "I bid you good even. Will you permit me . . . ?" She stepped onto the dais and a murmur passed across the hall.

Aislyn held up a hand, asking for silence. When it had fallen, she bowed to the king and queen. "I thank you for your courtesy in receiving me. A few moments of your time are all I ask—yours and this gentle company's." She smiled, gesturing toward the crowded hall. "Good people, I have come to tell you a marvelous tale. Some of it you know already, but if you will be patient, I think I may surprise you."

"Say on," Arthur said graciously. "You have our full attention."

"Thank you." Aislyn flashed him a smile that brought a warm glow to his cheeks. "This tale begins with you, my liege, and what befell you in Inglewood Forest one day last spring. As you all know, our good King Arthur was set upon by a knight calling himself Somer Gromer Jour, and overset. This knight demanded that in return for your king's life, he answer one simple question: what is it that all women desire? Was that not the condition, sire?"

Arthur nodded. "It was."

"King Arthur had one year in which to find the answer. During that year he—and his heir and nephew, Sir Gawain—traveled the kingdom over, asking many women to enlighten them. They sought high and low, and during their journey collected a great tome of answers to this question. Some of these answers were wise and some were foolish, but, alas, none was the one King Arthur sought. He and Sir Gawain suspected as much, though—being men—they had no real idea."

As Aislyn waited for the burst of laughter from the ladies to subside, she caught a flash of movement in the doorway at the far end of the hall, but it was only Sir Lancelot arriving late to the feast. Her heart lifted when she saw a tall, yellow-haired man behind him, but when he stepped into the light, his face was not Gawain's, but that of a stranger.

"They set out on the appointed day," she went on, "the king and Sir Gawain, with their book of answers. And I tell you, good people, I tell you in all honesty, that on that fine spring day, your king was riding to his death."

The last of the laughter died; the people watched her, rapt.

"But something happened on the way—as surely you have guessed, for here sits your king, alive and well. And what happened was this: they met an old woman in the forest, and she was a hideous creature. Her back was bent in a hump, her skin sagged, her teeth—well, there is no need to describe her fully. Suffice it to say that she was a most *loathly* lady. But as wretched and hideous as she was, she possessed the one thing the king needed: the answer to his question. And she offered this to him . . . but not freely. I regret to say that this loathly lady asked a grievous tithe. In return for this answer—the one thing that could save King Arthur's life, mind you, his only hope of escaping certain death—she demanded that his most loyal knight, his own nephew, Sir Gawain, take her to wife."

She waited a moment, allowing the startled murmurs to subside as she searched the hall, but if Gawain was there, she could not find him. At last she held up her hand, and when silence had fallen, she went on.

"That Sir Gawain agreed should come as no surprise to those of you who know him. But I ask you now—which of you fair knights would have done the same? For you have all seen her. She has lived among you, has she not? You knew not why Sir Gawain had chosen to wed this vile creature, for he, too, had a price for his part in saving King Arthur's life, and it was that none should know of the noble sacrifice he made—one that had not been made for any gain to himself, but purely for the love and loyalty he bore his king. Tell me, my liege, is that not how it befell that day?"

"It was," Arthur said. "Though I know not how you have divined such things."

"We shall come to that in time. Sir Gawain wed this loathly lady. You were all witness to his wedding. And many a jest was made at his expense during that wedding—and after, too. Good people, did you not laugh behind your hands? Did you not revile the lady he had wed? You knights of Camelot—sworn, every one of you, to protect the weak and respect the aged—how many of you were true to your vows?"

She looked at each in turn, her gaze resting on Sir Lancelot the longest. Only when he blushed and looked away did she move on, ending with Sir Dinadan. At him, she smiled, and he grinned, a speculative gleam in his eye.

"Not many, I regret to say. This horrid old woman—and she was a very horrid creature, I do not deny it—received little of charity at your hands. As for Sir Gawain . . ." She shook her head sadly. "You saw a man punished for no apparent cause, and because he bore it uncomplaining, you believed the punishment must be deserved. You forgot what he was—what he has always been—the truest and most honorable of knights, and assumed him guilty of some secret sin. You judged him and condemned him—" She looked straight at the queen. "And you reveled in his downfall."

Guinevere's eyes flashed, shame and anger warring on her face. "Lady," Arthur protested, "you are too hard—"

"Am I? Perhaps, my liege; I confess freely that I am not a judge impartial. For there is yet another secret hidden in this matter, and I will tell it to you now. That loathly lady Sir Gawain so generously took to wife was not a simple woman bent by age. She was an enchanted creature, a maiden cursed to bear a crone's form until a true knight could win her freedom. She was, in fact, none other than myself."

Cries of astonishment and disbelief greeted this pronouncement.

"Yes, I am Dame Ragnelle," Aislyn said, raising her voice to be heard above the tumult. "I have lived among you, unable to ask for help or reveal my grievous plight. The fell enchantments binding me could be broken only by one whose honor shines more brightly than the sun, and many tests and trials has Sir Gawain endured to prove himself that knight."

And then, when she least expected it, she saw Gawain, leaning against the wall, arms folded across his chest.

"Yet he won through," she went on, not daring to glance at him again. "Not for gain or profit, nor even out of pity for my state, for he knew no more of me than any man among you. Yet Sir Gawain—he, who above all others, had every reason to detest me—has shown me naught but gentle courtesy and kindness. I ask you, good people, to consider his plight. He bid farewell to all hope of a union befitting his station—yet that was only the beginning of his trials. How many of you could bear such scorn as he has suffered in silence, all the while knowing it to be completely undeserved? I tell you—I tell you in all honesty that my enchantments soon came to seem as nothing when compared to the vile aspersion cast upon the character of such a noble knight."

She stopped, her breath coming quick and short. Heads were turning now, and a low buzz ran across the hall as one pointed Gawain out to the other. If he was aware of the stir he was causing, he gave no sign. He merely watched Aislyn with hooded eyes, his face revealing nothing of his thoughts.

"If I consider him the finest knight in all the world, I think I have good cause. For here I stand before you, restored to my true state, and here sits your king, as hale and hearty as he ever was, and so he may continue with God's grace for many a long year."

Aislyn bowed again to the king and queen, and once more to the hall. "I thank you for your patience, and bid you all farewell."

"Farewell?" Arthur cried. "But—"

"Tell us how Sir Gawain broke the enchantment!" a lady called.

Aislyn's throat was tight with unshed tears, but she managed a laugh. "That is his tale to tell—or not, as he sees fit. For he, too, is free now. Our marriage was not a binding one, based on falsehoods as it was." At last she found the courage to meet his eyes across the hall. "So I declare with all of you as witness."

Gawain's expression did not alter. Aislyn whirled and made a hasty reverence to the king and queen before she fled the hall.

# Chapter 41

• • •

"YOU did rather well," Launfal said as they walked together into the courtyard. His words were light, but his arm was firm about her shoulders as he guided her across the cobbles. "Now, I spoke to Sir Dinadan before, and he agreed to lend me a horse. You wait right here, and I will bring it."

Aislyn sat down on a mounting block and rested her head in her hand. *Don't think,* she told herself, *not now. Just do what needs to be done and you can think about it later.* When she felt a light touch on her shoulder, she looked up, expecting to see her brother, but Gawain stood beside her.

"That," he said, "was humiliating beyond words."

She shrugged. "You could have left."

"I wanted to. It was like a nightmare I sometimes have." He sat down beside her on the mounting block. "Have you ever dreamed that you were having an ordinary day—that you were in the market, say, or in the hall—and suddenly you realize you are wearing nothing but your skin?"

Aislyn made a sound between laughter and a sob.

"It was like that," Gawain said. "I couldn't seem to move."

"I only spoke the truth."

"Part of it—"

"Of course! To tell the whole tale, I would have to go back to the moment of my birth. I doubt the court would sit the whole night through while I explained the whys and wherefores of every decision I have ever made!"

"You exaggerated shamelessly."

"I only gave back what I had taken from you," she said wearily.

"Do you expect me to thank you?"

"Don't bother. I wouldn't want you to do yourself a damage."

His eyes were dark in the flickering shadows cast by the torches above their heads. He touched her cheek where a teardrop still lingered. "Aislyn . . . You will not ever obey any man, will you?"

"No." She frowned down at the earth between her feet. "But if a man earned my respect, I would ask his opinion."

He caught her jaw and turned her face to his. "And would you heed it?"

"Always." She gave a choked laugh. "That doesn't mean I would *agree* with it. He could be wrong."

"What happened earlier—" Gawain shuddered. "It sickened me."

"I know. But I could think of no other way to stop her. The duchess of Cornwall once told me that there is more to magic than learning spells. After what I saw today, I know exactly what she means. That sort of power—I don't want it anymore."

"Then will you—?"

"But given the same circumstances," she finished sadly, "I would do the same again. I am sorry, Gawain, but that is the truth."

He nodded. "I knew you would say that. But I have come to see that there are times when sorcery can only be fought in kind. That does not mean I will ever like it, but if you were to ask my opinion first—and heed it—"

"So long as it is sensible," she put in, a smile tugging at her lips.

"Am I ever less than sensible? Don't forget, I am the finest knight in all the world, one whose honor shines more brightly than the—"

"You are right."

His smile was smug as he stroked a thumb across her lips. "Am I?"

"Yes. I *did* exaggerate."

His brows lifted. "I am not those things?"

"Some of them."

"Some? Which ones?"

"I haven't decided yet."

"Mmm." He regarded her through half-closed eyes. "When might you?"

"It could take some time."

He smiled slowly. "A long time? Perhaps . . . a lifetime?"

"It could be. That is, if—"

His gaze moved over her shoulder. "Ah," he said softly. "Morgana is here."

Aislyn stood. Her mouth went tinder-dry and her knees were trembling as the duchess walked from the direction of the stables.

"Morgana!" Gawain called.

"Oh, Gawain," the duchess said, holding out her hand to him. "I began to think I would never get here! My horse foundered in—Well! Dame Ragnelle, is it?"

"Sometimes," Aislyn replied, bowing. "But tonight, I am Aislyn."

"A vast improvement, I must say."

"I agree," Gawain said. "And you would oblige me very much if you were to make the change permanent."

Morgana's smile vanished. "That," she said, "I cannot do."

"Oh, but I have learned so much," Aislyn said. "Truly I have, Your Grace."

"I don't doubt it," Morgana answered. "But it is not in my power to release you."

"Of course it is!" Aislyn cried. "The spell was your own. You can reverse it."

Morgana touched her cheek. "I cannot. I am sorry, but that is the truth. You—like all of us—are in the hands of the Goddess now."

"Oh," Aislyn said faintly. Gawain pulled her hard against him and wrapped his arms around her. She rested her cheek against his chest until the world righted itself, then gently drew away.

"I will find a way to free you," Gawain said.

"But that could take—"

"I don't care how long it takes. Aislyn—" He cupped her cheek in one strong hand. "I would rather spend half my life with you than the whole of it with any other woman."

"You don't mean that," Aislyn cried. "I cannot give you children, or travel with you or—"

"I don't care."

"You do. Let me go away, Gawain—Launfal and I will go back to my cottage. You can visit me there when—when you like. That way you will be free, and if you decide—that is, if you meet someone—"

"No."

"But—"

"I said, *no*. You will stay here."

Aislyn glared at him. "And what if I don't *want* to stay?"

"Do you *want* to leave me? It would have been easier if you'd just said so from the first."

She struck a fist against his chest. "If you would only

*listen*, you would know that isn't true. But to go back to being . . . her . . . before all these people—How long could you bear it, Gawain? How long before you came to rue this night?"

"Never."

"You say that now, but in a year's time—ten years—you can find someone else, some clean-limbed maiden who will give you a dozen sons and never say you nay."

"Too late. I am already wed."

"You are *not*. You are *free*."

He pulled her hard against him. "I will never be free of you," he said roughly. "And you will never be free of me." He kissed her and she melted against him, her arms stealing round his neck.

Morgana cleared her throat. "It needn't be by day, you know."

Aislyn turned to her. "What?"

"The time you spend in the crone's form. It could be by night. That much, at least, I can grant you."

Aislyn laid her palms on Gawain's chest and looked up into his eyes. "Which shall it be?"

• • •

THE *night*.

Gawain nearly blurted out his answer; only the habit born of long years of negotiations stopped the words upon his lips.

If Aislyn was with him by day, he could share the better part of his life with her. He would wake beside her—well, so long as he took care not to wake too early. But he would certainly walk into the hall each morning with his lady on his arm, dine with her, ride with her—

"Aislyn?" Launfal appeared at the edge of the courtyard. "Shall we . . . ?"

"Oh!" Aislyn stepped back. "We will—that is, I think we will—"

"You are staying," Gawain said. "Launfal, I have not had the chance to tell you how pleased I am to see you again. Morgana—the duchess of Cornwall—this is Aislyn's brother, Launfal."

Morgana nodded to him. "Gawain, may we have your answer now?"

"I am sorry," Gawain said. "But I would like to think on it a little longer."

"Well, then, Launfal," Morgana said, "shall we leave Sir Gawain to his reflections and go in search of sustenance together?"

"I do not think I should—that is, it would not be proper for you—" Launfal looked away, his jaw tightening. "You see, Your Grace, I was the king's prisoner just this morning."

"Indeed?" Morgana's brows lifted. "What a very . . . interesting family you have married into, Gawain." Aislyn bristled, but before she could speak, Morgana went on. "Come here, my lad, let me see you." She drew Launfal into the circle of torchlight and gazed into his face. "You haven't the look of a felon to me," she said, holding out her hand and smiling. "Come, kinsman, you can tell me your adventures as we eat."

Launfal did not protest again, but gave the duchess his arm and went with her toward the hall. Aislyn started after them, but Gawain caught her hand. "Don't leave me," he said. "Morgana will look after him."

"Very well," Aislyn replied, sitting down upon the steps leading to the hall. "I will stay."

Gawain sat down beside her and took her hand in his, running his fingers through hers and smiling at the feeling of her smooth skin against his own callused hands. He had meant what he said to her before: he had no desire to wed any other woman. But his pride had been rubbed raw these past weeks, and though he refused to shrink from either the scorn or pity of his peers, he would not invite them, either.

Yes, that was it. He would—he must have her with him during the day.

And yet . . .

If Aislyn was with him by day, she would not be with him by night.

He glanced up to find her watching him anxiously. "Well?" she said.

"I am *thinking*."

"Does it always take this long?"

He put his arm around her and drew her close, resting his cheek against her hair. "Either way, it will not be forever. I *will* find the way to free you."

"Am I allowed to help? Or shall I sit with folded hands waiting for you to ride to my rescue?"

"You? Sit with folded hands? I'd like to see it." He tipped her face to his and kissed her once, and then, as it was over far too quickly, once again.

"Is this helping you to think?" she said a little breathlessly.

"Yes," he answered firmly, and soon her arms were round his neck, and his fingers were tangled in her bright hair as he bent to kiss her throat. She shivered, her head falling back against his arm, and—

"Sir Gawain?" a man's voice said.

Gawain sighed. "Yes?" he said. *Go away,* he did not say, but he might as well have done so, judging from the man's laughter.

"Forgive me. But there is someone who wants to meet you."

Gawain released Aislyn, who sat up, smoothing her hair, a rosy blush upon her cheeks. Dear God, but she was beautiful! He had to force his gaze from her to the man who had interrupted him. He was obviously a Saxon, but that mattered far less than the fact that he was staring straight at Aislyn without making the least attempt to hide his admiration.

*Perhaps it would be better to have Aislyn to myself at night.*

He dismissed the thought as unworthy, though Aislyn was staring straight back at the Saxon, frowning slightly as though trying to place him. Gawain thought he looked familiar, too, though he could not quite recall . . .

"Why, it is . . . Torquil, is it not?" Aislyn said, smiling.

"*Sir* Torquil," Sir Lancelot put in from behind the Saxon. "I met his party on the road; they were bound for Camelot and most anxious to speak to Sir Gawain."

Sir Torquil bowed to her. "And *you* are Dame Ragnelle?" He raised a brow skeptically and she laughed, standing and holding out her hand.

"You came to my cottage," she said, "and that young man, the one who dropped the battle-ax, said—well, never mind what he said," she added quickly. Gawain stood, as well. He wasn't sure he liked the way Sir Torquil laughed, as though he and Aislyn shared a private joke.

"Then *you*—" Aislyn sketched an arc before her belly. "And you said I was to come—though you were very nice about it. He even pretended I had a choice," she added, laughing to Gawain. "But now tell me how Lady Elga does! And the babe—is she well? Did the lady's mother arrive?"

"I did." A tall woman stepped from the shadows. "I am Mathilda, and I reached my daughter the next morning. She and the child are both well."

*Mathilda?* Gawain knew that name. She was . . . who was she? Someone of importance, or he would not have heard of her.

"Oh, I am glad to hear it! I'd never delivered a babe before," Aislyn said confidingly, "and I don't know how I would have managed if Lady Elga had not been so very brave."

Mathilda's eyes softened. "You are all she told me—yet nothing like. I do not understand this—enchantment?"

"It *is* confusing, isn't it?" Aislyn said. "May I present Sir Gawain to you, my lady?"

Gawain bowed deeply.

"Ah, Sir Gawain," the lady said. "I have heard of you, as well." She said no more, but smiled on him warmly.

"Sir Torquil, you have met Sir Gawain already," Aislyn went on, "though I don't think you were properly introduced."

"No, we were not," Gawain said. "You saw me at something of a disadvantage—"

"Really?" Torquil's teeth showed in a smile. "I would have said Gudrun was the one at a disadvantage."

"Peace, Torquil." An older man with a tired face and kind eyes stepped forward to take Aislyn's hand. "My lady, I am King Aesc."

"Good evening, sire. I am . . . honored to meet you."

"Sir Gawain." Aesc nodded to him. "I believe I owe you an apology. I relied upon my brother Gudrun's report of your encounter, which I now know to have been . . . incomplete."

Torquil snorted, but Gawain only bowed without speaking.

"Well, then," Sir Lancelot said brightly. "Now that the introductions have been made, shall we go and join the feast? I know the king is right eager to greet you for himself."

As they walked through the courtyard, Aislyn said to Mathilda, "I trust your journey was not too difficult?"

"Not very," the lady replied. "I came only from Wessex."

"Wessex?" Aislyn frowned slightly, then her face cleared as she, like Gawain, realized that these Saxons were King Aesc's troublesome Wessex kinfolk, the ones who had refused every invitation to King Arthur's court. "Oh, *Wessex*! King Ceredig rules there, does he not? Do you know him?"

"I should say so." Mathilda smiled. "He is my husband. And now, Sir Gawain," she said, laying a hand upon his arm. "Would you be so kind as to present me to your king?"

# Chapter 42

• • •

THE Saxon party seemed to enjoy the feast, which pleased Arthur. Gawain was pleased, as well, though he could not keep his mind fixed upon the Saxons at the moment. It was gratifying to have King Aesc beg his pardon, and Mathilda promise to persuade her husband to meet with King Arthur, though she could not guarantee the outcome. Still, it was something of a triumph, though of course it was not really Gawain's.

It was Aislyn's.

Unlike Guinevere, she did not set out to be deliberately charming. And though the queen was quite adept at putting her guests at ease, it was Aislyn who made them laugh when she gave a spirited description of Sir Torquil's visit to her woodland cabin. He obligingly repeated his imitation of a woman far gone in labor, which made Queen Mathilda cluck her tongue.

"You should not know these things!" she said, trying unsuccessfully to frown at her kinsman. "We must find you a bride—at once!"

"I have looked!" Torquil protested. "But the ladies I desire are all married," he added, casting a melting glance at Aislyn.

"So I hear," Mathilda retorted, and this time her frown looked far more genuine. "You will end by falling out a window and breaking your fool neck."

Torquil laughed. "*I* will end in battle, slain by a brave enemy." He raised his cup to Gawain. "Is there any better death?"

"Oh, don't let's talk of death," Aislyn said quickly. "It makes me sad."

"Forgive me," Torquil said at once, leaning forward to rest his hand upon her wrist. "What do *you* like to talk of?"

Gawain stiffened, but before he could react, Aislyn had slipped her hand from under the Saxon's. "Why, of Sir Gawain, of course!" she answered, laughing. "We have been wed such a short time, I can think of little else."

Mathilda looked on her with amused approval, and Torquil, with a good-natured bow to Gawain, subsided.

The talk went on to other things, but Gawain no longer listened. He leaned his chin on his fist, watching as Aislyn discussed herb lore with Mathilda.

He'd had enough of feasts and chatter. He wanted to sweep Aislyn off to their chamber. But first he must find Morgana before she disappeared again and tell her his decision.

He imagined Aislyn stretched out upon their bed with the moonlight gilding her sleek limbs. He thought of her walking proudly beside him with the sunlight in her hair.

How could any man make such a choice? Yet it must be made, and then endured, for once he had decided, no word of complaint would ever pass his lips.

At last the Saxons retired and soon after, the king and queen withdrew, as well.

"Shall we find the duchess?" Aislyn asked.

"Yes." Gawain sighed and gestured a page over. "I suppose we must."

"Do you care to tell me your decision?" she asked as they waited. "Or is it to be a surprise?"

"I will tell you." She looked at him expectantly and he scowled. "As soon as I know."

"Oh, Gawain," she said, slipping her hand into his. "It is awful, isn't it? Are you sure you want to be married to—"

"Quite." He kissed her fingers. "I just need to work out the details."

But he thought he had the answer now. He could not bear to sleep beside the crone each night, knowing he could have had Aislyn in his arms. He would just have to accept the fact that she would be the crone by day.

Instantly, an image formed in his mind of Dame Ragnelle capering in the garden. But it had been long since she had shamed him like that! Yes, it would be hard to face the court again with her at his side, but he could do it if he must. And Dame Ragnelle was not so very awful. She might be hideous, but she was kind. She had bound his wounds, made him laugh, helped him understand himself as he had never done before. He was really very fond of her.

And yet . . .

His mind went over it all again, turning and twisting the same pieces of the puzzle, but try as he might, he could not make them form a pleasant picture.

# Chapter 43

• • •

BY the time the page returned, Gawain was no closer to the answer, though had succeeded in giving himself a pounding headache.

*Oh, just pick one—night or day, what does it matter?* he thought impatiently, relieved that this ordeal must soon be finished.

"The duchess of Cornwall is with the king and queen," the page said. "She bids me have you join them."

"What now?" Gawain groaned, and Aislyn took his hand.

"Ah, Camelot! *Such* an entertaining place to live!"

"A bit too entertaining lately," Gawain grumbled, though he managed to compose his expression to one of polite interest as the page opened the door of Arthur's presence chamber and bowed them inside.

"Oh, good, you're here," Morgana said from the chair in which she was relaxing. Behind her stood Launfal, and he cast Aislyn a rather desperate look as she walked in.

Arthur sat at his long table with Guinevere beside him.

Though she had chatted brightly with the Saxons earlier, now the queen looked strained and weary, and though she, like Arthur, seemed ready to listen to what Morgana had to say, she looked as though she rather dreaded it.

"Launfal has been telling me the most interesting tales!" Morgana began. "I thought you two should be present when he repeated them to the king."

Aislyn stiffened and gave a little gasp. What now? Gawain wondered, looking from her to Launfal. Aislyn's hand clenched around Gawain's, but she gave her brother an encouraging smile, which seemed to hearten him, for he lifted his head and straightened his shoulders.

"Sire," Launfal began, "first, please allow me to thank you for getting to the truth of Sir Marrek's death. But there is something else you must know—part of the reason I was coming to Camelot in the first place was to tell you—" He swallowed nervously. "Sire, I am Somer Gromer Jour."

*Him?* Somer Gromer Jour? Gawain had seen nothing but a silver helm that day, but now he suddenly recalled what Somer Gromer Jour had said—"My sister told you that!"—and looked to Aislyn. She nodded and squeezed his hand, silently asking for his patience, and after a moment, he nodded in return. Arthur's expression did not change; only the slight widening of his eyes betrayed his surprise. "You?" he said. "But why?"

"Sire, at the time, I was in the service of the queen of Orkney," Launfal went on. "And she—"

"Are you speaking of me, Launfal?" Gawain sighed as his mother swept into the chamber. How did she always know when people were talking about her? Was it sorcery . . . or merely spies?

"Yes, madam," Launfal said evenly. "I was just telling the king about the adventure of Somer Gromer Jour."

"But that is my tale to tell!" Morgause protested.

"Then please do, madam," Arthur replied coldly. "For Launfal has told me nothing as yet, save that he was in your service at the time. I can only assume that *you* commanded him to challenge me, and it was by your order that I would have been slain had not Dame Ragnelle supplied me with the answer to your riddle."

"Oh, good, you do not know yet!" Morgause cried. "I was afraid that Launfal had spoiled my surprise!"

"Surprise?" Arthur said.

"Yes!" Morgause clasped her hands together like an eager child. "You see, Arthur, when I heard you had taken a bride, I wondered what gift I could possibly give you—you who have so much. I thought long upon the matter, and at last decided that nothing would do but to ensure your marriage would be a happy one. At first, I was puzzled as to how to accomplish such a goal, but at last I hit upon the answer—to send you on a quest so you might discover for yourself that which all women desire. Of course no man would undertake such a quest did not his very life depend on it," she added with a light laugh, "and so . . . Somer Gromer Jour!"

Launfal's lips parted, though he seemed incapable of speech as he stared at Morgause in astonishment.

"Poor Launfal was a bit uneasy about the role I asked him to play," she said confidingly to Arthur. "A bit confused," she added, tapping her brow. "Why, for a time, I do believe he actually feared I meant to do you harm! But tell us now, Launfal, on your honor—and remembering that the duchess of Cornwall will detect any falsehood you might utter—during your time as Somer Gromer Jour, did you ever, for a single moment, have the slightest intention of slaying the king or even causing him an injury?"

"No," Launfal said strongly. "I did not."

"I trusted Launfal implicitly," Morgause said, "for he comes of a very noble house, but just in case matters got out of hand—if you, Arthur, or my loyal Gawain decided on a bold attack—I had men-at-arms stationed close at hand to ensure that no one would be hurt. Is that not so, Launfal?"

"There were men-at-arms to hand," he answered neutrally.

Morgause spread her hands and smiled. "So there you have it, Arthur, my wedding gift to you—and particularly to dear Guinevere."

Guinevere looked at Morgause through shadowed eyes, her mouth set in a hard line. Nor did Arthur return Morgause's smile. Seemingly unaware of their cold silence, Morgause bowed. "And now I must to bed," she said lightly, "for I leave at dawn tomorrow. I am right anxious to get home to my children. No, don't bother to get up, Arthur," she added, though the king had shown no sign of doing so. "I shall see myself out."

With a wave of her hand, she swept from the chamber, leaving a rather stunned silence in her wake. "Exit the Queen of Air and Darkness," Morgana said drily. "Really, I think that might be her finest performance yet."

"Launfal," the king said. "Have you anything to add to what the queen of Orkney has just told us?"

"I—I cannot prove that anything she told you is not the truth," Launfal said carefully. "But I never did mean you any harm, sire, that much I *can* swear to."

"You already have," Morgana said, "and I, for one, believe you. Arthur, is it true that this lad bested you in a joust?"

"Handily," Arthur admitted wryly. "Gawain would have it that sorcery was involved . . . what say you to that, Launfal?"

Launfal looked down at the floor, flushing slightly. "No, sire. There was no sorcery. Had I seemed likely to lose, the queen of Orkney would have stepped in, but she did permit me to attempt it on my own."

"Sire," Aislyn said, "I know not if you have been told this, but Launfal is my brother."

"Is he really?" Arthur said. "No, I did not know. But now that you have told me, I can see that it is so."

Aislyn glanced up at Gawain, and he gave her a quick smile of understanding. "Then, sire, as Launfal is now my brother, too," he said, "I would take it as a great favor if you would make him one of your companions."

"He has certainly proved his fitness," Arthur said. "And if you, Gawain, will vouch for him—"

"With a good will."

"Then . . . would you like that, Launfal?"

"Sire—" Launfal dropped his gaze to the floor, biting his lip hard. Only when he had mastered himself did he look upon the king with his whole heart in his eyes. "It is what I have dreamed of all my life."

Like Gawain himself, the king seemed much moved by this simple declaration. "Young Gaheris is to receive his accolade tomorrow," Arthur said. "Do you go and join him in the chapel. Gawain will be standing up with him; I daresay he would do you the same service."

"Thank you, sire, but—would it be possible to ask Sir Dinadan? That is," Launfal added hastily, "if you do not mind, Sir Gawain."

"Not in the least. And I'm sure Dinadan will be honored."

"Run along, then, lad," Arthur said, "and I will see you on the morrow."

Launfal bowed without speaking, his face transfigured by a joy too deep for words.

"I think I will like that young man," Arthur remarked when he was gone.

"I am sure you will, sire," Aislyn answered. "He is quite—remarkable."

"A quality that seems to run in your family," Arthur said, a twinkle in his eye. "And I look forward to knowing you better. But not tonight," he added, stifling a yawn. "Shall we retire, my lady?"

Guinevere had been strangely silent this past while, and now she stood obediently without replying. Aislyn went to her and bowed. "Madam," she said, "if I said anything to offend you earlier, I do hope you will forgive me."

Guinevere regarded her, unsmiling. "Of course."

"My tongue runs away with me sometimes," Aislyn went on, "but I daresay you've noticed that before."

"Indeed I have." Guinevere nodded coolly to her, then to Gawain. "Congratulations on your marriage." And laying her hand lightly on the king's arm, she left the chamber with him.

"Oh, dear, I'm afraid I've gotten on her bad side," Aislyn said, a worried frown between her brows.

Gawain shrugged. "I've been there since she came to court."

"And did you see how she looked at Launfal?" Aislyn went on. "I hope she hasn't taken against him, too."

"He survived the Queen of Air and Darkness," Morgana remarked. "I daresay he'll bear up under Guinevere's dislike."

"If indeed she does dislike him and you aren't simply playing mother hen," Gawain said, slipping an arm around her waist.

Aislyn sighed and leaned her cheek against his shoulder. "I missed my chance to mother him," she said sadly. "And now it is too late."

Gawain gave her a comforting squeeze. "He is still your brother. You'll have plenty of chances to fuss over him."

"There *is* the matter of his marriage . . ." Aislyn said, brightening.

"Yes, but can it wait until tomorrow?" Morgana yawned. "I'm for bed. Come, Gawain, let us have your answer."

He looked into Aislyn's face, tipped expectantly to his. He must speak. It was not fair to keep her waiting any longer. No matter how lightly she pretended to take this, he could see the anxiety beneath her smile. But God help him, how could he decide? How could he bear to part from her for even half the day and have only Dame Ragnelle in her place? He looked into her clear green eyes, always so incongruous in Ragnelle's wrinkled face. How odd that he always thought of them as two separate women when really . . .

They were one. His mind had always known that, but only now did he feel it in his heart. It was *Aislyn* who had bound his wounds, *Aislyn* who had made him laugh as he had not done for years. And it was Dame Ragnelle who had enthralled the entire court tonight while she defended him as fiercely as a lioness. They were one, the maiden who had stolen his heart, the crone who had won his admiration, the woman who would heed his counsel, even if she would not promise to obey it. They were one, and all were his own love. She was infinitely changeable, yet she never could be other than herself—sometimes wise and sometimes foolish, brave and strong and loyal, the lover he had always dreamed of and the truest friend he'd ever known. The Goddess is in all women, Morgana had said to him, and though he had once flung those words mockingly in her face, now, at last, he understood their truth.

And with that understanding came his answer.

"I cannot choose," he said.

A quiver passed across Aislyn's mobile features, but when she spoke, her voice was firm. "I thought not. And you should not have to. It is all right, Gawain, I do not blame you for not wanting only half a life—"

He touched a finger to her lips. "I cannot choose because this choice does not belong to me. It must be yours."

"Oh!" Aislyn put a hand to her head. "I felt so strange . . . but it is past now."

Morgana laughed. "Yes, it is past now, and there *is* no choice for you to make. You are free of all enchantment. As you are now, so shall you be tomorrow, and tomorrow night, and so on."

*"What?"* Gawain rounded on his aunt. "You said you could not lift it!"

"I did not. *You* did."

"I?" he demanded. "How?"

"The last time I visited, when we sat together in the hall, I told you that if you wanted to find happiness with your lady, you only had to . . ."

"Solve that damned riddle," he finished, and Aislyn burst out laughing.

"Oh, Gawain, no! Why did you not *tell* me?"

"I forgot," he said honestly.

"Perhaps next time," Morgana said with some asperity, "you will give a bit more weight to my words. Can you guess now what it is that all women desire?"

"To have their own way?" Gawain said warily. "To rule men?"

Aislyn laughed. "What all women desire *is* sovereignty, but not over men, my love." She took his hand. "Over ourselves."

"That's *it*?" Gawain's laughter died abruptly as he looked from Morgana to Aislyn.

" 'Tis simply said," Aislyn began.

"But not so simply done," Gawain finished thoughtfully.

"Very good, Gawain," Morgana said. "There is hope for you yet." She looked as though she might say more, but in the end she only embraced him, and then Aislyn, too, and went away.

"Tell me," Aislyn said after a time, her hand against his cheek, "what made you say that I should choose?"

"You were the one who would have to bear the worst of it. It was only right you should decide. And, too, I realized that it did not really matter."

"Did not *matter*?"

He traced the delicate arch of her brow with one finger. "Your eyes are very beautiful, you know, but what I love most about them now is not their brilliance, but that they see straight through falsehood and pretension. And once you have seen a truth, you speak it in no uncertain terms."

He kissed her lips, then drew away, smiling as he stroked her hair. "You are the loveliest woman I have ever seen. Looking at you now—" He laughed. "You take my breath away. But it won't always be that way. Oh, not that I will tire of you—that could never happen!—but in time, we will grow accustomed to each other, and how you look will come to matter less than what you *are*."

"What am I, then?" she asked, half laughing.

"A woman whose spirit burns so bright that even age and illness could not damp it. You were alone in a strange place, imprisoned in a form that left you weak and weary and afflicted with all manner of aches and pains. Yet somehow you always found the strength to defend those who could not defend themselves. Look at how you stood up to Gudrun—and to Sir Lancelot—and to me when I deserved it. You showed me what true courage is—and you taught me how to laugh again—even at myself."

He took her hand and stroked it, a lock of fine golden hair falling over his brow. "To look upon your lovely face and hold you in my arms is more joy than I deserve. And it would be a lie to say I am not conscious of how other men admire you—and envy me your company, just as they pitied me before. I thought of those things earlier, but in the end, I came to see they did not matter. Even when you are the crone in truth, you will still be Aislyn." He raised his head to look into her eyes. "And I will still be yours."

# Chapter 44

• • •

THE torches were guttering in their holders as Aislyn and Gawain walked arm in arm down the deserted passageway. She had never known such happiness; indeed, she hardly dared believe that it was real. Yet once they had left the king's presence chamber for the shelter of the gardens, Gawain had proved his words of love in such a fashion as could leave her in no doubt of their truth.

"You are older than me," Aislyn remarked casually. "By the time I am a crone again, you will be *ancient*."

Gawain halted, then turning swiftly, bent her back across his arm. "And will you love me then?"

She pursed her lips. "Do you think you will grow ugly?"

"Undoubtedly."

"Liar. You are a man. You will merely be *distinguished*."

"I am distinguished now," he said, righting her and offering his arm. They rounded a corner, and light from the archway opening on the hall flooded the flagstones with gold.

"A bit *too* distinguished," she grumbled as they passed

by the entrance to the hall, where the sounds of pipes and drums drifted out into the corridor.

"What did you say?"

"You don't *dance*," she said, gazing wistfully over her shoulder.

Gawain laughed. "Oh, is *that* what you are muttering about! Well, Aislyn, I'll have you know that there was only one woman I ever cared to dance with. As she was . . . unavailable . . . I gave it up." He made her a flourishing bow. "My lady, will you do me the honor?"

"It would be my pleasure. But must we stop at one?"

"We can dance all night if that pleases you."

"Oh, yes, let's! Only—let us retire before dawn. If Morgana was wrong—not that I don't trust her, but . . . well, I'd rather be alone with you."

• • •

GAWAIN smiled without opening his eyes when something soft brushed his cheek, and sighed as warm breath stirred the hair at his temple. When a cold nose thrust into his ear, he bolted upright. "Sooty, get off me. Go!"

He yawned and stretched, then stilled abruptly and turned to draw back the coverlet beside him. Aislyn's hair caught the sunlight in a blaze of gold, spilling over the edge of the bed to brush the floor. He pushed it aside and kissed her neck.

" 'M I the crone?" she mumbled.

"Hmm, now, let me see. Well . . . I don't know, Aislyn, it's hard to say. Let me have a closer loo—"

His words ended in a muffled shout as a pillow hit him squarely in the face.

Sooty, denied her morning petting, cast them a disgusted look as she leapt through the window and stalked off to find her breakfast. Behind her, bright laughter spilled into the courtyard, fading into broken words and murmured endearments, and then, at last, to silence.